# It's a Desperate Life

## – PETER HAMMOND –

An environmentally friendly book printed and bound in England by
www.printondemand-worldwide.com

**Mixed Sources**
Product group from well-managed
forests, and other controlled sources
www.fsc.org Cert no. TT-COC-002641
© 1996 Forest Stewardship Council

PEFC Certified
This product is
from sustainably
managed forests
and controlled
sources
www.pefc.org
PEFC/16-33-415

This book is made entirely of chain-of-custody materials

www.fast-print.net/store.php

# IT'S A DESPERATE LIFE
Copyright © Peter Hammond 2013

A catalogue record for this book is available from the British Library

ISBN 978-178035-754-6

First published 2013 by Fastprint Publishing, Peterborough, England.

*Dedicated to my father, George Hammond, who delighted in Dublin – its places, its people and their humour. Also to Owen Nolan, who brought Frankie Flynn to life on stage in London and Dublin. God bless them both.*

# 1. McGowan's

Peggy detonated her bombshell without warning. There was no three minute warning, or even checking that I had adopted the brace position. In the middle of telling me off for leaving my shoes on the breadbin, she announced that we were moving to Sunnyside! It was done casually – callously – contemptuously even – like a Roman emperor deciding the fate of a noble gladiator by the whim of his thumb.

The Flynns had lived in the Daymo since the time of Brian Boru, and I was damned if I was going to move out to some miserable suburb of concrete, cars and kids just because Peggy said so. The problem was that Peggy's say-so was a powerful thing, and it would take more than my veto to stop it.

★ ★ ★

In Magowan's that evening, I sipped a pint and tried to put order on my thoughts. It was a Friday, and the problem with Magowan's on a Friday night is that it is not suited to quiet reflection. If you were looking for a good place to play chess or practice meditation, this was not it. Think about Dublin Airport on a bank holiday, or Arnott's sale, and you will have the idea.

Paddy Mulhall was talking, and although he was no more than three inches in front of me, and shouting his head off, I wasn't taking a single word in. The noise of the bar, on top of the effect of Peggy's earlier bombshell on my brain cells, made the business of receiving and decoding information difficult.

A further major distraction at this close range was Paddy's face. Paddy is not what you would call a handsome man. At this range, his features were like an ordnance survey map of rough countryside, packed with contour lines, embankments, marshes and winding paths going nowhere.

While Paddy was jabbering away, I was considering the best way to get from the tip of his nose to his left ear. I figured that the only way would be to do a zig-zag down his snout, up over his cheekbone, steering well clear of the shake-hole eye socket, through the sideburns, and you would be there. Every other way went too near his big fat gob, which would be madness.

"Frankie, are you listenin' to me at all?" he asked, looking at me suspiciously.

"Wha'?" I asked back.

"I said are ya listenin' to me? Ya're starin' at me like a feckin' mackerel up off a slab."

"I am listenin' to ya," I lied. "Go on."

I waved him ahead like a policeman, but I was still struggling. At the best of times, Paddy has a way of talking like a priest on a hot Sunday. No matter how hard I might try, my brain would wander off - almost like it had a mind of its own, if you know what I mean.

I hadn't the foggiest idea what he had been going on about, but somehow I did become aware that he had moved on to another item on the programme. When I realised what it was, I turned my concentration up to maximum. I squeezed my face into a ball to push out every other thought and noise, and cupped my hands around my hears like radars, to catch Paddy's words of wisdom.

"What're ya doin'?" he asked. "Ya look like a constipated elephant."

I ignored that.

"Wha' were ya sayin' about the Sky Sports?" I asked.

Paddy sighed, pretending that he was a man of infinite patience, and continued from where he had left off.

The topic under discussion was a frequent one in Magowan's: the best way to get Sky Sports for free.

There were various schools of thought. One was to have a next-door neighbour who had actually paid, and to plug into his box. The problem with this was that the signal became diluted - each house only got half. This created the prospect of a very pissed off neighbour, if he found out what you were up to. Therefore it could only be done the odd time, like for big matches, or if the neighbour was away. It was a non-starter for me, because the oul wan next door wasn't interested in football, and she would be too mean to get it, even if she was. In fact there were few enough people in the Daymo so lacking in resourcefulness that they would buy anything from a legitimate supplier.

The other more tried, tested and reliable method was to bung a few quid to the officially accredited engineer, who would install and fire up the necessary equipment, and all without troubling his employers with the information that he had done it.

Ginger Celtic - so called because he had a head of hair like a three bar electric fire, and because of his fanatical support for the Glasgow soccer team of that name - had hooked myself and most of the Daymo up. Don't ask me what his real name was - he didn't carry business cards, and I never got an invoice off him. He had one of those photofit faces that police always seem keen to interview, if only to eliminate from their enquiries, so it never seemed wise to pry too deeply into his affairs.

Ginger's normal place of business was the table to the left of the gents in Magowan's, and he could be found there most evenings. He was efficient, reliable and discreet. In terms of customer service and sheer value for money, it was hard to see how he could be beaten.

At least that was the consensus up to that time, but Paddy seemed to think that through the march of progress, Ginger's supremacy was in jeopardy. He was explaining the technical intricacies of a system he had discovered, which involved a Chinese satellite. Other than that, the details were a bit of a blur to me. I hadn't taken in Paddy's opening remarks, and it was like missing a week off school when they had done algebra, and I was struggling to catch up.

As I tried to formulate questions and challenges for Paddy, I was further put off by Miley Magee and Larry Edwards. They were to my left, loudly debating the Ireland football manager's credentials for scratching his own arse. Miley was strongly of the view that arse-scratching would be well beyond the man's capabilities, citing the team's recent poor performances in evidence. Larry appeared for the defence, saying that "even Jesus Christ down off the cross couldn't get that shower o' wankers to play football." This was an interesting and important debate, and I wanted to join in. I had several points to make, which I thought would help to resolve the matter, but I couldn't because I was juggling the satellite conundrum with sour thoughts of Sunnyside, which stayed with me like toothache.

Before I go any further, let me tell you about Magowan's. It's what I call a proper pub, laid out the way God decreed in His divine plan. It's divided into a lounge and a bar, with the serving area strategically placed down the middle, so that Betty Magowan (our Grand Mufti and Supreme Leader), and her staff can easily serve and police both sides.

To tell you nothing but the truth there was little to choose between the two options. In the old days, when my father was alive, the lounge was definitely more salubrious. It had a carpet, and the seats were upholstered. There were coloured lampshades, and a vase of plastic flowers in the window. It hadn't been decorated for a while – a long while – so, while these features were still there, their initial glory and magnificence had faded.

The bar had none of the lounge's refinements. If a workhouse had a bar, this would be it. There was no carpet, and the furniture was functional - wooden chairs and stools to sit on, and wooden tables to put pints on. The walls were bare, other than for some ancient notices setting out various prohibitions – singing, swearing, selling, begging and children. There was also a catch-all notice giving the management the right to sling you out on your ear, if the management, in its considered opinion, regarded you as not being conducive to peace, harmony and the public good.

The lighting was the same as you would get in a factory. It allowed you to see what you were drinking, but no interior designer would have chosen it for its soothing qualities.

The most that could be said for the bar was that you were not actually outside in the street. The other main attraction was that women didn't come into it - other than one or two mad oul wans, who nobody minded.

Of course these days the ladies are free to go wherever they like, and to hell with what anyone thinks. There's no sanctum sanctorum for the gentleman drinker anymore. We've just had to learn to put up with it. You would be a brave man to say anything. I remember Hughie Nelson suggesting to a couple of lady visitors that they might be more comfortable in the lounge, and they nearly filleted and stuffed the poor bastard. Don't get me wrong, I don't mind. I'm a modern man. I'm all for progress, equality and all that rubbish.

The bar had what estate agents would call 'many original features', in that it hadn't seen a redecoration for generations, if ever. It was just about warm enough to take your coat off in the winter. There was no food, cocktails or shite like that. There was a telly for watching football, the pints were sound, and the toilets had somehow been passed by the health inspector. What more could you ask for?

The clientele were decent local people like myself – the salt of the earth, backbone of the community. Mature family men. Younger people wouldn't go into Magowan's to save their lives - thanks be to God. It was off the beaten track for tourists and culchies, and Betty Magowan wouldn't tolerate scag heads, chancers, bowsies, gougers or anyone looking to drink on credit.

Betty presided over the Magowan's emporium seven days a week. A good Dublin barman (sorry - person) needs to be a combination of philosopher, encyclopaedia and bouncer and Betty had it all. She was friendly enough. You could pull her leg, but you wouldn't want to take the piss. I've seen her personally assist customers to leave the premises, and I can tell you that she wasn't too fussed which bit of them hit the pavement first.

So that's Magowan's. Plain, simple and straightforward - a home away from home.

"So wha' do ya think?" Paddy asked.

He looked at me like a dog waiting for someone to throw him a stick. I think 'expectantly' is the word I'm looking for.

On top of the problems I already had concentrating, it was getting on in the evening, and the pints were having their effect on me. Let's just say that I was no longer in a state to operate complicated machinery. I probably couldn't have accurately hit a wall with a hammer. I was working my way outside pint number five, and was weighing up whether six mightn't be pushing it a bit. I had just concluded that indeed it would not, when Paddy had interrupted his flow with his probing question.

"Eh?" I asked.

I was playing for time, hoping to get further and better particulars, so that I might be able to play a meaningful part in the discussion.

Paddy rearranged his map so that the hills and valleys took on a look of extreme irritation.

"Have ya been listenin' to me at all?" he wanted to know.

"I have," I said. "Yeah. About the Chinese satellite."

The hills and valleys relaxed a bit.

"So wha' do ya think?"

What I thought didn't really add up to a fully formed view, but I could see that I would have to make a stab at an answer - at least something to get the ball back into Paddy's court, and set him off again.

"I suppose there could be somethin' in it right enough," I ventured.

"What do ya mean 'somethin' in it'? Sure wha' could be wrong with it?"

He had me there. I scratched around amongst the miniscule collection of 'facts' that I had gathered for something sensible to say. There was little enough to go on. All I came up with was 'Chinese satellite'.

"Well, it's Chinese isn't it?" I pointed out.

"So wha'?" he challenged.

I took another tiny step forward onto the thin ice.

"Well, wha' would it be doin' over Ireland?"

"Wha' are ya talkin' abou'? It's a feckin' satellite. It'd be in outer space, not hangin' off a bleedin' chimney up the Cabra Road."

"Yeah, bu' Chinese, ya know. The programmes mightn't even be in English."

I knew that there was probably something wrong with this point even as I put it forward, but at the time I couldn't think what. And under pressure I had nothing else to contribute.

There was the start of a serious eruption on Paddy's map.

"Ah, for feck's sake! Amn't I after explainin' to ya tha' it's all the same channels tha' we get already, an' a pile more. Ya don't think tha' we're goin' to get Mícheál O'Muirtheartaigh's commentary on the Sunday Game in Chinese, do ya?"

"Well no, bu'..."

We were interrupted by Betty Magowan floating into focus with two fresh pints. Paddy had ordered them with a flicker of an eyebrow, while he was berating me.

"Here yis are gents," she said.

Paddy fished out the do-re-mi and handed it over. While he waited for Betty to bring him whatever he was due back, I took the opportunity to change the subject.

"Peggy wants us to move house," I said.

Paddy was a man with strong local affiliations, and I knew that this would get his interest.

"Why in the name o' Jaysus would she want to move? Wha's wrong with where yis are?"

"Sure wha' isn't wrong? The road is too noisy. The neighbours are too common. The kitchen is too small. The garden is the wrong shape. An' we don't have an en suite bathroom," I explained.

"An en suite!"

He spat the words out like they tasted bad.

"She's been watchin' too many o' them property programmes," he said. "Tha's the problem. Them bloody things'd fill yer head full o' shite. Master bedrooms. kitchen diners, an' en feckin' suites..."

The hills and valleys registered something between nausea and disgust.

"Mary was the same for a while," he said. "She wanted me to go an' look at some new development out in the arse end o' Donlee. I told her she could forget about it. Wha' would we be doin' out there? Eh? I said to her we'd be up to our oxsters in newlyweds an' screamin' feckin' kids."

"An' sure there's not a decent pub for miles around," I reminded him.

Paddy shuddered at the thought of the peril averted.

"I wouldn't mind bu' there's only me an' her in the house now since the girls left," I said. "An' the bathroom is slap bang next door to the bedroom. But accordin' to her tha's not the same thing as an en suite. She says tha's the family bathroom, an' should be free for guests to use. Guests! Apart from Peggy's nephew - who couldn't care less - the last guest we had was her mother - Lord a mercy on the oul cow. Tha' mus' be over twenty years ago, an' I never remember her washin' herself anytime she came near us."

"It's a load o' bollix," Paddy agreed. "In our day the only en suite we ever had was the poe under the bed. They should bring them back in again. They were handy."

Paddy looked like he was wondering where he might buy one.

"Thanks Paddy," I said. "I'll suggest tha' to Peggy when I get in."

Paddy warmed to his great idea.

"What ya want to do is get a poe, stick a bunch o' flowers in it, an' gift wrap it for Peggy in cellophane an' a red ribbon. Inject a bit o' romance into the lady's life, an' sort out her ablution needs in one go. She'll be delighted with ya, an' the house move'll be history."

Paddy laughed, delighted with his genius. He knew Peggy well, and he knew that the chance of her being put off her stride by any such bullshit was zero.

And I knew from grim experience that when Peggy gets an idea into her head, the options available to me are a) give in immediately, or b) lay low and hope that she might forget about it. Arguing only gets me where the Charge of the Light Brigade got Lord Raglan, so I have learned to keep my mouth shut. My strategy has developed into staying non-committal. I might fake a tiny bit of interest, but I do nothing. I hunker down, cover my head, and hope that she gets bored and goes away.

You won't be surprised to hear that she has wised up to this. Einstein she isn't, but she's not a complete daw either. She knows that my motto is: 'If it ain't broke, don't fix it; and if it is broke, don't fix it either.' Nowadays when Peggy gets something into her noodle, she comes after me like a Jack Russell after a rat. She wants to know what I think about it, how I'm going to do it, and when, when, bloody when. I do my best with "I'll see," "let me think about it," and "maybe when the weather gets better." (You can rely on the weather never getting better for long enough in Dublin). But it's a struggle - an endless bloody struggle.

Hiding in Magowan's is my other tactic. The more she sees me, the more she thinks of things for me to do, so staying out of sight is important.

Since that morning, when I had first heard of her bloody Sunnyside plan, she had been constantly bashing away at me.

It was like an artillery bombardment to confuse and demoralise the enemy, and I was expecting a final charge to mop up any remaining resistance imminently.

★ ★ ★

Later that evening - much later - I arrived back at the happy home. The place was in darkness, and I surmised that Mrs F had taken herself off to bed.

Quietly opening the front door, I tiptoed in. Bertie, our pedigree dog, wagged his tail to salute the return of the Master, but otherwise he stayed put on the sofa.

I thought about having a little nip from the Jemmy bottle in the press, but I am a man who knows when he has had enough, and I had had enough.

I crept out to the kitchen to see if I might find the makings of a sandwich, and was stealthily rummaging in all the likely places, when there was a roar from the top of the stairs.

"Wha' the hell are ya doin' down there, crashin' aroun' like a rhino on a feckin' skateboard?"

I whispered an apology, and Peggy - for it was she - returned to bed, banging the bedroom door shut.

I gave up the culinary treasure hunt. The challenge of finding bread, butter, ham, mustard and the necessary hardware, would have defeated me at the best of times. At this hour, and tired as I was, I had no chance, so I headed up the wooden hill.

After using the not-en-suite facilities, I snuck into the bedroom. I could make out a mound in the bed. Peggy appeared to be sleeping. Having difficulty with navigation, and after tripping over something, I thought she wouldn't mind if I put the light on for a minute. I hit the switch, and held my breath. But she was grand. There wasn't a stir out of her.

I sat on my side of the bed, wrestling with my socks, which seemed to have welded themselves onto my feet. Eventually I managed to divest myself of them, and the rest of my evening wear. After turning off the light, I dived in under the duvet, and found myself warbling that old standard "I'm in the mood for love."

"I'm in the mood for love .....

...simply because you're near me....

Funny, but when you're near me ....

...I'm in the mood for love...."

I was keeping it low and soulful - after all, it was late. I reached across and gently patted where I thought Peggy's hip might be.

"Frank, if ya come near me, I'll kill ya stone dead. I swear to God I will," she said.

I tried a bit of the old Maurice Chevalier.

"Ah ma sherrie. Voolay voo cooshay aveck mwah?"

"FRANK. FECK. OFF. Ya stink o' beer."

To make sure that I didn't misunderstand the message, she turned around and somehow managed to punch, knee and kick me, all at the same time. I took the point, and crawled over to the touchline to nurse my injuries, and eventually to dream about getting physio from the blondie one in the Spice Girls.

# 2. Peggy

P eggy and me have been locked together in wedded bliss for just on thirty years. We met in the Savoy Cinema in O'Connell Street. She was with a pal that she used to work with in the County Council, and I was with Joe Horgan. The film was Conan the Barbarian.

They were seated a few rows in front of us, and for some reason I took a fancy to her. I can't imagine why. Even in her prime, she was no Marilyn Monroe. But in all fairness to me, it was dark.

I started throwing popcorn at her to get her attention.

I don't know if you've ever used popcorn for target practice, but if not, I can tell you not to bother. It's useless. There's not enough weight in it, and it's probably the wrong shape. I mean if you compare popcorn with a javelin or a dart, you'll see what I mean. The grip, the shape and the balance of a dart are all spot on and just what you want. You would have your work cut out to design something more crap for throwing than bloody popcorn.

But my motto is that you have to play the hand that you are dealt. All I had in my hand was popcorn, and I had to make the best of it.

I was pleased enough that, after I had found the range, about sixty percent was landing in or around the target area, i.e. Peggy's head. Unfortunately the rest of the stuff was landing amongst the general public, and while most of these good citizens were suffering in silence, one cranky bastard decided to object.

I wouldn't mind, but I hadn't hit him at all. He was with this mousey-haired young wan who had taken a few direct hits. In fairness to her, she had said nothing, but if she was willing to laugh it off as part of a jolly night out in Dublin, he wasn't.

He was a huge bugger, with a head like a turnip on steroids. I would have believed it if you told me that he had come to audition for the lead role in the film, and that he was pissed off to find that they had given it to a scrawny little fart like Schwarzenegger. Social workers would have sussed him out immediately as a man with anger management issues.

He turned around and suggested where I might shove the popcorn, using language and gestures not suitable for a mixed social gathering. I considered telling him where to go, but weighing the pros and cons, I came down on the side of self-preservation, and decided on an immediate ceasefire. Anyway, I figured that I had done enough to establish the initial relationship with Peggy, and negotiations could be continued at our leisure after the film.

I gave my full attention to the screen, and thus engrossed, was not paying attention when Joe fired off a zinger – beginner's luck, I called it - which caught yer man square on the back of his fat neck.

The first I knew of this, was the sensation of being dragged out of my seat, and being repeatedly punched in the head.

To add insult to injury, the cinema authorities arrived, and after conducting a brief enquiry - during which my own statements and complaints seemed to count for nothing - they turfed me out on my ear.

Afterwards Peggy, her pal and Joe thought the whole thing was hysterical. The fact that I had suffered assault and battery at the hands of the man-ape didn't dampen their amusement one little bit.

Over the years since, I have noticed a nasty tendency in Peggy to be amused every time I come a cropper. It is not the attitude you would hope from your soul mate and the love of your life. The time I fell off my bike into the canal, and nearly drowned, she actually wet herself laughing - and I can tell you that it was not part of any gesture of comradely solidarity.

After the Savoy, we got chips from Forte's, and they had great gas telling me to throw them at people in the street. Joe set himself up to throw one at the back of a couple of Guards in Abbey Street, but I put him off with a good root up the arse.

We left the women down to their bus, and made some arrangement to meet up again. I think we went out to Howth on the train the following Sunday. Or it might have been Bray. I can't remember. All I know is that Joe didn't get on with his one, and that was the end of that. But with me and Peggy, one thing led to another, and the rest, as they say, is history.

Peggy was brought up on a farm in County Carlow, but at this stage she has been so well marinated in Dublin coddle, that you would not be able to pick her out from the native ingredients.

She wasn't always like that of course. When I met her first, she was a hick, a hillbilly and a bog-trotter of the first order - totally out of her depth in the big city. I felt it my duty to smooth off the rougher edges and to polish her up a bit, to stop her making an eejit out of herself - and out of me.

I was like Professor Higgins with Eliza Doolittle. There was the dopey flat accent to get rid of, and the stupid sayings. I mean what exactly is a 'rake of shpuds'? You can't be going around Dublin saying "I had a mighty feed last night - a plate o' mate an' a rake o' shpuds."

I wasn't planning on introducing her to Leopardstown society. I just wanted her to be able to get through a night at the dogs at Shelbourne Park, without looking like an agricultural exhibit.

I still wonder what I thought I was up to when I remember the look of her back in those days. There were the shoes that were probably Red Army surplus, dresses like the one they buried my grandmother in, and a hairdo that a sheep shearer would have been ashamed of. It took all of my tact and diplomacy to be able to point out to her nicely - without hurting her feelings - that in Dublin she stood out like shite on an iceberg.

It was one step forward and two steps backward for a long time. We would be going along fine, then she would disappear back down to the bog for the weekend, and on Monday we would be back where we started.

Why I kept at it, I will never know. They say that love is blind, but in my case, it was blind, deaf and pure stupid. Joe Horgan said that I was fascinated by Peggy's fine child-bearing hips. Night after night we sat in Sheary's Bar or in the Smithfield Inn, soaking up the ambience for her benefit. Joe and Barney Pugh did more than their fair share, giving master classes in that unique form of Dublin wit known as slagging. If you are unfamilar with the term, it is basically insulting people to their faces for a laugh.

Perseverance won out in the end. I can still remember the night at the bus stop when she said to me: "Keep dem hands to yerself, unless ya want to be in tomorrow's paper." I could have cried - I was so proud. By George, she'd got it, at last!

She'd got it, and I'd had it. Before I had fully weighed up what I might be committing to, I was in front of a clergyman, pledging all my worldly goods, and plighting my troth.

Fast-forward through the years, and Peggy's fine child-bearing hips have disappeared under a generous blanket of blubber. The chances of her ever succumbing to anorexia are nil. She has a voice to match her impressive proportions. Where others bring light to where there is darkness, Peggy's specialism is to bring noise to where there is silence. I would be staggered if she has ever had an unuttered opinion.

★ ★ ★

On the Saturday morning, after the night in Magowan's with Paddy Mulhall, I wasn't feeling at my brightest and best. When I woke up, there was a lump of something heavy loose in the back of my head. If I budged at all, it crashed around like a pin-ball. My continuing existence was only made bearable by lying absolutely flat in the bed, with the top of my head jammed up against the headboard, and with my chin pointed up at the ceiling. My stomach felt like it had been used to mix concrete, and my mouth was as dry as a camel's arse, that had been facing into the desert sun all day.

The peace - if you can call it that - was broken by Peggy bawling at me from close range.

"Frank," she barked. "Get up. Half the mornin' is gone, an' there's things to be done."

I could think of several replies to this, but it would have hurt me to speak, so I settled for a moan that would have wrung sympathy out of a Christian Brother. Peggy came to the side of the bed, and looked down at me. There was a kindly light in her eyes, with which I was unfamiliar. She gently rested the backs of her fingers on my forehead.

"Aah, are ya not well?" she asked. "Ya poor thing. Will I go down an' make ya a cup o' tea? An' maybe a rasher an' an egg?"

That sounded like it might help. I was going to suggest that she might throw in a bit of buttered toast, when she flung back the duvet, and started manhandling me.

"Get out of tha' bed, ya lazy fecker. Ya think ya can sit in Magowan's all night turnin' beer into lard, and sleep in here half the day. Well y'ave another thing comin'. It's nearly half ten, an' there's a man comin' from the estate agents at eleven."

"Would ya leave ...?"

I wrestled to keep hold of the duvet to maintain my dignity, but it was no good. Peggy spent her formative years lassoing and branding cattle, so for her, grabbing the side of a mattress, and tipping a sick man onto the floor was child's play. My pain and misery were complete. The pinball was ringing all the bells and lighting all the lights in my head, and my stomach was lurching and heaving like a ship in a hurricane. I decided to stay lying where I had been dumped on the floor. I reasoned that she couldn't tip me any further. But she could kick me, and she did, opening up with a couple of juicy ones to the small of my back. I know when I am beaten, and I ran up the white flag.

"Give over," I said. "Give over, will ya? I'm goin'. Leave off."

"Get into that bathroom an' get yerself shaved, washed and dressed. If ya're not downstairs, an' lookin' respectable in ten minutes, I'll be dug outta ya."

I struggled into the bathroom. At least I would get a few minutes' peace and sanctuary behind the locked door. I turned on the shower, sat on the toilet and closed my eyes. The pain and nausea subsided, and I managed to get my legs under me, so that I could stand up and examine the damage in the mirror. I didn't look great – I will admit that. The hair was standing on end, the skin was the colour of porridge, and the eyes looked like stab wounds. If the dog's dinner looked like me, Bertie would have gone on hunger strike.

"Jaysus Frankie, where is the youthful bloom of yesteryear?" I asked my reflection, and it looked back at me, stumped for an answer.

I turned off the shower - I figured that it had been on long enough to keep her happy - and applied shaving foam to the chin. The razor was one of those five bladed things that you could supposedly use on a babby's arse. If so, F. Flynn Esq. is more delicate than any babby. After taking a lump out of my earlobe, I swore that I would sue the razor company for millions. For a second I thought that all was well. Then the blood began to flow like spilt ink on a blotter. I was sure that I was after slashing my jugular. The blood was getting mixed up with the soap and the water, until the sink looked like the shower scene in Psycho.

When I came downstairs, Peggy was giving tea to a young fella in a putty-coloured Penney's suit. He was probably about twenty, but if you told me he was twelve, I would have believed you. The cheap suit was set off by a grey shirt and stripey tie, which I was glad to see were doing their best to strangle him. The ensemble was completed by a pair of grey winkle pickers, that could have been classed as offensive weapons. He got up out of the chair - my chair - to greet me. He had the handshake of a month-old corpse.

"Good mornin', Mr Flynn," he said. "How are ya? A grand day, isn't it?"

I said 'howya'. There's no harm in being civil. I manoeuvred him so that I could claim my chair back.

"Frank, this is John-Paul O'Driscoll, from Hannigans. He's come to look at the house."

John-Paul, for feck's sake!

"Pleased to meet ya, Mr Flynn," he said. "I understand that ya're plannin' on movin' out o' the city. Very wise. I'm gettin' married meself next year, and we're hopin' to buy a place out near Sunnyside."

Peggy seemed pleased with this news.

"Is that righ'?" she asked. "Tha's where we're lookin', isn't it Frank?"

I felt that it would be best for me to keep my strong views on the subject of Sunnyside and similar hell holes to myself for the moment. Hold your fire until you see the whites of the enemy's eyes - that's my motto. Anyway, I was still digesting the news that some female had agreed to have her children fathered by this drip.

At the time, Dublin city and county planners were in a race to cover every bit of green with concrete. New houses and flats were the thing, and the more the merrier. People who already had one to live in, were buying another two or three, just for the hell of it. I would have minded less if the new places were well put together, but they were not. They were no more than boxes made of concrete blocks and plasterboard. There were lads out in Africa making a better job of house-building using sticks and mud.

"Tha's great," John-Paul said. "We might be neighbours."

I tried to arrange my features into something which expressed, if not delight, then at least contentment at this happy prospect.

"I'll take some measurements as I go aroun', if tha's alright?"

"Oh, you fire ahead," I said.

He pulled a biro, a writing pad and one of those electronic measuring gizmos out of his arse or somewhere.

"So this is the front reception in here. Then there's the kitchen. An' it's three bedrooms and the family bathroom upstairs. Is tha' right?" he wanted to know.

The front reception! Where did he think he was? The Mansion House?

"Yeah, tha's right," Peggy confirmed. "It's quite compact, but it's a very good family home. We raised our two daughters here - although they've both flown the nest now. Our eldest - Angela - is married with three little ones, an' with another one on the way, an' Marian – she's the other one - has a lovely apartment over in Ballsbridge."

John-Paul seemed to be overwhelmed by all this information. I could see that he wasn't sure whether he was supposed to write it down on his pad or what.

"Oh well," he said. "This part o' Dublin has certainly seen a few generations pass through it, right enough. But people are movin' out all the time. These properties are popular with people wantin' to invest in buy-to-lets. There should be great interest in one like this. With the original character of the property intact like it is - new owners will be able to modernise an' put their own stamp on it."

What he was trying to say was that he thought that the place was a dump, and anybody coming in would have a job on their hands. I could see that Peggy wasn't sure whether she should be delighted or insulted. There was a silence, and I felt that I needed to say something to keep the jolly chit-chat on the boil. The onerous burden of being a host!

"Do ya folley the football at all?" I asked, not really giving much of a shite whether he did or not.

"Oh yeah," he said. "Manchester United is my team."

I warmed to him slightly. There might be hidden depths to this John-Paul.

"Good man," I said. "The same as meself. Did ya see them the other day?"

"Yeah," he said. "Tha' referee was a disgrace."

"Fergie certainly thought so. He looked like he'd burst a blood vessel. If he got his hands on him, he'd a wrung his feckin' neck."

"We're away to Liverpool on Monday night, Mr Flynn," he said. "Tha's always a tough place to go."

"Not at all," I said. "We'll wipe the floor with them. 'This is Anfield,' my arse. Them days are gone. There was a time, when ya had Shanks or Bob Paisley there, when ya might be wettin' yerself, but not any more."

Peggy called the meeting back to order, giving me a look that would freeze gin.

"Do ya want to look upstairs now, John-Paul?" she asked.

"Thanks, Mrs Flynn. I'll do tha' in a minute. Can I jus' ask yis how far back the garden goes? It's kinda hard to tell."

"Tha's wha' ya call a natural meadow," I explained. "There was a thing on the telly about the importance o' leavin' a bit o' yer garden to grow wild. It's a habitat for the little animals an' the birds."

I said 'ha-bi-tat' slowly, as I figured the word would be new to him.

"A bit o' yer garden, yeah - not the whole feckin' thing," Peggy said.

Although she was raised in the wilderness, her father only grew potatoes and turf, so she knew sweet FA about the subtleties of environmental management. I tried to explain.

"Ya see the problem is tha' most o' them aroun' here don't give up enough space to house an earwig. They've every square inch covered in grass, an' patios an' flower beds. I'm jus' tryin' to make up for them, tha's all."

"Ya're talkin' shite," Peggy said.

John-Paul looked like he had wandered into the deep end without his armbands.

"It's all about the ecosystem," I explained to him, regarding Peggy as a lost cause.

He nodded, but I could tell that he hadn't a clue what I was talking about. Pearls before swine, I thought. I gave up and went back to simple facts that he might understand.

"The garden goes back as far as the shed ya can see through the bushy things. Tha' black thing. D'ya see it?"

John-Paul nodded. I felt like patting him on the head and giving him a biscuit. He wrote something down.

"Tha's Iggie Farrell's shed - or his workshop, as he calls it. Workshop me arse. He sleeps in there more often than he does in the house."

John-Paul looked blank, so I gave him further details.

"Iggie's missus doesn't let him in the house if he's jarred, an' he's jarred most o' the time."

He wandered out to do a tour of the Flynn demesne, and I pushed the door shut behind him. If he got lost and was never heard of again, that would have been fine by me. I got up and shuffled over to the table to see if I could find tea. Peggy was watching me as I footered about. I detected irritation.

"What are ya after?" she snapped.

"Tea," I said.

"The pot is there on the table."

I found the vessel as indicated, hidden behind the corncrakes, and poured myself a cup. It was not very hot, and was the colour of black pudding. I was going to ask her where the milk was, but like Macbeth in the story, I couldn't bring my courage to the sticking point, so I went back to my chair, and drank it black.

Peggy pointed at the lump of toilet paper hanging off my ear.

"What are ya after doin'?" she asked – I'd like to say with concern, but it wasn't.

"I was tryin' to cut me throat," I said.

"Jus' my luck tha' ya didn't manage it. I hope ya left tha' bathroom in a reasonable condition for John-Paul."

"Ah, would ya relax. He's only lookin'. He's not havin' a bath."

John-Paul found his way back to the ranch house, and Peggy took him up to check out the upstairs accommodation. When he came back down he looked shook - like a boy sent to do man's work. He was drawn towards the door, like a dog to a lamp post. He had seen enough, and wanted to find his way back to civilisation, as soon as he could manage it.

"Well tha's all fine Mr and Mrs Flynn. I'll do up the particulars back at the office, and I'll let yis know wha' askin' price we'd recommend, after I've had a word with Mr Hannigan. I jus' need yis to sign the agreement appointin' us as your sellin' agents, and we'll put all the wheels in motion."

I was going to tell him where to stick his agreement, when Peggy's eye froze me back into position. I figured that on balance I could let this battle go, but that I would win the war. Under this duress, I signed my name, so did Peggy, and John-Paul added his mark.

"Tha's great," he said. "We'll send the photographer aroun' durin' the week."

He paused and looked nervous.

"Jus' a little piece of advice: We find that the more you can reduce the clutter, the better rooms look, and the better the response ya get."

"Is that a fact now?" I said.

I wanted him to know that Frankie Flynn is always open to new ideas from a professional man like himself.

"We'll get stuck into it John-Paul, don't you worry," Peggy said. "Won't we Frank?"

"Definitely," I said, hoping that I sounded like I meant it.

# 3. Daughters

As you may have gathered, the union of Peggy and me has been blessed with two daughters: viz Angela and Marian. You would never guess that they were from the same family. They hardly look like they are from the same species. I always explain it by saying that it was due to a change in milkman, which always gets a laugh, except from Peggy, who has a sense of humour bypass.

Angela is the older one. She is a very sociable, easy-going, friendly kind of person. She would do anything for her family and friends, up to and including murder. I often think that she is a bit like Duffy's Circus: big, loud and colourful. You are always pleased when she arrives, and delighted when she goes. If I was to be picky, I would say that her only failing is a slight tendency to get a bit foul-mouthed when she is pissed. But none of us are perfect.

The major cloud in Angela's life - although she would not agree - is Tommy Doyle. Tommy is Angela's husband, and if there is a bigger waster in Dublin, I have yet to come across him. Tommy enjoys the best of bad health. There is always something wrong with the bugger. If it isn't his back, it's his stomach, or his nerves. He does nothing. He doesn't work. He doesn't drink. He doesn't smoke. What the point of him is at all, I don't know - other than getting Angela pregnant, which he somehow manages at regular intervals. At the time I am talking about, they had three urchins - aged five, three, and fifteen months - and there was another one ordered, and due any minute.

Angela's normal fighting weight would be somewhere between welter and middle. If she played rugby she would be a mainstay of the scrum, rather than one of the little ferrety ones running up and down the wing. But when she is up the duff, she takes on juggernaught proportions, and needs flashing lights and a motorcycle escort whenever she leaves the house.

Peggy and Angela are very close, and similar in many ways. They complement one another like opposite sides of a pick-axe. Either one of them on her own is a force, but together they are unstoppable. Angela is something like her mother was when I knew her first. Before Peggy turned into what she is now, she used to be more friendly and relaxed. They say that if you want to know how a girl will turn out, you should take a look at her mother, and all I can say is that Tommy's days of wine and roses are numbered. It will serve the malingering little bastard well enough.

They live just around the corner from us, so Angela and the kids spend nearly as much time in our place as they do in their own. I sometimes mind the sprogs - if Angela and Peggy are out together at the bingo, or their zombie dancing - and sure they're no bother at all. I just put Willie Wanker on the video, give them a load of crisps and cola, and you would hardly know they were there.

In fact, one time it turned out that they weren't. I left them parked in front of the telly, and I must have nodded off reading the paper. The next thing I knew, all hell was breaking loose - shouting, running, crying, doors banging and general commotion. Angela and Peggy had come back, and the roll call had found only one present and correct - me. Needless to say, they were a bit put out - especially Angela. Mothers are like that when their kids go missing. I understand that. It's a natural thing.

Apparently what happened was that the film had come to an end, and the little buggers decided that they would take Bertie for a walk. So off they went, the two bigger ones pushing the little one in the pram, and Bertie roped on somewhere like a husky. He isn't a husky. He's a pure bred sheep dog crossed with pure bred cocker spaniel, with some other pure bred blood in him as well.

In the end there was no harm done. After the hue and cry was raised, someone found them playing beside the canal, and not a bother on them. We all had a great laugh about it afterwards - or maybe it was just me who had the laugh - I can't remember.

Then there is Marian, who is not a bit like Angela. Chalk and cheese. Sweet and sour. Laurel and Hardy. Marian is a marketing manager - whatever that is - working for some international insurance shysters down in the docks. She has explained it to me more than once, but I can't get my head around it. All I know is that it is basically a tax scam, but she swears that it's all tickety-boo, approved and above board. The job is to sit in front of a computer, go to meetings, and travel all over the place. And I am not talking about Dublin, or even Ireland - I'm talking about London, Frankfurt and New York. They pay her a small fortune. She has an apartment in Ballsbridge that Zsa Zsa Gabor wouldn't have sniffed at, and a car that has got more knobs and switches on it than a spaceship.

Unlike her sister, Marian is built like a racing weasel, which is just as well, with all the running around that she does. Her brain works the same way - like a machine gun on a hair trigger. Before you even have a chance to open your gob, she is telling you what you're supposed to think. Even the most innocent remark can have you with your back against the wall with a chair and a whip, trying to keep her off. I remember one time saying, in all innocence, that I thought that black guys would be better at breaking and entering because they would be harder to see in the dark - which is nothing but a scientific fact. The next thing I know, I am being accused of everything from starting slavery to shooting Martin Luther King.

I remember one evening, in the course of having a few quiet pints, telling Betty Magowan all about Marian, and her high-flying career.

"Ah, that'll all come to an end when she meets a nice fella," Betty said.

"Yeah, I suppose ya're right," I agreed. "Then she can relax and settle down to a life o' Riley, like Angela an' her mother."

But Betty didn't see it that way.

"Wha' are ya talkin' about? Hasn't your Angela got a gang o' little ones - an' another one on the way? It's not my idea of the life o' Riley."

"Will ya go away out o' tha'," I fired back, warming to the debate. "Sure women today are on the pig's back, with their washin' machines an' microwaves an' dishwashers an' boil-in-the-bag dinners. Sure they don't know they're born."

I thought that would have been the end of the argument, but Betty was not having it.

"Well Frankie, there's plenty tha' wouldn't agree with ya. The young women today have it all to do. They're lookin' after the home, bringin' up the children, and they have to go out and bring in a wage to help pay the mortgage as well. Tha's no bed o' roses."

I dismissed that nit-picking nonsense, as not even going near scuppering the essence of my thesis.

"A rose by any other name is still a handy number in my book, Betty. When I think o' the things me mother had to do. All the washin' done be hand, an' wrung through a mangle. God knows how she dried it. Hangin' it on a clothes horse in front o' the fire. Even on a dry day ya couldn't leave clothes out on the line in Mountjoy Square. Ya'd be lucky if even the pegs'd be there when ya got back. They'd rob the knickers off a nun goin' past on a motorbike, they would. The young women today would never manage all tha'."

I felt that I had won on points, and drew the proceedings to a close. There was no need to humiliate the woman.

"Anyway, Betty, I have to go," I said, downing the last of my pint. "I need my beauty sleep. These looks don't happen by accident, y'know."

"No?" she asked. "I always assumed tha's wha' it was!"

I remember that conversation very well, because it was the same evening that I arrived back at barracks to find that I had no key. As usual, Peggy had gone to bed, so to get in I had to do some energetic knocking.

Here's a tip for you. If you want to meet Peggy at her brightest and sunniest, don't go banging on the door and getting her out of bed at a late hour. She doesn't respond well to it. The likelihood of meeting Peggy the genial and welcoming hostess would be limited in any event, but in these circumstances would be zero. What you get would be similar to the three hags Macbeth used to bump into on the blasted heath.

"Wha' the hell are ya doin' makin' a racket at this hour o' the night?" she asked, flinging the door open, so that it bounced off the wall. "Where's yer feckin' key?"

At least I was sure that I had come to the right house. I might have wittily replied that I had it in my pocket, but wanted my darling to come and share the moonlight with me. But luckily I hadn't enough drink taken, so I muttered something about leaving it on the mantelpiece, and scurried indoors before she banged the door in my kisser.

"Y'ave half the road up with yer bangin'," she said.

"It's not my fault tha' ya sleep like the dead," I said, which was only true.

"You'll be sleepin' like the feckin' dead if ya go out without yer key again," she replied.

While this witty banter was going on, to my surprise, she followed me into the living room, rather than going straight back to her crypt. This was a shame, as I had been considering a little digestif, which would now be firmly off the agenda.

I parked myself in the Master's armchair - a magnificent piece of furniture, which I have personally moulded over the years into my particular shape. It is strategically placed in front of the telly, and comes equipped with wide arms, handy for essentials like tea, sandwiches, occasional nips and the remote control.

"Were there many in Magowan's?" she asked.

This was very unusual. Peggy's interest in chit-chat with me is limited at the best of times. At this hour of the night it was bizarre. But I was game if she was.

"No," I said. "The place was nearly empty. D'ya know I sometimes wonder why I bother meself."

"Sure aren't you the backbone o' the economy?" she replied. "If you didn't go to Magowan's every night, the country'd shut down altogether. The Minister for Finance said on the radio the other day: 'The country may be in shite, but while Frankie Flynn is out swallowin' pints like a camel at a waterin' hole, there's still hope for us all.'"

"I don't go out on Thursdays," I pointed out, just to keep the records straight.

"No, ya don't go out," she agreed. "But ya don't do without either. I hear ya at tha' press when I'm gone to bed. Ya mus' think I'm a right eejit."

"Tha's wha' it's there for, isn't it?" I said – as always being the voice of reason.

"I'm goin' to tell Marian to stop bringin' bottles back here. Everywhere she goes, she's luggin' back duty free. The arse'll fall out o' tha' press, with all the bottles tha's in it. Ya'd think we were runnin' a distillery."

"Well, ya can tell her to stop bringin' back your duty free fags as well, before they kill ya," I said.

"They might kill me, but they've saved your life many a time," she fired back.

"Ya have me gassed out o' the place. I have to go down to Magowan's to get a breath o' fresh air."

I gave a little cough, and put on an injured expression.

"Magowan's!" she spat. "Tha' manky, festerin' dirt hole. Ya're takin' yer life in yer hands every time ya go in there. It's a wonder ya haven't got dysentry or somethin' out of it already. Though ya're prob'ly immune to the place at this stage."

"There's nothin' wrong with Magowan's," I said in its defence. "It's a good old-fashioned, family-run public house."

"It's a sewer."

"It's got the best pint around here."

"Wha' would you know? Ya'd lick it off a scabby leg."

Peggy paused to light up a cigarette. I don't think she really wanted one. She was just doing it to annoy me. But I can maintain the sang-froid when required, and I ignored the provocation.

"Betty Magowan asked me once why I never come in on a Thursday, and do y'know wha' I told her?"

Peggy looked less than agog at the prospect of hearing my witty reply.

"I told her I didn't want people to think tha' I'm an alcoholic."

I had a good laugh at the joke. I think it's a good one. I've used it before, and I'll use it again.

Peggy didn't join in the merriment. As I explained to you earlier, her sense of humour is restricted to occasions when I suffer a misfortune. Severe embarrassment gets a happy smile, while contusions, breaks and blood loss have her laughing her head off.

She looked down at me like I was an idiot child, and blew smoke in my face - and you're not supposed to blow smoke at children, idiot or not. At least the nicotine seemed to be calming her down.

"Angela was over earlier with the kids," she announced.

'Hold the front page,' I thought.

"Yeah?" I asked, beyond grateful that I had missed them.

"Yeah, she brought them out after their tea to give poor Tommy a break."

"Whassup wi' him?" I tried not to gush too much with concern.

"It's his stomach. Angela says he's havin' an awful time with it. He can't keep anythin' up or down. She's been feedin' him milky tapioca. She says it's all he can manage."

I could have done without the medical update on Tommy's innards. It was making me queasy myself. Milky tapioca! I tried changing the subject.

"How's she keepin' herself?" I asked.

"Ah, she's grand. Only a month to go now! She says she's nearly finished decoratin' the box room. She jus' has to gloss the skirtin' boards."

"She's a great girl, right enough," I said.

There was a silence - a rare enough thing with Peggy. I was thinking that the meeting might be concluded, and that she might feck off to bed. That little nip might be possible after all. But she lingered in the room like a porter fart. I could tell that she had something on her mind, but it seemed to be stuck there, and that was fine with me. I was not curious, and I doubted that whatever it was, that it would be in my interests. Eventually, she cleared her throat and started to spit it out.

"I was talkin' to Marian this evenin' - on the phone," she said.

"Yeah?" I asked, getting ready to close the brain down, as Peggy's conversations with her daughters rarely contain items of much interest to me.

"She's comin' up on Thursday," she said. "For her tea."

"Right," I said, hoping that there was no further business, and that we could declare the meeting closed. But there was, and we couldn't.

"She's bringin' a friend," she said. "Susan. Ya've heard her talkin' about Susan before."

If I had, I had forgotten.

"Have I?"

"She's bringin' Susan up for her tea. I thought tha' I'd do lamb chops."

"Grand," I replied, hoping that now that we had discussed and agreed Thursday's guest list and menu, that she might go away and leave me alone.

"I think Susan is a vet. They've been friends since they were in Trinity together. I think she was at the graduation, but she would have been doin' science, and Marian was in the Business Studies."

As the more academically inclined of our two, Marian flew through school, Junior Cert, Leaving Cert, the lot, and the next thing we knew, she had a degree from Trinity College. Angela only got a certificate in geography because she just about managed to find the school once or twice.

Peggy had heard my views on Trinity College many times before, but as the topic had come up, I thought that I would give her a quick reminder.

"Trinity College!" I said. "A load o' crap. Marian never learned anythin' useful in tha' place. Psychology! Technology! Boloxology! I used to tell her: 'Get yerself a job in a shop or a bar. Ya'll learn more off the people o' Dublin, than ya'll ever learn in any feckin' university'. Trinity College my arse!"

"Yeah, yeah, yeah," Peggy said. "Oh, an' if only she'd listened to ya. She could have a great job now washin' glasses an' sweepin' floors. She wouldn't be stuck in tha' nice air-conditioned office - livin' in Ballsbridge – an' drivin' aroun' in her Audi."

"Feckin' motorin' cars have the town gone mad. Ya can't move with them," I said, throwing in a quick update on my view of the Dublin traffic situation.

"Well, you don't mind plantin' yer fat arse in Marian's car when it suits ya," Peggy said, managing to accuse me of hypocrisy and laziness in one swipe.

I grunted and moved back to the main item under discussion.

"Anyway, wha's she bringin' this Susan one up here for?" I wanted to know.

"I told ya. They're friends. People bring friends for tea."

"Well me an' Joe Horgan have been friends since we were in short trousers, but ya don't see me draggin' him up here an' stuffin' him full o' chops," I replied.

"Joe Horgan has never eaten anythin' in his life tha' needed cutlery. He wouldn't know what to do with a chop."

I decided against a riposte, as I still had not given up on the chance of a moment of reflection involving man and whiskey bottle. But Peggy the mind-reader thwarted me.

"Stop eyein' tha' press. Ya've had enough. When ya open yer mouth I can see the beer lappin' up against yer back teeth. Get yerself up to bed."

I indignantly protested my innocence. I think it was indignantly - I protested it anyway.

"I don't know wha' ya're talkin' about. I'd've been gone up ages ago, only for ya goin' on about Marian an' Angela an' feckin' Tommy."

"Jus' go to bed," she said. "Now!"

I could see that further resistance would get me nowhere, so I hauled myself out of the chair and set a course for the stairs. She eyed me like a floorwalker watching a well-known shoplifter.

"Chops!" I sneered, for he who has the last word is king.

# 4. Susan

That Thursday afternoon I decided to go on a little tour of the highways and byways of this great city. Somebody once said: "A man who is tired of Dublin is tired of life," and whoever he was, he never said a truer word. I often think they could charge people just for looking at it. For centuries Dublin has been an open-air entertainment centre, with its cast of dealers, drunks and down-and-outs. But nowadays it's even better. To add to the home grown lunatics, we have thrown the gates open to the world, and they have sent us nothing but their best. We have Africans preaching the gospel on street corners - after us sending out money and missionaries for years to convert them! And Lithuanians and Albanians doing our bricklaying and labouring! Talk about bringing coals to Newcastle!

It is a truth universally acknowledged that a man in possession of a few bob, must be in need of a bookmaker and a pint. I was in just such a position that Thursday as I strolled down Capel Street. I took a sharp left into the premises of J P Twomey, Turf Accountant, and sidled up to the boards on the wall which give information on the day's runners and riders.

I saw that a horse called Gorgeous Julie was running in the 4.40 at Brighton. I had taken several financial interests in this animal's previous career, but so far without return. But we learn from our mistakes, and the earlier disappointments had taught me much. For example, I had learned that running her over seven furlongs on a right handed track was no good. Into the last furlong, her interest in the contest seemed to fade, her thoughts probably turning to oats and hay. She also seemed to have a steering problem, and you could see the jockey struggling to keep her from veering off into the middle of the track. I suspected that the cause of it was that her left legs were shorter than her right. But Brighton asks horses only to swing downhill to the left, and the 4.40 needed her only to stick to the business for six furlongs. I also had a feeling that the sea air might have a bracing effect on her. All the signs were good, and the TV screens told me that the bookies were not up to speed with my thinking. They were foolishly offering fourteen to one for a win. This was worth ten euro of Frankie's money any day, so I put the cash down, and retired next door to Burke's to watch the action.

I remember my father telling me a story about him and his pal Timmy Cronin getting a tip on a horse from someone who had something to do with a stable near Newbridge. This was the proverbial 'sure thing' at a big price, but they hadn't got a make between them. Timmy was wearing a good wool suit in reasonable condition, and they had an idea. The two of them went into the public toilet in Stephen's Green, and Timmy retired to one of the cubicles, handing his suit out to me Da, who brought it around to Silverman's the pawnbrokers, who advanced ten bob on it. This was put on the horse to win, and to make a long story short, the animal obliged. The winnings were collected, the suit redeemed, and the anxious Timmy released from his confinement. They went out on the lash on the strength of it, and weren't seen again for days.

I had less luck with Gorgeous bloody Julie. All was well coming into the last, with her nicely in the slipstream of the leader. The jockey put his foot on the accelerator and away she went. Money in the bank I thought, when out of the seaside mists some other thing emerged with a rocket up its arse. Julie lost it on the line by the width of a nose hair – possibly pausing to pose for the photograph, being female.

I had come into Burke's to watch the race, and I had a pint to observe the local customs, and to contribute to the establishment's overheads. I got talking to the barman, who turned out to have gone to the same school as me. We were reminiscing about the thugs and sadists who passed for teachers in our day. In particular we were remembering one saintly man of the cloth known, not affectionately, as 'The Blister' for his prowess in raising them. This man had heard a calling from on high to come and knock the bejasus out of Dublin's youth, and he did it with commendable zeal. We swapped stories of this great educator's colourful career, in between my new friend serving other customers.

When Dubliners start telling stories, it becomes a competition, where you lose if the other guy gets to tell two in a row. So with one story leading to another, the first pint was soon gone. I reasoned that a bird never flew on one wing, so I had another. That went the way of the first, and I thought it might be interesting to see a bird flying on three wings. I got the last word in with an amusing story about the Blister throwing some argumentative student of history through a window. This young fool had put forward the blasphemous view that the English can't have been all bad. If there was any truth in that crazy idea, the Blister hadn't heard it, or wasn't having it. Don't worry – we were only on the first floor, and there was a bicycle shed outside for the scholar to bounce off.

\* \* \*

In spite of the time spent in Burke's, I arrived home in plenty of time for the tea, pausing en route to pick up the Evening Herald from the huxster shop around the corner. I was greeted with the disdain that I might get from a receptionist in a five star hotel – you know that you are lowering the tone, but they can't think of an immediate reason for chucking you out. Peggy eyed me up and down with disapproval. She clearly wasn't ecstatic to find herself once again in my presence.

"Hi honey, I'm home!" I said, not giving a shite.

I took up position in my chair, and shook the paper into the reading position.

"Do ya know wha' I'm goin 'to tell ya'?" I said, as Peggy made a nuisance of herself banging plates and cutlery onto the table.

She didn't answer.

"Tha' young fella aroun' in the shop needs a good kick up the arse," I said.

"Is tha' a fact?" she asked, without much interest.

"It is a fact," I told her.

"I asked him if this was the late edition, and he said 'No, it was here on time.' I said to him 'You're so sharp ya'll cut yerself one o' these days.'"

"Did ya now?"

Peggy was less horrified by the collapse of service standards than I was. She moved on to other business.

"Ya haven't forgotten tha' Marian is comin' up for her tea?" she asked.

I was looking at the deaths in the paper.

"Ha!" I said. "Ya'll never guess who's after dyin'."

"I don't know. It's not you anyway."

I detected disappointment.

"Will ya listen to me?" she said. "Marian is comin' up, an' she's bringin' her friend Susan."

"It's oul Matty Maguire. Dead! I wonder what he died of? It jus' says 'at his residence after a short illness.' Residence!

Tha' kip! He prob'ly died as a result o' his residence. Still, the funeral will be good. The Maguires are all great singers."

"Look, I don't care if every Maguire in Ireland is dead," she said. "Marian an' Susan are comin' up. They'll be here any minute, an' I want ya to try an' behave like a civilised human bein'."

She started to sniff like an airport security dog detecting a consignment of contraband.

"Have you been boozin'?" she asked.

"I had one," I said, which was true, if only partially.

She fired a look at me which combined disbelief, contempt and irritation. Not bad considering that she was still busy juggling knives, forks and spoons.

"Will ya make sure tha' my chop is well done?" I asked. "The one ya gave me last week still had a pulse. Only for I had a hold of it with me fork, it would have been up an' out o' here."

The security dog growled, and might have bitten me, but we were interrupted by a sudden tattoo from the door-knocker. She was going to ask me to go and deal with it, but thought better of it. She scurried out, whipping off her apron as she went, shoving it behind my back out of sight. She came back with Marian and some young wan.

Marian wasn't wearing one of her usual superwoman business outfits, which make her look like the Fine Gael member for Dublin South-Central. She was in some sort of jeans and shirt combo bearing brand names, which signify that you have overpaid for the privilege of acting as a free advertising space. Her pal was wearing a Dublin football jersey, track suit bottoms and trainers. She was bouncing around on the balls of her feet, like she was waiting for someone to blow the whistle and start the game.

"Hello, Mrs Flynn. Howya, Mr Flynn. It's great to meet yis," she said.

She shook Peggy' s hand, then grabbed my arm and had a go at ripping it out of its socket.

"Da, this is Susan," Marian said.

"Oh yeah, right, howya," I said, retrieving my arm and checking it for damage.

"How are yis girls?" Peggy asked. "Sit down. Sit down. I've a bit o' dinner on. It'll be ready in a while. Will yis have a cuppa tea while ya're waitin'? Or coffee? Ya can have coffee."

I was wondering where the coffee had come from.

"Tea would be great Mrs Flynn," Susan said.

"Yeah, Ma. Tea, thanks," Marian said. "I'll come an' give ya a hand."

Peggy and Marian traipsed off to the kitchen, leaving me with Susan. I checked that she had sat down, and wasn't likely to attack me again. Satisfied that she was calm, and at a safe distance, I went back to my Herald to see who else had died.

"Is this a picture o' the girls when they were little, Mr Flynn?"

I looked up. She had picked up a photograph that lives on top of the press.

"Yeah," I said. "It's one o' them school ones. Tha's Marian with her sister Angela."

"Oh will ya look at them," she said. "The little dotes. All neat and tidy in their school uniforms."

"Yeah, the pair o' them were always well turned out," I said. "Mind you, only after they'd left a trail o' destruction behind them in the bathroom. Youse women are all the same. Sure even with jus' meself an' herself in the house, the bathroom above is full o' lotions an' potions – nearly every bit of it hers. Wha' it's all for beats me. I only have me razor an' me toothbrush. When I wash me hair, I use a bit o' Persil."

Susan laughed.

"Oh, Mr Flynn! Ya do not! Persil!"

"Tha's a fact," I said. "It gives it a lovely shine. Give it a go yerself."

She didn't say whether she would take up the suggestion.

"Ya're prob'ly right about the bathroom, Mr Flynn," she said. "Sure Marian never picks up a towel or a..."

Marian came back from the kitchen carrying a tray of cups and accessories.

"How many sugars, Da?" she asked me.

"I don't know," I said. "Ask yer Ma."

Peggy was bringing up the rear, carrying a plate of biscuits.

"Give him two sugars, an' a dollop o' arsenic."

Susan laughed, I hope out of politeness, rather than thinking that Peggy was funny. I could do without Peggy's humour taking hold.

"So tell us Susan," I said. "How do ya make a crust yerself?"

I was just making conversation. I was less interested in this young woman's doings, than I was in the contents of Peggy's handbag.

"I'm a vet, Mr Flynn," she said. "I work in a practice over near Firhouse. We get the lot - everything from hamsters to horses."

"Susan is very dedicated, Da," Marian said. "Even on her day off she's ringin' in to check up on some sick rabbit."

"A career girl like our Marian then, are ya?" I asked. "Not married with a gang o' chisslers or anythin'?"

"No, not married, Mr Flynn," she said.

"An' are ya livin' out tha' way?" I asked.

"Well, I used to live in Rathmines, but now o' course..."

Peggy butted in: "Frank, will ya stop interrogatin' the girl. I'm sorry Susan. He thinks he's Gay Byrne."

"Gay Byrne, me arse," I said.

Marian had been sitting, lapping up her tea. She got up and stood beside Susan.

"Da, tha's wha' me an' Susan came to tell ya," she said.

Peggy knocked her cup over.

"Oh God, look wha' I'm after doin'," she said. "I'll get a cloth."

"Leave it, Ma," ordered Marian. "Look Da, Susan is livin' with me in the apartment now."

I didn't think Marian needed to take in a lodger, but if she wanted to share with a pal, that was up to her. If you said that I didn't give a fiddler's fart on the issue, you wouldn't have been far wrong.

"Grand," I said. "Tha's grand."

Susan opened her mouth to speak, but Marian got in in front of her.

"Da, I don't think ya understand. Me an' Susan are LIVING TOGETHER."

The three of them were staring at me like they were expecting me to do a trick or something.

"Yeah," I said. "I suppose it's company for ya. I often thought ..."

"No, Da," Marian was nearly shouting now.

"Me an' Susan are a couple. Like you an' Ma. We are makin' our lives together. Da, we are in love."

Did you ever notice that time goes into slow motion, when things that you are not expecting to happen, go and happen? Like the time when I fell into the canal, or when I was cutting a slice of bread, and the knife slipped and nearly cut the thumb off me. I remember seeing the blood, and it being like one of them out-of-body experiences. I was quite calm, cool and collected as I assessed the situation, and formulated my plan of action - which was to roar for Peggy to come and sort it out. It was the same then with Marian. There we were drinking tea and talking about rabbits, and the next thing she's telling me that she's a whatyamacallit.

The three of them were still staring at me.

"I knew there was somethin' up," I said. "I knew it."

"Ya knew feck all," Peggy said.

"How long have you known about this carry-on?" I asked her.

Susan decided to put her tuppence-worth in.

"Mr Flynn, I'm sure that it must be a bit of a surprise, but when you've got used to the idea..."

"Look Susan," I said. "Ya seem like a grand girl, an' you an' Marian can be great friends, but this..."

"No, Da!"

Marian was definitely shouting now, like I was in another room.

"Me an' Susan are a couple. Jus' like you an' Ma. We are lovers. We share the same bed. We even..."

"Marian!" Peggy interrupted. "Thanks. I think we understand. Don't we Frank?"

"No, we bloody well don't," I said. "We don't feckin' understand at all. This sort o' thing might be all the rage over in Ballsbridge an' in feckin' Rathmines. Nothin'd surprise me abou' the goin's on over there, but in this part o' the world, we have different standards. I have a position to uphold."

"Wha' position would you be upholdin', unless ya're talkin' about hangin' onto the counter in Magowan's," Peggy put in unhelpfully.

I ignored her and carried on.

"Tha' sanctimonious oul cow next door will have her knees red raw prayin' for us," I said.

"Feck her," Peggy said. "Feck them all. Not tha' it matters wha' any o' them think, but we're movin' away from this bloody place, so I don't give a damn about their opinions."

Peggy paused to catch her breath.

"Ah Frank," she said. "Won't ya give the girls yer best wishes?"

"No, I feckin' well will not," I said, mystified at her attitude. "Will ya get a grip on yerself, woman? The next thing is ya'll have us crackin' open the champagne, an' singin' 'Here Come the Feckin' Brides."

Susan piped up again: "Why don't we all calm down? We can talk about it over dinner."

"I don't want any dinner," I said. "I'm goin' down to Magowan's."

"Bu' the chops are nearly ready," Peggy said. "An' it's Thursday. Ya never go out on a Thursday."

I got up and made for the door.

"I don't care wha' feckin' day it is," I said. "I'm goin' out, an' tha's tha'."

And apart from tripping over bloody Bertie, which spoiled the dignified exit I had hoped for, that is exactly what I did.

★ ★ ★

Betty Magowan welcomed me, as I came in to dock at a stool by the bar.

"There ya're Frankie. The usual is it?"

I confirmed that it was, and that I would have a small Jemmy alongside it.

No one has antennae like Betty Magowan. She is like Sherlock Holmes when it comes to spotting the smallest trace of evidence, and deducing the whole story. She might see a complete stranger at the end of the bar and say: "Do ya see yer man? I'd say tha' he used to be in the merchant navy, he's got piles, and a dog called Monty." And she would be right.

Although I was my usual debonair self, she sensed immediately that all was not well with Frankie.

"It's not like you to be in on a Thursday," she observed.

"No," I said. "But didn't the heroes o' 1916 fight an' die for our right to go out whenever we damn well wanted?"

"They did indeed. They did indeed", she agreed. "But everythin's alright is it?"

"Couldn't be better," I said. "Right as raindrops!"

Betty was not having it, and we both knew it. She stood in front of me polishing a glass, waiting for me to tell all in my own time. It was still early, and the bar was empty. Most of the regulars wouldn't be in for hours yet.

"Can I tell ya somethin' in confidence, Betty?" I asked, looking around to make sure there was definitely nobody within hearing range.

The pub is like the confessional, and a good barman does everything a priest would except dispense forgiveness. Peggy leaned over the counter, and lowered her voice.

"Wha's the matter?" she asked.

"Betty, I'm after gettin' an awful shock," I told her. "An awful shock altogether."

She was instant concern: "Oh God - a bereavement is it?"

"Ah no," I said. "Nothin' like tha' - but tha' reminds me about Matty Maguire - he's after dyin'."

"Yeah, I saw it in the Herald," she said. "The Lorda mercy on him."

Having dealt with the matter of Matty's demise, I now had her full attention.

"It's our Marian," I said. "The younger one."

"Yeah?" she asked. "Wha's wrong with her?"

I leaned further over the counter, so that we were nearly cheek to cheek.

"She's after goin' quare," I said.

"Wha'?"

Betty seemed confused, so I elaborated.

"Quare! Gay! A fairy lady! On the bus goin' the wrong way!"

I could hardly have been any plainer. Betty seemed to be choking on something. She poured herself a glass of water, and had a swig to get herself right.

"My God, Frankie! Wha' happened?"

"Nothin' much", I said. "She barrelled into the house this evenin' with this other young wan, an' the two o' them announce tha' they're a couple. Like Fred an' bleedin' Ginger."

"Or Morecambe and Wise," Betty added, showing that our two minds were as one.

"Exactly – now ya have me," I said.

I felt better that I had told her. 'A problem shared is a problem halved' has always been my motto.

"So wha' did ya say?"

"Sure wha' could I say?" I said. "I took it all very calmly, an' maintained me composure. But I had to come out o' the house, in case I said somethin' I might regret."

"Good man, Frankie," she said.

"I mean to say - it's not natural, is it?"

"Oh, I dunno", she said. "Ya see it all in this game. My view is tha' everyone is equal in the eyes o' the Lord, an' in Magowan's pub. Ya have to keep an open mind. As long as they pay for their drink an' behave themselves, I don't concern meself with their private arrangements. Anyway – if ya haven't tried it, don't knock it, Frankie. Do ya know wha' I mean?"

She winked at me. Surely she wouldn't, I thought, and dismissed the idea. No, not Betty Magowan! One shock in a day was enough.

\* \* \*

When I arrived back chez nous, Peggy was on her own. Luckily enough she was still up, because I had forgotten my key in my hurried exit. But she didn't bother with her usual guff about how all the trouble in the world is caused by me going out without a key. In fact she said very little, but I knew that there would be no escape from some form of spirited conversation, when she had worked herself up to it. Resigned to whatever fate had in store, and fortified by grain and spirit, I opened proceedings.

"Wha' time did Marian an' tha' other young wan go off?" I asked.

"Her name is Susan," Peggy said. "An' she's a very nice girl. Jaysus Frank, ya coulda bin a bit more civil to them."

"How long have you known about this?"

I put on my best barrister for the prosecution voice.

"Not tha' long, but tha' doesn't matter."

"I had a feelin' there was somethin' goin' on," I said.

"Don't be ridiculous. You! I could give ya yer dinner stark naked, painted blue an' with a feather up me arse, an' ya wouldn't notice."

"Well, I don't know wha' to make of it. I don't, an' tha' a fact," I said.

"Sure how would ya? How would ya know about anythin', when yer only view o' the world is through the bottom of a pint glass?"

I wasn't having that.

"I know wha's goin' on," I said. "I watch the telly. I read the paper. I'm out an' about every day." I tapped my nose. "There's not much that gets past Frankie Flynn."

"Go away outta tha'. If ya were any more narrow-minded I'd be able to pick me teeth with the top o' yer head."

"There was never any o' tha' in the Flynns," I said.

"Oh, we're not goin' to have the lecture on the royal an' noble clan o' the Flynns, are we? The aristocrats o' Cork Street. A shower o' robbers an' rapists, more like."

"My father was a very sophisticated man," I said.

"Don't be ridiculous," she fired back.

"He was," I said. "There was nothin' he didn't know. I've seen money changin' hands on his word alone. They'd say:

'wait til Jimmy Flynn comes in – he'll settle it'. An' he could speak Russian."

"Ah, for feck's sake - he could hardly speak English."

Peggy was never my father's biggest fan.

"He could," I said. "He learned it off a sailor. A Russian sailor."

I thought that would put the thing beyond doubt, but it did not.

"A Russian sailor!" she snorted. "An' who in the name of all tha's good an' holy would he be talkin' Russian to?"

"Well, to anybody," I said. "Sometimes the lads would ask him how to say somethin' in Russian, an' he'd tell them."

"God help us," she wailed. "I sometimes wonder if ya really can be as thick as ya make out. Tell me tha' it's a game ya're playin'. Please!"

I picked up the Herald. I had been interrupted earlier in the evening, and hadn't been able to finish it. Peggy stayed where she was. It seemed that she wasn't finished with me either.

"Marian an' Susan have invited us over to the apartment for lunch on Sunday," she said. "Angela an' Tommy are comin' too."

I saw the trap immediately, and took avoiding action.

"Tha' sounds like a very fine gatherin'," I said. "Ya can leave me somethin' on a plate before ya go."

Peggy got to her feet, and pointed a finger into my face, in case I might think that she was talking to somebody else.

"You listen to me, Frank Flynn," she said. "Ya're comin' over to yer daughter's home on Sunday. Ya'll behave like a respectable adult for once in yer life. An' another thing - ya can get yerself down to town tomorrow an' buy a new suit. Tha' blue one is a disgrace."

"Wha?" I said. "There's nothin' wrong with tha' suit. There's plenty o' wear left in it."

"Ya bought it for your Georgie's weddin'. Tha' was years ago. The bloody thing is threadbare. I wouldn't mind, but it doesn't even fit ya anymore. So ya can go an' get a new one before Sunday, an' not be makin' a show o' me."

"Pigs'll fly," I said.

"They will," she agreed.

With that rare moment of agreement, she banged off upstairs, and peace rained down on me at last like a warming soup.

# 5. Sickness

On the Saturday, I went to Matty Maguire's funeral, and it was great. The church was jam packed. The priest spoke movingly about Matty's devotion to Jesus, and about how great it was that the two of them were together now in heaven. He said that the big turnout showed how loved Matty was, and how much he would be missed by his friends and family. He must have got his notes mixed up with someone else's, because Matty hadn't been through the doors of the church in years, and probably wouldn't have been there then, only for they had put him in a box, and nailed the lid down. As for him being missed, I guessed that would be by all the people he owed money to. Even Mrs Matty looked like a woman who had already gotten over the worst of her grief.

Dubliners love a funeral, and it doesn't matter whether the departed was the greatest bollix ever to draw breath. We will still go to celebrate the sad or not-so-sad loss, and to have a few scoops on the strength of it.

Funerals are much better than weddings. You can wear what you like. You can come and go when you want. You don't have to bring a present. And there are no bloody photographs.

The priest said that Jesus was waiting to welcome Matty back into his heavenly kingdom. If so, Jesus was in for a shock. I could not imagine how he would even recognise the fat fecker. Maybe Saint Peter makes announcements as you come in, or organises name badges. I could see Matty waddling through the Pearly Gates and Jesus saying: "Matty, will ya look at the state o' ya. Ya left here a pink little baby, and ya come back lookin' like a sack o' shite. Did ya never even think o' tryin' a salad? If ya're plannin' on sittin' at the right hand o' the Father, we'll have to get half a dozen skinny saints to move out o' the way."

Matty was planted in Glasnevin Cemetary with all due honours. On the way, the convoy paused outside his residence, as is traditional, but I thought that it would be better to have stopped outside all the pubs in the Daymo, because Matty spent more time in them than he ever did at home.

If you have to be buried, Glasnevin is as good a place as anywhere. It is now a proper leisure attraction. There is a museum, a shop, a restaurant, and guided tours of the graves of all the great Irish men and women, who put the country into the state that it is in today. May the Lord forgive them and have mercy on their souls. My advice is to go there now, while you can still enjoy the facilities, before you are booked in on a one-way ticket.

We all went back to Kinsella's in Dorset Street. The Maguires had laid on the necessary soup and sandwiches, and they stood us a few pints to toast Matty. After that we were on our own, which was fair enough.

There's a certain decorum that has to be maintained at funeral gatherings. You can't go barging in and giving them your Tom Jones straight off. Even though you have been to the church and the grave yard, you still have to sidle up to the chief mourners, and mutter something about being sorry for their loss. Then you speak quietly with whatever of your cronies that might be there assembled. The conversation should be about the recently departed, and what a fine fellow he was, or at least that he probably wasn't the worst. No talk of football or other routine business is allowed at this stage of the proceedings.

After a pint or two, things start to lighten up. The noise in the room grows. Kids get bored and start to run around, smokers nip outside for a fix, and there is the odd burst of laughter that still gets choked off out of politeness.

Eventually someone will start up the singing. The first couple of songs will be sad ones in deference to the occasion. But Dubs can't put up with misery for long, and they will be followed in short order by a few livelier ones. The organisation of all this takes on a life of its own. There is no need for any master of ceremonies, and everyone knows what's what. You can see the usual suspects being lined up, as though by some invisible force.

"Eh Frankie, will ya sing 'Whiskey in the Jar' like a good man?" someone asked me.

"Ah no," I said. "It's a bit early yet."

"Fair enough," the somebody said. "But ya'll sing it in a bit?"

"I will," I said.

It's usually considered bad form for the wife or husband of the deceased to sing anything too cheerful - especially if it gets people up dancing. However, there are exceptions to every rule, and Matty's do was a case in point. Mrs Matty, aka Bridie Maguire, has a fine contralto voice, and it would have been a shame if she didn't do something. Her repertoire is full of barnstormers from the Hollywood musicals. After she had had enough vodka and tonic poured into her to float a medium-sized boat, she was persuaded to let rip with 'I'm just a girl who can't say no'. She said afterwards that maybe it was too much, with poor oul Matty hardly cold in his grave, but we assured her that it was what he would have wanted.

I did 'Whisky in the Jar,' 'Strangers in the Night,' and 'Monto', and I would have done 'Delilah' as well, only Mickser Maguire (Matty's brother) got in before me with it.

We kept it going nice and steady through the afternoon and into the late evening. The Maguires put out plates of sandwiches to keep our strength up, so I didn't have to go home for Peggy's meat and two veg. It was as fine a send-off as any man could hope for. All Matty's family and friends were there – even friends who couldn't stand him. Everybody agreed that the Maguires had done a great job, and could be proud of themselves, even though we knew that normally the lot of them would live in your ear, and not pay the rent.

★ ★ ★

The first thing I was conscious of the following morning was Peggy's sweet voice.

"This room stinks to high heaven. It's like a brewery in here."

She was dressed in what I took to be her Sunday best. She had probably been up for ages, doing whatever it is she does in the early morning. She flung all the windows open as wide as they would go. I groaned and hid under the duvet, hoping that she might feck off, after she felt that she had annoyed me enough.

"Are ya comin' over to Marian's or not?" she asked.

"Not," I said.

"Right," she said back - making it sound like a threat – like I would have only myself to blame for whatever dire consequences she might inflict on me.

She banged around the room for a bit, and after saying 'right' again, she exited, hopping the door off its frame. A minute later, the front door was also slammed in a thorough and meaningful way, and I sensed the shadow of her broomstick crossing the window.

Some considerable time later, like Ratty's pal Moley, I poked my head out into the light. I felt strong enough to push myself to the vertical, and to get the day under starter's orders. After attending to the ablutions, I climbed into shirt, trousers and accessories, and ambled downstairs. Bertie wagged his tail to salute the Master's arrival, and looked at me hoping that a stroll might be on the cards.

"Not now, Bertie oul son," I told him. "If ya need the jacks, ya'll have to do it in the garden."

Knowing that my word on these matters is final, he put the tail away, and lay down with his head on his paws. He fixed me with one of those looks – reproachful, I think you might call it – designed to make the average dog owner feel like a louse. But I am not a man to be psyched out by a dog - even a pedigree one - so Bertie stayed ignored.

There was no sign of any meal left for me, and I knew exactly what she was at. She thought that she would starve me into submission, and that I would come over to Ballsbridge begging for nourishment. Well, she had another thing coming. My motto is 'look after number one, because no one else will.' A trawl of the fridge and the kitchen presses produced sausages, rashers, black and white pudding, eggs and tomatoes. With tea and half a batch loaf, I had the makings of a feast.

I slung the fryables onto the big black pan with a wedge of dripping, and fired up the gas. In a few minutes it was all sizzling nicely, and there was that lovely smell that signals that the full Irish is in production. If Peggy Flynn thought that she was indispensable, she was very much mistaken. I don't know what the Queen of England gets for her breakfast on a Sunday, but whatever it was wouldn't have beaten this. I ate every scrap, except for half a sausage which I offered to Bertie, but he was still sulking about the walk, and he turned his nose up at it.

The weather being fine, I thought that a gentle stroll to Magowan's, followed by a libation or two in the company of friends and neighbours, would be the thing. The rest of the planned programme of activities was to return to a peaceful home, and watch the football on the telly for the afternoon. As far as I was concerned, God was in His heaven and all was right with the world. If Bertie had given me a loan of his tail, I'd have wagged it.

★ ★ ★

Later in Magowan's, I was telling Betty about Matty's funeral when I felt the first twinge. Well, it was more of a right royal kick in the knackers, than a twinge. It settled down, and I was okay for a bit, but then it came back with reinforcements. Only that I was braced up against the bar, I would have fallen off the stool onto the floor.

"Are ya alright, Frankie?" Betty asked.

"I'm not sure," I said, because I wasn't. "I feel a bit queasy. I was alright earlier. It might be the pint."

"There's nothin' wrong with the pint," Betty said.

I should have recognised the sound of a warning shot across my bow, when I heard it. The pain must have done something to my brain. Telling a publican of Betty's standing that there's something wrong with her pints, is like telling a fond mother that her kids are ugly. A proud woman will tend not to take it well. But I was not in my right mind, so I carried on regardless.

"It tastes funny," I said. "When was the last time ya cleaned out the pipes?"

"Listen here to me now, Frankie Flynn," she said. "Them pipes are as clean as the barrel of a gun. If you think tha' ya can come in here…"

I don't know what she went on to say, because my insides had turned into Vesuvius, and an eruption was imminent from any or all available orifices. With one hand over my mouth and the other trying to hold the cheeks of my arse together, I ran for the jacks.

I will draw a veil over what happened next, as you won't want to hear the painful and undignified details. I will just say that at one point I thought that I was going to die, and soon after I thought that I was never going to die. I was barely able to drag myself back out to the bar, I was that weak. I felt cold and clammy, and hadn't the energy of a half-starved kitten. I got back and collapsed onto a chair by the wall. I might have been moaning or crying out. I can't remember exactly.

Betty was not looking too sympathetic, but she could not ignore a customer passing away in front of her. People would talk, and it might be bad for trade. She came out from behind the bar, over to where I was lying in a heap. A circle of entertainment seekers had gathered around me.

"How are ya feelin', Frankie?" she asked.

"Peggy said tha' I'd get dysentery in this bloody place," I said - the lunacy not having left me. "She did. Dysentry!" I added for effect.

Peggy snorted like a horse, ready for the charge.

"Are ya goin' to tell me how ya are, or are ya not?" she asked me again.

"I'm not great," I said. "It's like there's a rusty knife cuttin' through me."

"Ya don't look too hot, right enough," she said, not making me feel any better.

"Will I call ya an ambulance?"

"Do not," I said, alarmed. "They'd only take me to the Northside, an' ya'd want to be in the full o' yer health before chancin' tha' place. I never heard o' anyone goin' in there tha' didn't come out worse."

"Dr Lawlor, then?" she asked. "Will I call Dr Lawlor?"

"Don't be ridiculous," I said. "Tha' eejit couldn't cure a ham."

Betty looked exasperated, and happy to abandon me to whatever the Good Lord might have in mind. She was turning to go back to her duties.

"Hold on. Hold on," I said.

I fished around in my wallet, and found one of Marian's business cards, which had her mobile number on it.

"Here," I said. "Ring Marian an' ask her to come an' bring me home out o' here. An' tell her to hurry, if she wants to see me again in this life."

Betty went off and made the call. I don't know how long it was before the cavalry arrived. I stayed where I was, wondering if each breath I took would be my last. The lads around me weren't sure how far they could take the piss, in case I did die. Miley Magee even offered to buy me a brandy, but I was so bad that I said no.

When Marian arrived, she had the whole entourage in tow - apart from Tommy who had cried off the lunch with something from his own extensive repertoire of ailments. They had been in the middle of eating, when Betty called. Angela told me afterwards that Susan was a bit of a cordon blue cook, and had made them roasted duck in a lime sauce, with courgettes and sautéed potatoes. I was pig sick that I had missed that, I don't think! Marian is well used to that kind of fodder, but Peggy and Angela like their potatoes boiled or chipped as God intended. So, they were happy enough to have an excuse to throw down their knives and forks, and get out of there.

By the time they arrived, I was sort of lying across three chairs. By now the clientele had decided that I would probably survive, and that slagging me would be fine, and might even be good for me. When Marian arrived in with Peggy, Angela and Susan, there was a general chorus of 'Nee Naw, Nee Naw.'

In fact, Angela led the way - the others couldn't get past her.

"Da, wha's wrong with ya?" she asked, sounding gratifyingly concerned.

"It was a bad pint, love," I moaned, "a bad pint."

If this was to be my last breath, I wanted to be sure to finger the perpetrator.

"It was not a bad pint," shouted Betty from behind the despatch box of her pint pumping station.

"He keeps sayin' tha'. There's nothin' wrong with the pints. There's plenty have drunk pints in here today, an' there's not a bother on any one else."

She addressed the congregation: "Has anyone had a problem with their pint?"

Everyone looked too terrified to speak. Larry Edwards thought of something funny to say, but held on to it when he caught Betty's eye. Feeling suitably vindicated, she rested the case for the defence.

"Now!" she said, making it sound like 'game, set and match.'

"Let me have a look at ya, Mr Flynn," Susan said, all business-like.

Dr Dolittle rolled up her sleeves, and before I could tell her to feck off, she was prodding and poking me like she was examining an expectant heifer.

"Does it hurt here?" she wanted to know.

I yelped.

"What about here?"

I yelped again.

"Is it a sharp, or a dull pain?" she asked, and like an eejit I was trying to answer her.

"It hurts all over," I said, "an' you're not helpin' by kneadin' me like a lump o' dough. Anyway, wha' am I talkin' to you for? I'm not plannin' on runnin' in the feckin' Derby."

Marian stuck her oar in: "Da, will ya listen to Susan? She knows a lot about anatomy an' physiology." And I heard her adding to the others: "...and there won't be much difference between his insides and a rat's," but I hadn't the strength to tell her off.

"I don't think it can be his appendix, or an ulcer," Susan said.

"Have ya eaten anythin' today, Mr Flynn?" she asked me.

"He won't have," Peggy said. "I didn't leave him anythin'."

She didn't show the slightest embarrassment or remorse that she had gone out, and left her husband with nothing to eat. I called up my last reserves of strength to tell the world of my self-reliance in the face of this neglect.

"No," I said. "Ya didn't. I made a fry-up meself."

Even in my weakened state I felt a swelling of pride. I expected Peggy to be impressed, and maybe even abashed, but she just laughed.

"You!" she said. "You made yerself a fry-up? Sure ya can't even slice bread withou' nearly cuttin' yer arm off!"

"Wha' was in it, Mr Flynn?" Susan wanted to know.

Here was I, trusting my life to this horse doctor, and she didn't even know what was in a fry up.

"Wha' do ya think was in it?" I asked. "Sausages, an' rashers an' eggs."

"An' was it all cooked properly?" she asked.

"O' course it was. Didn't I tell ya tha' I cooked it meself."

Susan looked at the others in what I took to be a meaningful way.

"I think the best thing is to get him home," she said. "Can ya stand, Mr Flynn?"

"I'll try," I said. "I'm a bit wobbly."

"Come on, Da", Angela said, manoeuvring herself into position like a heavy-lifting crane. "We'll give ya a hand."

I struggled to my feet, and with Marian on one side, and Angela on the other, I limped towards the door.

"All the best now, Frankie," Betty shouted after me. "We'll prob'ly see ya in durin' the week?"

"Ya will an' yer eye," I shouted back. "I'm not comin' in here to be poisoned – not at your prices anyway."

"Well ya can feck off then, ya cranky oul bastard," she shouted back. "I've enough o' ya. Ya can consider yerself barred."

"Come on girls," I said. "Let's get out o' this dump before we catch somethin' worse."

In the circumstances, with me being half-carried, and Angela barely fitting through the door, I think we managed a dignified exit.

★　★　★

My motto is: 'anything that doesn't kill you makes you stronger.' When you have a near-death experience like I had, it has a profound effect on you.

Kneeling on the floor of the toilet in Magowan's that Sunday, I was in a bad way. If I was not actually breathing my last, then I was certainly throwing up my last. I puked up everything I had eaten for days, a few things I had never eaten in my life, and probably a few body parts. I definitely saw something that looked like a kidney in there. I was like road-kill, splattered across the floor tiles. In my delirium, my whole life passed before my eyes like the trailer for a film. There was my early life under the Christian Brothers' lash, the Christmases, and the days by the seaside. There was my wedding day, the years slaving away for Sinnotts, and celebrating in Mooney's when the girls were born.

I could feel myself being drawn to a bright white light. It was like cotton wool with a bulb in it. I could see my father - the Lord have mercy on him – and he seemed to be calling to me. It was hard to hear him over the noise from the telly in the bar. He didn't seem too pleased to see me.

"Wha' are you doin' here?" he asked.

I said that I had come to join him, and that I would be with him for all time.

"Ya will an' yer arse," he said. "Ya're not due here for ages, an' anyway, ya still have work to do."

He might have said 'much work', and called me 'my son'. I'm not sure. As I say it was hard to hear him over the racket in the bar. But I realised that he was right. I was not done yet. I had a family, and a community that needed me.

With a super-human effort, I turned my back on the white light, and my surroundings swam back into focus. At forehead level, there was the toilet bowl with which I had recently done significant business. Above me were the semi-literate inscriptions on the wall, and the shiny toilet paper that had the same effect on your arse as a sockful of broken glass.

I was explaining all this to Peggy and Angela on the Monday evening, when Marian and Susan arrived in.

"Howya, Da?" Marian asked. "Ya're lookin' a bit better."

"Ah yeah," I said. "I'm grand now, thanks."

"Ya mean, thanks to Susan," Marian said.

"Ah yeah - credit where credit is due," I said. "Thanks very much Susan. Tha' was a great tip with the hot water bottle. An' them banana yoghurts – they were gorgeous. Why do we never have yoghurt, Peggy?"

"Yoghurt!" Peggy said. "I bought yoghurt before an' ya put it in the bin."

She turned to the girls.

"He said I was tryin' to poison him."

"Ya're better at poisonin' yerself, aren't ya, Da?"

This was from Angela who rarely misses an opportunity for lobbing in a barb.

"Wha' are ya talkin' abou'?" I asked her. "It was a bad pint."

"It wasn't a bad pint," Peggy said. "It was them sausages. I was goin' to put them in the bin. They were well past their sell-by date."

"There was nothin' wrong with the sausages," I said. "They only put sell-by dates on to get ya to go an' buy more. It's just a con."

Peggy pointed her finger into my face, like it was a loaded gun.

"They put sell-by dates on to stop feckin' eejits like you from poisonin' themselves."

"It was a bad pint, I'm tellin' ya," I said, standing my ground. "Ya said it yerself abou' Magowan's. I've a good mind to report them to the authorities."

"Will yis listen to him, girls?" Peggy said. "As if the authorities don't know already wha' a kip it is. Isn't tha' wha' attracts them to it. Like flies to shite."

I let it pass. Arguing with Peggy is like wrestling with an octopus in the dark.

"But thanks Susan for sortin' him out," Peggy continued. "Do yis ever come across tha' kind o' thing in yer practice?"

"We do indeed, Mrs Flynn," Susan said. "Animals often eat things tha' they shouldn't, an' the treatment is more or less the same. Get rid o' the offendin' material. Keep the patient warm an' quiet. Give them plenty o' fluids, an' somethin' to put back the salts an' minerals. Tha's where the banana yoghurts come in."

"I'm sure tha' animals don't act up the way me Da did," Marian said.

"Well, sometimes they do," Susan said. "But we have a special way o' dealin' with them."

"Wha's tha' love?" Peggy asked.

"We shoot them."

They all laughed - Peggy loudest of all, of course.

"Tha's wha' we'll do the next time," she said. "You bring yer humane killer Susan, an' we'll put him out o' his misery. It'd end mine anyway."

"Haw, haw, haw," I said. "Very funny! Yis are all very funny indeed."

After the hilarity had died down, Marian asked Angela how Tommy had been since he had declared himself a non-runner at the lunch. Angela lowered her voice - probably a first for her.

"Ya're not goin' to believe this," she said. "He's goin' over to some place in Merrion Square for a colonic irrigation."

Marian and Peggy laughed. Susan put her hand to her mouth.

"Yeah," Angela was nearly whispering now. "He read somewhere tha' it was a great way o' purgin' the system, so nothin'd do him but to have it done. I told him tha' he mus' be mad, but ya know wha' he's like, once he gets an idea in his head."

"Mad is right," Peggy said. "Ya'd have to tie me down."

"Wha's a chronic irritation," I asked.

The three of them turned to look at me.

"It's a colonic irrigation," Marian said. "Ya know ........... a colonic irrigation."

She looked at me, waiting for me to nod or something, but I didn't because I didn't know what she was talking about. She could repeat it all night if she liked.

"Ya know wha' it is, don't ya?" she asked, like she was checking with an Eskimo whether he had ever heard of snow.

I wasn't bothered. I am always happy to learn new things. If you don't know something, you don't know it. There is no such thing as a stupid question in my book, so you have to ask it.

"No, I don't," I said. "I never heard of it. Wha' is it?"

"Ah Jaysus, Frank," Peggy said. "Ya mus' know."

"I said tha' I don't," I repeated.

The four ladies looked at each other.

Marian spoke: "You tell him Susan."

Susan looked uncomfortable.

"Well it's a kind of a purgin', Mr Flynn," she said. "O' the large intestine. They use a warm saline solution."

My face must have been registering that the penny was stuck in the slot. Peggy gave it a shove.

"They stick a hose up yer arse, and turn the tap on," she said.

"Feck off," I said. "Ya're pullin' me leg."

I found this really hard to believe - the only shred of plausibility being that Tommy was involved.

"Tha's wha' they do, Da," Marian said. "It's very popular with the beautiful people. They say it's very good for yer skin – an' tha' it brings a sparkle to yer eye."

"I could see it makin' yer eyes water, right enough," I said.

I shook my head, not for the first time amazed at humanity's ability to do stupid and painful things in pursuit of health and beauty.

"And ya say tha' Tommy's gone in for it?" I asked. "The feckin' gobshite."

Angela leapt to his defence.

"Da! Ya know tha' Tommy hasn't been well. He's jus' tryin' to sort himself out. Tha's all."

"Don't mind him, Angela," Peggy said, always willing to vote black if I say white. "Let's hope it does the poor divil some good."

"I hear tha' ya're movin', Mr Flynn," Susan said.

She probably thought that changing the subject would be welcomed, but I would rather have talked about Tommy and his bowels all night. Careful evasive action was called for.

"We're thinkin' about it," I said.

"The house is goin' on the market next week, Susan," Peggy corrected me, firing off a dirty look that ricocheted off the wall and caught me bang between the two eyes.

"We had the estate agent aroun', and he's done the valuation. He thinks we should have no bother sellin'.'"

Although talking to Susan, Peggy was eyeing me, daring me to disagree. I stayed shtum.

"An' yis're looking at Sunnyside?" Susan asked. "I hear tha' the houses are lovely out there."

She might have worked up credits with F. Flynn in the matter of the hot water bottle and the yoghurts, but they were evaporating now like a puddle in the desert. Peggy filled her in on the delights of Stalag Dublin West.

"Ah yeah, Susan," she said. "They're gorgeous. They all have huge kitchen diners, and the master bedrooms are all en suite."

En feckin' shite, I thought.

"Not like these oul places," she went on. "Sure they're no more than dog boxes."

I felt stirred to defend the honour of the noble and historic Daymo.

"Hold on a minute," I said. "Generations have been raised in these 'dog boxes' as ya call them. Often with ten or twelve kids under the roof."

"It's no wonder tha' they're all midgets then," Peggy heckled, but I continued.

"An' they were well built, these houses. Built to last, they were. They'll prob'ly be protected in a few years, as a valuable part o' the city's history. There might be a bit of wear an' tear on them now, but nothin' tha' a lick o' paint wouldn't sort out."

Peggy wasn't having that.

"A lick o' paint! A bulldozer more like! An' wha' about the location? Eh? We're buried here under the dirt an' noise o' the city. We want to get out to where there's a bit o' fresh air."

I thought of objecting to the liberal use she was making of the word 'we'. I didn't remember signing any power of attorney, but my self-preservation over-ride kicked in, and I kept my trap shut. It was time to escape before I got further mired in her plans. I got up from my chair, and reached for my coat.

"Where are ya goin'?" Peggy asked.

"I'm goin' down to Magowan's for a pint," I informed her.

"Wha'?" she enquired, feigning the sort of disbelief that St Thomas specialised in.

"Five minutes ago, ya were reportin' Magowan's to the authorities. Now ya're headin' down there like a homin' pigeon. An' c'mere - there's also the small matter o' ya bein' barred."

"Barred, me arse," I replied.

"I heard the woman with me own ears. Youse heard her too, didn't yis girls?"

Peggy appealed for witnesses, and a row of heads nodded in confirmation.

"Yeah, yeah, yeah," I said, accepting that the point was technically correct. "Betty is always barrin' people. It doesn't mean anythin'. It's jus' a turn o' phrase."

"I never in all me life," Peggy said.

I left her to reflect on her new learning, if new learning it was. I gathered up coat, cap and currency, and in one bound I was free. Ambling McGowanwards, I realised that there would have to be some nifty footwork to restore the entente cordiale between myself and Betty. I had been dismissive of the being barred issue in front of Peggy and the girls, but I realised that Betty was a professional, with enormous pride in her craft. My stream of insults vis-a-vis her pints would have cut her to the quick. She was also a female, which added further complexity. Nevertheless, I was confident that I would manage my way through the delicate situation.

When the order goes out for charm and diplomacy, it is a well-known fact that you need look no further than Frankie Flynn.

# 6. PJ

Actually getting barred from Magowan's would have been a very serious matter. It is true that there are many other pubs in the Daymo, one or two of which are okay for an occasional extra-curricular or emergency pint. All the others have been taken over by youngsters and other undesirables.

I would not patronise establishments like 'Foxy's' or 'The Inn Place' if the drink was free. The inhabitants of such hellholes either have their noses permanently stuck into their mobile phones, or are watching crap music videos on the telly. The result is that they are as thick as suet, with personalities to match. These wannabe Californians, with their marzipan tans and skimpy clothes, have a command of the English language that would embarrass Bertie. When I hear young Dubs spewing drivel like "Oh my God like … in my whole life … I never saw anything SO amazing like," I want to hit them with something very hard and heavy. Pubs attracting such trade know that allowing for conversation is about as necessary as a tie on a wetsuit. Therefore they have music systems loud enough to melt paint. And then there's the drink! These pubs are really only glorified sweet shops, selling coloured bottles of gloop infused with industrial alcohol. They could not produce a decent pint at the point of a gun. In summary, they are not designed to provide Frankie with the refreshment, peace and intellectual stimulation which he craves, and are therefore not an option.

I was confident that the meeting with Betty would go okay, but on a bad day she could be stubborn. Ideally I would like to have had some intelligence on how the land lay. Most of the time Betty is as mild and mellow as a vicar on wacky-baccy, but sometimes she is a roaring demon, and she would not serve Jesus if he came straight in from a forty-day shift in the desert.

I said a little prayer to Saint Anthony, the patron saint of bacon, asking that he might save mine. I took a deep breath and slipped in to the bar. It was quiet. Betty had her back to me, as she messed around with bottles and glasses, in the manner beloved of bar keeps. I parked myself on a stool, and coughed politely. She turned around, and in a micro-flicker her face dropped from a ten to a one on the welcoming scale.

"Howya, Betty," I ventured.

I probably sounded more chipper than I felt. She looked at me like I was something unpleasant that she had stepped in. But, so far so good - at least she wasn't screaming at me to get out.

"Do ya want somethin'?" she asked.

I thought of diving straight in and ordering a pint, but instinctively I knew that there was some ceremonial to be gone through first.

"I did," I said. "I mean I do. I want to have a word."

"Do ya?" she asked.

"Yeah," I confirmed.

"Well, go ahead", she said, and she stood with her arms folded, waiting for me to say something.

It was like being twelve years old again, in front of the Blister, giving evidence at his enquiry into who had filled all the inkwells with piss.

"I might've said somethin' yesterday," I said.

"Might ya now?"

"Yeah," I said. "But I didn't mean it. I wasn't well. I wasn't feelin' meself. I'm okay now."

"I heard it was sausages," she said, not sounding too pleased that I had been snatched back from the brink of death.

"So Peggy says," I said.

"So it wasn't the pint here then?" she asked.

"Ah no!" I said, trying to do the effusive thing. "Sure the pints in here are like mother's milk."

"So ya'll have one then, will ya?" she asked.

I beamed with gratitude. The prodigal son was back in the fold.

"I will, Betty," I said. "I will. Fair play to ya."

While Peggy was creating the piece of artistic genius that is the perfect pint, a man I had never seen before came in and sat down near me at the bar. He was mid-forties, gawky, tall and thin – a real sniper's nightmare. He had a face that looked like it had been abandoned outside for the winter by an uncaring owner. He wore a suit that flapped around him like washing on a windy day. When he spoke it was confirmed that he was not a local boy. The accent identified him as a son of the soil, probably visiting the great metropolis for a hurling match or similar entertainment. I figured that he must be lost. Magowan's didn't normally attract much in the way of passing trade from tourists or visitors.

"Yerra, that's great weather we're having," he said, or words to that effect. I'm not great on accents. One culchie sounds pretty much like another to me. I can tell Northerners, who make a sound like a drill going through tin, and people from the West who speak in bursts of machine-gun fire.

My guess was that this particular yokel was from the deep south – Kerry maybe - where they sing instead of talk, and it comes out of the side of the mouth, like everything they tell you is a secret.

I agreed with him on the weather, and we exchanged further thoughts regarding the traffic, the news headlines, and - when he had been equipped - on the excellent quality of the pint.

I asked him if he was visiting, and to my surprise he said that he was not, but that he was living locally. The story was that his older sister had died, and left him a little cottage somewhere in the neighborhood. He said that he had only just moved in, and that he was starting into doing it up. He added that he had always wanted to live in this part of Dublin, and I felt myself warming to the man.

"Sure you have great character around here," he said. "This is the real Dublin. Sure where else would a body want to be?"

I asked him if he would not rather live out in one of the new estates, and he passed my test with honours.

"Yerra, not at all," he said. "Sure they're making them houses out of shtring and elastic bands. A half daecent wind would blow the lot away."

I could have kissed his hand. I only wished that Peggy could have been here to listen to him. He told me that his name was P J O'Connor.

"Well Mr O'Connor," I said. "It's a real pleasure to make yer acquaintance."

"PJ, PJ, PJ please," he said. "Everybody calls me PJ. Can I get you another one of those Mr emm?"

"Good man," I said. "Tha's very good of ya. Frank is the name. Frank Flynn, but they call me Frankie."

As we settled into the pints, I was telling PJ about the family, where we were living, and about Peggy wanting to move out to bloody Sunnyside. In fairness to him, he seemed properly shocked at the idea.

"You're not serious!" he said. "But sure why would she want to do that?"

"I'm fecked if I know," I said. "They say tha' far off grass is always greener, an' there'd be an element of tha' in it for Peggy. She's a culch...she's from the country herself, an' maybe she sees herself gettin' back to nature or somethin'. I dunno."

"Well, if it's country life the woman wants, why don't you give it to her where you are?" he asked.

"Wha' do ya mean PJ?" I asked, because I hadn't the foggiest idea what he meant.

"Sure haven't you just told me that you have a garden, man? Why don't you have a go at growing a few veg? Give your lady wife what she's after – the taste of country living, but in the city. And sure you'll have great produce - much better than the rubbish they sell in the supermarkets. Sure all that stuff is tasteless. It's not fit for feeding pigs."

I was slowly warming to PJ's idea. I would save money – Peggy was a dedicated fritterer of the Flynn wealth, and veg was one of the things that she liked to fritter it on. It would be good exercise for me too. Although I was in fairly good condition for a man of my age, I would accept that a little toning would do no harm. I could see it all coming together nicely - a lean and fit Frankie bringing in bushels of carrots and cabbages, and Peggy so delighted that she would forget all about Sunnyside. I could see only one problem, and I shared it with PJ.

"It'd all be new to me though," I said. "I've never bothered much with the gardenin'. To be honest with ya, I wouldn't know where to start."

"Sure ya needn't worry about that, Frankie oul shtock," PJ said, and I think he may have squeezed my shoulder in a comradely way. "I can give you a steer there, boy. Where I was brought up, we grew everything. There's not much that I haven't had a hand in growing, and that's a fact."

He went on to explain some of the secrets of growing things, passed from gnarled hand to gnarled hand down the generations. He assured me that, even though the year was well advanced, there were plenty of winter varieties that could still be planted. Even better, he said that he had a big collection of seeds, and that he would be happy to let me have whatever I might need, free gratis and for nothing.

I don't mind telling you that I was moved. I felt like Jesus when the guy gave him a hand with the cross - except the circumstances were significantly different: Jesus hadn't married Peggy.

"Ya're very good," I said. "Do ya know wha'? I'll give it a go. I will. I'll re-make the Hangin' Garden o' bleedin' Babylon, if it stops Peggy in her gallop."

I shook PJ's hand to emphasise my commitment to the project.

"Betty, give us two more pints like a good woman, will ya," I said.

"Arra, no," PJ said. "No thanks, Frankie. Another time, maybe. I better go and get the tea. I'm going to Agnelli's to get myself some nice fish and chips."

"Oh, I wouldn't do that PJ," I said.

Betty was hovering on the periphery of the conversation.

"Isn't that right Betty?" I asked.

Betty nodded.

"I wouldn't go in there meself," she said.

"Why not?" PJ asked. "Sure their chips are beautiful."

"Aha," I said. "Tha's wha' we all used to say - until we found out about their secret ingredient."

I tapped the side of my nose.

"What do you mean 'secret ingredient'?" PJ asked. "Sure chips are just chips."

"Betty, you tell him," I said, yielding her the floor.

"Well ya see, it's like this," she explained. "The Agnelli's live in the flat over the chipper."

"Yes," PJ said, showing that he was following the story closely so far.

"An' they keep the chips upstairs in the flat until they need them," I added, feeling that this point was important.

"They keep them in the bathroom," Betty explained. "In the bath."

PJ hadn't put the necessary two and two together yet, so I added further details.

"Our Marian worked there the odd time when she was a student, an' she told us. The Agnelli's have a couple o' kids, an' when they need to go – well they go in, an' piss on the chips."

"You're not serious!" PJ looked sick, probably remembering Agnelli chips he had already consumed.

"Tha's the secret ingredient now for ya, PJ," I said. "I'd steer clear if I was you."

"Go home an' boil yerself an egg," Betty advised.

"I think I might do that. Thanks very much."

PJ looked like a man who had discovered new and hitherto unimagined caverns in the depths of human depravity.

"Good night to you both," he said, exiting stage left.

"Who's yer new friend?" Betty asked.

I told her all I knew about PJ, the house his sister left him, and about the great veg growing enterprise.

"I'm not sure where he said tha' he's from," I said. "Bally feckin' somewhere. I don't know. It'd be all the one to me, anyway. Anywhere beyond Finglas is a closed book to me."

"He'll be like an exotic bird o' paradise in here," Betty said.

I laughed more than the remark was worth, as I was still conscious of the need to re-cement myself into Betty's select inner circle.

"Yeah," I said. "I don't know wha' Barney Pugh an' Joe Horgan'll make out o' him. Still, if he helps me to turn the back yard into vegutopia, an' gets Peggy to give up on her house movin' ideas, he'll do for me."

★ ★ ★

You know when you first wake up in the morning? When you're trying to establish the basics, like who you are, where you are, and what might be on the agenda? Well, the morning after meeting PJ, as I tried to figure these things out, I got a horrible feeling that I had lost the use of my arms and legs. I tried to move them, and I couldn't – not an inch, or even one of the new centimetre things. I was sure that I had had a stroke. I had visions of Joe Horgan holding up a pint for me, so that I could drink it through a straw. So it was with enormous relief that I gradually figured out what was going on.

Peggy was piling the contents of the wardrobe and the drawers on top of the bed. I was being buried alive under a mountain of coats, shirts and dresses. I thought that I should remind her of my presence, before I was suffocated.

"Wha' in the name o' God…," I babbled.

In replying, Peggy dropped an armful of brassieres on my head.

"I've started the clear-out like John-Paul said. Ya can get up an' give me a hand."

"How can I get up?" I spluttered, choking on a bra strap. "I can't move a feckin' muscle. Will ya get some o' this stuff off o' me?"

Peggy made a casual swipe, and an avalanche of schmutter toppled onto the floor. I could feel the blood starting to flow into my legs again. I wiggled a few toes to test that all systems were returning to normal. Then I hooshed myself up, so that I could better observe the changes that she had inflicted on the landscape.

"Wha' did ya say tha' ya're doin'?" I asked.

"I told ya. We're havin' a clear-out, so tha' the place might look a bit more respectable for anyone mad enough to think o' buyin' it. Everythin' tha's in tha' pile on the floor is goin' in the recyclin', or the charity shop."

I peered at the heap that Peggy indicated, and shot up several inches. Well, maybe an inch, because I was still caught like a rat in a trap. The pile indicated was mostly made up of my clothes, and included many cherished garments, which had served me well over the years.

"They are not," I objected. "They're my clothes."

"They're rags," Peggy corrected.

"They are not," I said, correcting the correction.

Stimulated by rage, I gathered the strength to kick myself loose of the bed, and went to examine the pile of clothes that Peggy was planning to dump. I started to pick items from it.

"Tha's goin' nowhere," I said, dragging a favourite shirt free. "An' neither is tha'."

A pullover that had enjoyed many nights on my back in Magowan's was saved from a change in career, warming a Romanian goat herder.

In fact, as far as I could see, there wasn't anything in the death-pile that deserved to be there, and I set to re-organising matters to that effect.

Peggy came at me like a full back intercepting a definite goal.

"Put them back where they were, or I won't be responsible for me actions. I've used better rags to mop the floor."

"There's nothin' wrong with tha' shirt," I said. "I wore tha' to Matty Maguire's funeral."

"I know ya did," she said. "Y'ave no shame."

"Wha's wrong with it?" I asked, genuinely puzzled.

"'Wha's wrong with it?'" she echoed. "Wha's not wrong with it? The colour is so faded tha' ya couldn't even begin to guess wha' it started out as. The collar is worn away to nothin'. An' if it ever fitted ya, it doesn't even come close now."

"Ya could sew up the collar," I countered.

The suggestion wasn't well received.

"I'll sew up yer gob."

"An' me pullover," I said. "Ya can pu' tha' back."

"I will not," she said. "I've washed tha' thing, an' washed it, an' I can't get the stains out of it. Wha' do ya be doin' down in Magowan's? Lyin' on the floor, or wha'? Ya'd think it belonged to a four-year-old."

"Ya could throw some o' yer own stuff out," I said. "Most o' the space in here is taken up with your clothes – not mine."

In Peggy's tiny brain every skirt and dress has to have matching shoes, but she's not very good at it. She buys shoes that don't match the clothes that she has, and when they don't, she has to buy new clothes to match the shoes. But they don't. So we end up with wardrobes full of Peggy's gear, nothing of which matches anything else, and she says that she has nothing to wear.

I had only said the thing about throwing her stuff out, when I regretted it. She might throw them out alright, but then she would be off buying more. I decided to take a different tack.

"Wha' if we were to jus' tidy things up a bit?" I wheedled. "Make it a bit neater like. We don't have to throw good stuff away."

I was aware that I was pleading, and was not presenting my usual authoritative master of the house figure. It is hard when you are in your pyjamas, unshaved and un-toileted. Even Napoleon's generals probably wouldn't have taken him seriously, until after he'd had a boiled egg and got his hat on. Peggy sensed the power vacuum, and stepped in.

"Get yerself dressed, and go down an' get yer breakfast," she barked.

I was reluctant to leave her with a free hand in editing the Flynn sartorial collection, but other than resorting to hand-to-hand combat, my only option was a strategic withdrawal. My motto is: 'live to fight another day.' I drew myself up to my full height, gave her a look that told her that I had not closed the file on the issue, and I stumbled off to the bathroom. Again, just for the record, let me point out that although it lacked en-suiteness, the journey took no time at all.

Over the cornflakes, I told Peggy about PJ, and the plan to turn the Flynn estate into a vegetarian's paradise. I was waiting for her to tear the tripe out of the idea, but to my surprise she didn't.

"Well," she said. "John-Paul said tha' we should clear the garden."

"Exactly!"

I was shocked to hear myself agreeing so enthusiastically with John-Paul.

"So ya're goin' to go out there, clear away the jungle, an' plant vegetables?" Peggy asked.

A clearer summation of the facts could not have been produced by a High Court judge. I nodded.

"But ya've never grown anythin' in yer life - other than mould, maybe," she said.

Always the bitter word. I spoke coldly.

"I will be takin' advice an' guidance from an expert. Mr O'Connor has been at it since he was a schoolboy, so it'll be no bother. No bother at all."

She still seemed dubious.

"When are ya goin' to start?" she wanted to know.

I sensed the time-honoured trap. As I explained earlier, I prefer to leave myself leeway in making plans, and not make commitments that Peggy can use to batter me.

"I'll need tools," I said. "A spade, a fork, an' somethin' to hack down them bushes."

"No problem," she said. "I'll go around to the Farrell's in a minute. They have all tha' kind o' thing, and Marie will loan them to me."

Peggy is not one for mulling things over. With her, to think is to act. And so it was that half an hour later, I was out in the back flailing away at generations of undergrowth, like that chap who was trying to find the source of the Nile. If I had any notion that gardening was going to be easy, that notion soon disappeared. This was serious back-breaking work. The autumn sun still had strength in it, and I was like a steak on a grill. I sat down for a second to mop the sweat from my brow.

"When are ya goin' to start?"

Peggy had appeared at my shoulder like Duncan's ghost - which you may recall put Macbeth right off his dinner.

"Are ya waitin' for someone to blow a whistle or wha'?"

"I've been at it for ages," I complained. "I'm entitled to a break ya know. Even galley slaves got a break."

"I can't see tha' ya've done anythin'," she said. "Wha' have ya done?"

I sometimes dream about being presented with an award, and I'm thanking my wife, without whose encouragement, loyalty and respect none of this would have been possible. It's just a dream.

"It's not easy y'know," I said. "You try it."

"I take it we won't be havin' fresh veg anytime soon then?" she sneered.

The woman has the tongue of a viper, that is particularly noted for its sarcastic attitude. Now I knew how the lads must have felt on the Burma railway. I got back onto my feet, and lashed into the undergrowth again, like a Scotsman trying to find a lost fiver.

When Peggy had fecked off about her business, I slackened the pace a bit. I knew if I was too quick in turning this wilderness into a Capability Brown paradise, Peggy would be on to John-Paul, and the house-moving wheels would begin to roll in earnest. I needed time for the idea to germinate with her that this nirvana was not for parting with. Delay was called for. 'Up here for thinking, and down there for dancing,' is my motto.

So I reduced the rate of work into something a bit more public sector. I also reasoned that Frankie was not put on this earth to work like a conveyor belt operative. I am a skilled artisan, with a strong creative flair. My best work takes time. I decided to give another half hour to gentle hacking, and then to slope off for my daily constitutional, which might encompass a pit stop at Magowan's to restore essential fluids.

Abandoning a work assignment which has been set by Peggy is like busting out of Colditz. You have to check that she isn't manning a machine gun post, and that Bertie is asleep, and not likely to give the game away by howling to join in the breakout. Mind you, Bertie is not so fond of coming walkies with me anymore. Being tied up outside Magowan's annoys him at the best of times. It certainly does ever since I left him there overnight once, after I forgot that I had brought him.

On this occasion, Bertie happily ignored me, and Peggy had returned to the business of reducing my wardrobe to a spare sock and a tie for special occasions. I shot through the gate, and legged it for freedom. Each second, I expected the cry of 'Achtung! Halt!' and a shot to ring out, but it didn't. Soon, I was safely in Switzerland (aka McGowan's) in the care of the Red Cross (aka Betty).

# 7. Health

PJ was as good as his word. He was in Magowan's most evenings in the week or two after I met him, and he seemed to take a delight in sharing everything he knew about matters agricultural. By the end of it, I knew more about cabbage varieties and crop rotation than I knew that there was to know.

John-Paul came around to see how we were getting on, but thanks to a just and merciful Lord, Peggy wasn't there, so I gave him the bum's rush. 'Don't call us - we'll call you,' was my message.

Funnily enough I was noticing a slight mellowing in Peggy. She was not being the same menace to my peace and contentment at all. Mind you, I wasn't turning my back on her. A lioness may look all sleepy and cuddly, but she can still take the top of your head off with a swipe.

I was suggesting to her one day that there was a better way to organise the tins and packets in the kitchen cupboards. I started showing her what I meant, taking things out and scattering them all over the worktop. To be honest I couldn't really give a gnat's mickey where stuff went. I was only doing it to get a rise out of her, but it didn't work. Normally such interference would not be tolerated for a second. I would be catapulted out of the room, with a tin of beans hopping off the back of my head. But not that day. She just sat there, sucking on a cigarette, and staring out the window.

"Wha'? Yeah. Do whatever ya like," she said - which threw me a bit. I had been going to suggest an alphabetical organisation, with apples next to aspro, and soap next to soup, and so on. But she had taken the wind out of my sails. I shoved the things back to where I thought I had found them.

"Are ya alright?" I asked her.

"Yeah," she said. "Well no. I feel a bit off."

"A dose o' syrup o' figs is wha' ya need," I said.

I have always found that oiling the machinery works wonders, and if it doesn't, it takes your mind off whatever it was that was bothering you.

"No," she said. "It's not tha'. I might make an appointment an' go an' see Lawlor."

I may have mentioned this Lawlor quack before. He was the local medic, or at least that was what the sign outside his premises claimed. I never saw a diploma, or any evidence that he knew anything about healing the sick. He was a little half pint of a man – all beard, nose and glasses. From my own experience, and from talking to members of the Daymo lame and infirm community, he never once examined anybody. His m.o. was to lurk behind a desk, with a prescription pad in front of him, and a pen in his hand, poised and ready for action.

His solution to everything was some combination of a small selection of pills. He prescribed blue ones, pink ones and brown ones. That's all. Nothing else, ever. In his book there was no condition known to man, that could not be tackled with some combination of the blue ones, the pink ones and the brown ones.

His main purpose in the Daymo was to provide employers, and the Department of Social Protection, with certificates to evidence citizens' inability to get out of bed and go to work. Anyone who was really sick would stick with prayer, or might chance the A&E in the Northside.

Peggy's dealings with the medical profession to date had been confined to her confinements. Therefore, her announcement that she was going to place herself in the hands of the Quack Lawlor surprised me. But if that was what she wanted, that was fine and dandy with me.

As expected, some of the usual multicoloured medication was prescribed, but very unusually for him, he also referred her for a blood test. These things take time, and between the jigs and the reels, with the garden and all, it went out of my mind. It was Angela who reminded me. Peggy was out somewhere, and Angela had come around with the kids. I was reading an article about mulching that PJ had given me. Like her mother, Angela was not easily ignored.

"Jaysus Da, ya could give me Ma a bit more of a hand," she said, derailing my train of thought.

"Wha'?" I enquired. "Wha' are ya talkin' about'?"

"Ya could run aroun' with the hoover," she elaborated. "Or peel a few potatoes. She's not well ya know."

"Yeah, I know," I said. "She's waitin' for the results of a blood test."

"Ya need to look after her," Angela went on, haranguing me. I felt harangued anyway.

"I do look after her," I said, kind of automatically.

Angela turned ten degrees in my direction, like a dreadnought called to battle stations.

"Do ya?" she asked.

She laughed, but it was one of those laughs you do when you think that something is not funny. 'Mirthless' I think they call it.

"Wha' in the name o' God do ya do to look after her?"

Put on the spot like that, I struggled to come up with actual specifics. Mentally I ran through Peggy's job description – cooking, cleaning, ironing, shopping, etc., and I had to put them all down as 'not applicable' as far as my intervention was concerned. Stuck for any better answer, I went for a combination of the old Dunkirk spirit – we're all in this together – and changing the subject .

"Ah, me an' you, Angela," I said. "Sure, we're a pair o' saints, the two of us. You with Tommy, an' me with yer Ma. How is Tommy anyway? Is the stomach still at him?"

I didn't care, but the diversionary tactic did the trick.

"No," she said. "His stomach is grand. It's his back tha's botherin' him now. He's in agony with it. He can hardly move. I nearly had to carry him down the stairs to his breakfast this mornin'."

The lazy malingering little ghet, I thought - and her going to have another babby any minute.

"Ah, God love him," I said. "A bad back is a terrible thing."

"He's a martyr to it, Da," she sympathised. "He's had back trouble for years."

"Yeah," I agreed, thinking that his trouble was getting it off the bed.

"Maybe if he tried a bit o' exercise," I offered, knowing that there was as much chance of him taking exercise, as of him shitting gold bars.

"He couldn't, Da. Rest is the only thing tha' does him any good."

I thought that a good kick up the arse might do wonders for him too, but I kept it to myself.

"But me Ma … will ya try an' give her a hand," Angela said, finding her way back on track. "She really isn't right ya know."

★ ★ ★

I suppose Angela's words must have lodged somewhere in my noodle, because that evening I heard myself saying: "Would ya like to go out for a change? To the pictures maybe?"

There was a silence. I thought that I had screwed up, and that I was about to reap the consequences. I braced myself for incoming shellfire, but all was well.

"Hmm," Peggy said. "That'd be nice. Wha's on the pictures?"

I picked up the Herald and had a look.

"There's a new Harry Potter," I said.

"No."

"Or Planet o' the Apes?"

"No."

"Ya can get all the monkey business ya want at home, wha'?" I gave her an open goal with the gag, but she wasn't in the mood.

"Or there's one tha' looks like a thriller – guns an' car chases, an' tha' class o' thing."

"No."

"I suppose ya can get tha' in the Daymo too, eh?"

"Maybe another time," she said. "I want to see Coronation Street anyway."

Bloody Coronation Street!

"Right ya're," I said. "How've ya been feelin' since?"

"Not great, "she said. "A bit flat."

"Maybe a bottle o' stout would do ya good. I'll bring a few back when I'm out."

I reasoned that even if she didn't drink them, they would not go to waste.

"I'm goin' up to Lawlor in the mornin' for the results o' the blood test," she said. "Will ya come?"

This caused the Frankie eyebrows to shoot so far up the forehead that they nearly flew off the top of my head. Peggy would normally keep such arrangements absolutely to herself, or at a push she might involve Angela.

"Sure," I said. "Yeah, I'll trot along."

It gave me cause for concern though. I was so bothered that I didn't even stay in Magowan's until closing time.

★  ★  ★

The next morning, off we went, the two of us, around to Lawlor's.

The surgery was a one-man band, and as I have explained, the pip-squeak in question hardly merited the description. The premises consisted of a reception area, and Lawlor's private caboose. There was no receptionist. The door from the street was always unlocked when he was in session, so the public could come and go as they pleased. He answered the phone himself, even if he was with a paying customer.

It was obvious that he had never spent a penny on a cleaner or a decorator in all the years that he had been there. The seats were a collection of unmatched plastic school hall chairs that he probably found on a skip. There were piles of old newspapers and magazines, so that you could still read updates on the progress of the Vietnam War. The walls were covered with notices. It seemed that every time he got sent a poster, he stuck it up, and never took anything down.

Rapid turnover and low costs were the key elements of Lawlor's business model. Very little time was allowed for each customer. All it would take to generate a queue around the block, would be for one windbag to go on about their ailments for even a few minutes. Lawlor facilitated speedy processing by sticking to his no examination policy, by allowing patients nowhere to sit, and by rarely saying anything himself.

There was an appointments system, but it was not meant to be taken seriously. The etiquette amongst the clientele was very well developed. You went in to see Lawlor in strict turn, regardless of any appointment time you thought you might have. If you were dumb enough to try to march in to Lawlor in front of people who had been there before you, you would hardly make it to your feet, before you would be back on your arse.

When we arrived, there were about a dozen in front of us. They moved along the conveyor belt at a fair clip, and in no time we were going in to see the great man.

His inner office was even worse than the waiting room. His desk was buried in papers, and the floor was an obstacle course of boxes and parcels. On the walls, posters scrummaged for space with notices. As Peggy was the main attraction, she stepped forward, and I could hang back and look around. I was surprised to spot that there actually was an examination couch, but it served only as a storage shelf for boxes and papers.

Lawlor was in his usual position, crouched behind the desk, like a furry animal with anxiety issues. It was hard to put an age on him. He was certainly well past his prime, if he ever had one. My best guess was that the next time he would see sixty would be on a door. His clothes looked even older than him, probably inherited from his father - who was clearly a bigger man. A first year forensic science student could have given you chapter and verse on his diet, through an examination of his tie. He badly needed a haircut. The lower half of his face was hidden, under what I assumed to be a beard, but looked like he had stopped halfway through eating a rat. A pair of heavy black glasses balanced on a nose, which was half the size again of his head.

As we came through the door, he looked up at us through the hair and the glasses. He seemed surprised to be interrupted, and not too pleased about it, like a man finding strangers disturbing him while he was taking a bath. He clearly had no idea who we were. The fact that we had been on his books for years, and had an appointment for around that time, did not seem to help him.

"Name?" he barked.

His world record for a doctor getting through most patients in a day, was not won by wasting time on idle chitchat.

"Mrs Flynn," Peggy said. "Margaret Flynn." Margaret is Peggy's real name.

"What seems to be the problem?"

The pen hovered, ready for action over blank prescription and certificate forms.

"You sent me for a test," Peggy said. "A blood test it was."

"Ah yes," he said.

He clearly had no recollection of doing anything of the sort. She could have told him that he had sent her up to the zoo to get him a parrot, and he would have said 'ah yes.' He burrowed into a tower of documents, and after a while came out with what I took to be Peggy's results. He stared at a sheet of paper for a few seconds, chewing thoughtfully on his rat. I wondered how complicated it could be to decide on the right combination of blue ones, pink ones and brown ones.

"There appears to be a problem, Mrs …"

"Flynn," Peggy supplied.

"Yes," he confirmed.

"I sent you for a blood test," he told her, and she nodded.

It was great that we were all up to speed on that.

"And the hospital has sent me the results."

I found these insights into the mysterious ways of the medical profession fascinating. I was hugely impressed that he could explain them in a way that even lay people could understand.

"So wha's up, Doc?" I asked, not being able to resist it, and feeling up on the briefing so far, and ready to take in the next piece of information.

He looked at me like he had not noticed me before. There was a short pause, during which he was either considering the ethics of continuing the conversation in my presence, or was trying to remember who he was, and what the hell he was doing there.

"Most of the results are normal," he said eventually. "But there's a problem in the gallbladder. There is evidence of a build-up of what is called biliary sludge."

This was a new one on me.

"Biliary sludge," I repeated, to get the feel of it. "It sounds like someone outta Dickens. 'Mr Micawber, may I present Mr Biliary Sludge'."

I laughed. Pretty good, I thought. Peggy and Lawlor ignored me.

"It is sometimes called biliary sand, or pseudolithiasis," he said.

"Oh right," I said, not wanting to give him the satisfaction of being impressed by his babble.

"It is crystals formed from cholesterol in the bile," he said - making everything as clear as crystals. He started to scribble.

Now we were back in known territory. He handed Peggy a prescription.

"Take one of those three times a day before food," he said. "We'll get you to go back to the hospital to see Mr McCormick. You may need a cholecystectomy."

By the way, I only know that word and the other ones, because I saw them in the consultant's letter afterwards.

"I may need a wha', Doctor?" Peggy asked - she is notoriously nosy.

"It is the removal of the gallbladder," he said.

"Removal?" I asked. "Ya mean tha' they'd take it out?"

"Yes," he said. "That's right. It is a routine surgical procedure."

He was like a man patiently explaining trigonometry to a sheep.

"Bu' will she be able to manage without it," I wanted to know.

"Yes," he said. "It will not be a problem. The bile can flow from the liver to the intestine without any trouble."

"Tha's ridiculous," I said. "Wha's it in there for, in the first place then?"

Lawlor looked like a failed teacher of trigonometry, wondering how to explain the rules of chess to the sheep. He didn't even try.

"Is it a big operation, Doctor?" Peggy wanted to know.

"It is a fairly routine procedure, and Mr McCormick is very experienced," he said. "But all surgery carries some risk. They will explain all that to you in the hospital."

Our time was well past being up, and he wanted us to feck off. When we got to the door, I turned back to him, like

Columbo does when he's leaving the bad guy, and asks the question that catches him out.

"Jus' one thing I wanted to ask ya," I said.

He looked up at me, like he was having an attack of biliary sludge himself.

"Yes?" he asked, and it was not patiently.

"This Mr McCormick fella," I said. "Is he not a doctor?"

"Surgeons are called 'Mister'," he said.

"Ah yeah," I said. "Right, thanks. I thought ya might a bin sendin' her to a plumber!"

I laughed, before falling over something, and Peggy thumped me. Lawlor returned to staring at his pad.

★ ★ ★

That evening there was a full gathering of the Flynn privy council to consider Peggy's health, viz Angela, Marian and now Susan, who had been co-opted. They were trying to outdo one another with sympathy and concern. There was an endless chorus of 'are ya warm enough?' 'would ya like a drink?' 'ya look tired,' 'ya look a bit pale,' 'would ya like to lie down?' I went up to the jacks at one point, to strain the potatoes, and when I came back, they had planted Peggy in my chair – my chair - and they had her feet up on the coffee table! I risked losing a foot any time I put one near that prestigious article of furniture.

"How are ya feelin' now, Ma?" Angela asked.

"I'm grand thanks," Peggy replied. "The pain comes an' goes, but it's fine now."

"Did ya take yer tablet?" Marian wanted to know.

"I did, yeah, before me dinner."

"Will I make ya a cup o' tea, Mrs Flynn?" The horse doctor was not going to be left out.

"Do," I said, "an' ya can make me one as well."

"Tell us again wha' Lawlor said it was, Ma," Marian said.

"Biliary sludge," Peggy said. "In the gallbladder."

Angela had news of the start of an epidemic.

"Like an eejit, I told Tommy abou' it, an' now he thinks he's got it. I said to him: 'Ah Tommy, this mornin' ya didn't even know ya had a gallbladder, an' now ya think tha' yours is banjaxed, an' tha' it's goin' to be the end of ya! Would ya ever cop onto yerself?'"

"Ah, poor Tommy," Peggy said.

Poor Tommy! Ten million sperm, and his was the one to make it through! What the hell were the other ones doing?

Marian, the great organiser, started marshalling the battalions. "Ya're goin' to have to take it much easier Ma. Rest. Keep yer feet up. Me Da can do any cleanin' tha' needs to be done. Can't ya Da?"

I wanted to tell her to mind her own bloody business.

"Ah yeah," I said. "No bother. Leave it to me."

"Ya need to eat on a regular schedule, Mrs Flynn," Dr Dolittle advised. "No skippin' meals. An' make sure that ya eat meals tha' contain very little fat, but plenty o' whole grains, fibre an' calcium."

What that would look like on a plate was anybody's guess. I feared that in future we would be getting our groceries from the pet shop.

"An' ya can forget about the house move until ya're right," Angela said. "It's too much for ya. Da, will ya ring tha' estate agent fella, an' tell him tha' he'll have to wait."

I said that I would take on that regrettable task - trying not to look as deliriously happy as I felt.

"Which hospital are ya goin' to, Ma?" Angela asked.

"The Northside," she said.

My blood ran cold. I knew too many people who had walked in the front door of that place with hardly a bother on them, and had come out the back door in a box. My Uncle Joe, who was as fit as a flea on a butcher's dog, was admitted with a bit of a cough, and a week later he was under six feet of Dublin clay. Once I was sitting in A&E myself, minding my own business. I was there with some kid off the football team, the time when I was head coach of the under tens. A drunk took a dislike to me, and hit me with a crutch. He nearly took the leg off me. That's a fact. The bloody place is dangerous. The only way you would get me in there now, would be by giving me a general anaesthetic in the car park.

"Ya'll need to get yerself transferred away from tha' kip," I said.

"I can't," Peggy said. "Ya have to go to where ya're sent. It's not like choosin' a holiday, ya know. Tha's where Mr McCormick is, so tha's where I have to go."

"No, ya don't," I said. "There are other consultants. Thanks Susan."

Susan had made tea, and handed me a cup. At least I think it was tea. It tasted like a mixture of cabbage water and Agnelli's secret ingredient.

"Tha's not our usual tea, is it?" I enquired, keen to identify and blacklist this muck.

"No. It's camomile," she said, as though this was a small matter. "I thought that it might relax Mrs Flynn. Marian and I quite like it."

Peggy was either happy enough with this slurry, or she was sicker than I thought, and beyond caring.

"Thanks Susan," she said. "Yes, it's very nice. Very aromatic."

"Do you like it, Mr Flynn?" Susan asked.

I felt like spewing a mouthful of it at her, but the Flynns can wear the mask.

"It's prob'ly an acquired taste, like stout," I said, although if there was anything less like stout, I had yet to come across it.

"Do ya know tha' when I started drinkin', I didn't like it," I said.

Although it may be shocking, this was true.

"It's jus' as well tha' alcohol doesn't taste nice," Peggy said. "If it was palatable, ya would've killed yerself years ago."

"But I persevered," I said. "I stuck at it. It must've been months before I got the hang of it."

"Tha's a very inspirational story, Da," Marian said. "Ya're like Scott o' th' Antartic, boldly goin' forward into the frozen wastes o' pints."

Angela joined in the slagging. "One small step for man – one giant step for mankind. Who was it tha' said tha'?"

"Armstrong – the astronaut," Susan said.

"Tha's right," I said. "Louis Armstrong."

I don't know why, but they seemed to think that was hilarious.

"Do ya want us to come with ya when ya go to see the consultant, Ma?" Angela asked.

"No thanks, Angela", Peggy replied. "Ya've enough to be doin' - in your condition, lookin' after the kids, an' with poor Tommy the way he is. An' Marian an' Susan, yis've yer jobs to go to. I'll be fine. It's only a consultation. Yer Da will come with me. I'll be fine."

They looked doubtful, and not too assured that she was in safe hands, and I was less than keen on visiting the disease and pestilence centre of Ireland. But I knew my duty.

"Yer Ma'll be grand with me," I said, trying to sound like Vinnie Jones, but it came out more like Corporal Jones. "But if I've to go into tha' bloody hospital, I'm goin' to scrub meself from head to foot with their handwash."

"Jus' don't drink it, Da. Ya might get to like it," Angela said.

"Thanks, Frank," Peggy said, and I felt better. Nobody could say that Frankie Flynn went awol when the call went out for volunteers.

The camomile tea was stinking the house out, and I needed fresh air.

"I'm goin' out for an hour," I said, and we all knew that an hour was a very rough approximation.

"Bring me back twenty cigarettes," Peggy said.

So much for healthy living, fibre and camomile tea, I thought.

# 8. Welcome

I am a glass half-full man - everyone will tell you that. A born cock-eyed optimist! The cornerstones of my philosophy are a) leave well-enough alone, and matters eventually sort themselves out to everyone's satisfaction, and b) there's no point in worrying about things that may never happen. But this business about Peggy's sludge was getting to me. You sail along in life thinking that everything is grand, and that it's going to stay that way. There are dinners on the table, socks in the drawer, and the presence of your soulmate to keep you on the straight and narrow. Then a ten ton weight drops out of the sky and puts the mokkers on the dinners, socks and everything.

I had no trust in Lawlor, the Northside or this McCormick plumber. As a sportsman, I felt like we were betting everything on a twenty to one shot, with the stable known to be out of form. I searched my brain for some other way to tackle the problem, but came up empty. So, I thought that I would lay the problem before PJ – a man of the world who might have some new idea. And when I arrived at Magowan's, who was sitting in front of a nearly empty pint but that very man.

"There ya're PJ," I said, in case he had been wondering. "Will ya have another one o' them?"

"That's very decent of you, Frankie," he said. "I will thanks."

Betty was hovering like a well-trained butler, and I gave her the details of the mission I wished her to undertake on our behalf: "Betty, two please."

"Coming up," she said, leaping into action like a fireman at the sound of the alarm bell.

She pulled the two pints simultaneously with her right hand, holding the two glasses up with her left. She paused as she reached the three quarters mark, as per the method passed down from one master pintpuller to another. Like the view of Dublin Bay from Howth Head, I could never get tired of the magical sight of the birth of a new pint.

"How have you been?" PJ asked. "And how is Mrs Flynn?" he added, showing the decent caring man that he was.

He knew that Peggy had been on the sick list, and that she had been scheduled to see the quack. I filled him in on the latest developments, and on the concerns that I had, sparing no detail in case it might be important.

"Yerra, I'm sorry to hear that," he said. "Ah sure maybe she won't need the surgery at all."

"Please God she won't PJ," I said. "Please God she won't."

Betty had been multi-tasking, attending to the pint pouring, while tuning in to PJ and me. It is an implied term of the contract between barman and customer, that the the barman may listen in on, and join any conversation involving the customer.

"I hate to tell ya this Frankie, but once they say surgery, tha's usually wha' they mean," she said. "They only tell ya tha' it mightn't be necessary, so tha' ya don't leg it."

"They wouldn't do tha', would they?" I asked, fearing that it was probably exactly what the bastards would do.

"Lawlor says it's up to the consultant, an' he hasn't even seen her yet," I said, without much conviction.

"All them fellas are paid by piecework," Peggy said. "If they don't do the job, they don't get paid. It's like a mechanic lookin' at a car. They're always goin' to find work tha' needs to be done. It stands to reason."

This sounded like gospel truth to me, and I didn't like it. Peggy was not in the first flush of youth. We had probably seen the end of her first, second and third flushes. Any further flushes would need several energetic yanks on the handle. If she was the car that Betty alluded to, you wouldn't even think of fixing her. She would be declared unroadworthy, a danger to the public, and she would be hauled off to the scrapyard. When McCormick had a good look at her, he would find enough work to keep him going for years.

I needed help, and I turned to the oracle.

"Wha' do ya think PJ? Have ya come across this type o' thing before?"

"I have," he said.

Here was hope at last.

"Sure my old mother was a martyr to the gallstones, and she never went next nor near a doctor. She used to make herself a stew of nettle leaves and chickweed. It always settled her."

This was the kind of stuff I wanted to hear. If he had been wearing a cloak, I would have stooped to kiss its hem.

"There are still plenty o' weeds in the garden," I said, thanking my foresight for keeping the clearance operation in low gear.

"You need to be careful with weeds, Frankie," he said. "You have to have the right ones for the job. Any old thing won't do."

The hope dimmed from a hundred, down to forty watts.

"Yeah, I suppose," I said, wondering how I could identify the right weeds, and whether it would be safe to ingest anything that had been subjected to relentless fertilising by Bertie.

"Listen, Frankie," PJ said, seeming to read my mind. "I'll tell you what. I'll take a stroll up to the Phoenix Park tomorrow, and I'll see what I can find for you."

"Ah no," I said. "That'd be too much trouble," I protested - but only a bit.

"It'd be no trouble at all, boy," he said. "Sure, I often take myself up there for a walk. And I need to look for a guesthouse or something for myself. There's a few of them up that way."

"Wha'?" I asked. "Wha' for? Wha's wrong with yer own gaff?"

"Ah, it's the builders," he said. "They've to re-wire the place, and it'll be unliveable in for a few days. I'll have to get out."

"Not at all!" I heard myself saying. "Ya can come an' stop with us."

Well, it was the least I could do, after him offering to go collecting weeds for Peggy.

"Ah no, I couldn't do that," he said. "Sure Mrs Flynn has never laid eyes on me – and the poor woman not well on top of it."

"Peggy'll be delighted to have ya," I said. "Sure it'll cheer her up no end to have someone else in the house. She's always complainin' tha' I don't talk to her. Now she'll have you to natter to as well."

"But would ye have the space?" he asked. "Anyone else I know wouldn't have the room to swing a cat."

"Swing a cat? Ya'll be able to swing a feckin' elephant," I assured him. "There's only ourselves in it, since the girls moved out. We've loads o' space."

"You see I've a lot of old bits and pieces," he said. "Things my father left me. I wouldn't want to leave them in the builders' way, in case they'd be damaged like."

"Bring the lot," I said. "We'll find room, no bother."

"Oh, I don't know, Frankie," he said. "It seems like an awful imposition. Shouldn't you have a word with Mrs Flynn first?"

"Not at all," I said. "I'm tellin' ya, she'll be delighted."

"Well, if you're sure," he said. "The builders are anxious to get in and make a start."

"Well, tell them to start away then, an' up ya come."

"Well, okay," PJ said, still not sounding too sure. "You're a good man all the same. I'll come up tomorrow evening if that's alright so. And I'll bring some flowers, as well as the other plants, for Mrs Flynn."

"Flowers?" I laughed. "Ya will not! Sure Peggy wouldn't know what to do with flowers."

"Ah, I can't come empty-handed," he said, and to help him out I suggested bringing a little bottle of something instead.

"The very thing," he said. "Mrs Flynn will have the finest bottle of medicinal brandy I can lay my hands on."

I knew that Peggy wouldn't drink more than a teaspoon of brandy in a lifetime, but I was sure that we would find a use for it.

"Sound as a bell, PJ," I said. "Come up by seven, and we'll have the fatted calf on the boil."

★ ★ ★

PJ's stay with us was settled as easily as that. What with getting in late that night, and Peggy going out at dawn to do whatever she gets up to, I didn't get a chance to break the news to her until nearly lunchtime.

Angela had come around, and the kids were running around like creatures possessed. The eldest fella, Chandler, and me were practicing headers. I was throwing a football to him, and he was trying to head it back to me, but it was going all over the place. I had high hopes of him playing for Man United and Ireland one day. He had enthusiasm and the competitive spirit of a Nazi, but he needed expert coaching. In particular, his heading was crap, and I was in the process of addressing that weakness.

"Frank, will ya go outside with tha' ball?" Peggy asked.

"We're grand where we are," I replied.

I was happy enough in my chair, and the young fella wasn't hurting himself much, making diving headers onto the carpet.

"Chandler, keep yer eye on the ball, an' throw yerself at it," I instructed. "Fling yerself! There's only five minutes left in the game, and Man U is losin' one-nil. So, come on, give it all y'ave got."

I threw the ball again, and I will admit that it was not my finest work. It was too high, and a good yard to the left of where he might have expected it. But fair do's to him, he was a game little bugger, and he took a wild dive at it. He met the ball with his ear or shoulder. It flew across the room, deflecting off Peggy's face, before knocking some china ornament off the mantelpiece. This hit the hearth, and exploded into so many bits, that it could now be safely removed from the list of items needing to be packed and carted to Sunnyside. Rather than seeing this - the brighter side of things - Peggy went into mourning and catterwauling.

"Ah no," she wailed, rubbing her face. "For feck's sake - not me china dog!"

She bent and picked up some of the late dog's entrails.

"Language, Peggy," I reminded her. "Not in front o' the children."

She often gave it to me in the neck for effing and blinding in front of the little ones, so I thought that she would appreciate the feedback. She growled and bit her lip, looking like she would rather bite my head off.

"Chandler love, why don't ya take tha' ball outside, an' I'll give yis all some ice cream in a bit?" Peggy said.

Chandler was already every inch the professional footballer - available to the highest bidder, with not an iota of loyalty to the team. He was gone through the door faster than a Ronaldo dive.

Angela swept up the remains of the china dog, as Peggy eulogised its history and its enormous sentimental value. I would have sworn on a stack of bibles that I had never seen it in my life before.

"Wha's for the dinner," I asked, trying to take her mind off her bereavement.

"Cows' rowdies an' bullock's banjos," Peggy replied - a stock response to such enquiries.

"Ah no, seriously," I said. "Wha' is it?"

"Why d'ya want to know?" Peggy asked.

The Spanish Inquisition would have had their work cut out getting information out of Peggy.

"I've invited someone to stay for a day or two," I explained. "An' I said he should come up this evenin' in time to have a bit o' dinner. Tha's all."

Apart from the two kids brawling on the floor, a dead silence descended. It was like one of those scenes in cowboy pictures when the bad guy comes into the saloon - the piano player stops playing, and the barman starts worrying about his furniture.

"Wha' do ya mean?" Peggy asked, seeming to be having difficulty understanding simple phrases.

I was wondering if some of the sludge had reached her brain. I spoke more slowly.

"I said tha' someone's comin' to stay for a day or two. It's jus' PJ O'Connor. I told ya about PJ before. From Magowans. The veg man. It's him."

I thought that this should have done it, but I could see that we were having a communication breakdown. Angela and Peggy sat staring at me. Peggy's jaw was hanging down and to the left, like she had had a stroke. Angela looked like a tanker abandoned on a calm sea, with all its power turned off. I dredged up more details, to paint as complete a picture for them as possible.

"He has builders in, an' he needs somewhere to stay. Tha's all. It's no big deal. He'll be no trouble."

They still seemed to be having difficulty grasping the concept. Peggy found her voice.

"Let me get this straight," she said. "Ya've invited someone to come an' stay here. In this house? Today. This evenin'. An' ya're tellin' me now?"

I considered her presentation of the facts, and found them to be correct in every detail.

"Yeah," I said.

"Someone we hardly know," she said. "Someone out o' Magowan's."

She made 'Magowan's' sound like 'Black Hole of Calcutta', but otherwise, once again, I could find no fault with her summation of the main elements of the situation.

"Yeah, bu' PJ's alright," I said. "He's a quiet fella. Ya'll hardly even know tha' he's here."

Angela joined in the discussion: "Bu' Da, ya never invite anyone up here. Not even for a cup o' tea."

"Yeah," I agreed. "Bu' everyone I know aroun' here has their own place, and they can make their own tea. PJ has nowhere to go. So I said tha' he could come here. Tha's all."

"I never heard the like of it," Peggy said.

"Look, I said he'd be no bother," I said. "Jus' throw up the usual oul grub, and he'll be fine."

Peggy seemed stung. She regained some of her usual fighting spirit.

"Did ya hear tha', Angela?" she said. "'Jus' throw up the usual oul grub'! 'Jus' throw up the usual oul grub'! Jaysus, when he sweet talks me like tha', I'd do anythin' for him. I would. I'm like putty in his hands."

Her tone changed from sarcastic to threatening.

"Listen you," she said. "I've a good mind to beat yer head in with the fryin' pan, bu' it'd prob'ly only damage the pan."

Angela was laughing like a container ship in a force eight.

"I'm goin' to call Marian an' get her to come over this evenin'," she said. "An' I'm comin' too. This we have to see. Me Da an' a house guest!"

"Do," Peggy said. "Wha's rare is wonderful. We may as well make an evenin' out of it."

"Wha's for the feckin' dinner anyway?" I asked again.

"Bacon an' cabbage," Peggy said. "An' he can like it or lump it."

"Tha'll be great," I said. "All culchies love bacon an' cabbage."

"Don't tell me he's a culchie as well!" Angela said. "This is gettin' better an' better. Me Da has invited a culchie to come an' stay! Where's me phone til I ring Marian."

"You jus' make sure tha' he's gone in two days," Peggy said, stabbing her finger into my chest. "Here we are tryin' to tidy the place up, an' yer man is draggin' in every waif an' stray he can find in the Daymo!"

"I'm tellin' ya tha' ya won't even know that the man is here," I said.

★ ★ ★

That evening, PJ arrived at seven on the dot. He came in one of those taxis that are like small vans. It's amazing how much they can hold. At least, I was amazed at the number of bags and boxes that came out of it. It looked like PJ had brought everything apart from the cooker and the bath. I gave him and the taxi driver a hand with unloading and getting the stuff through the garden gate.

"Leave the stuff there for a minute – it'll be alright," I said. "Come in an' meet the family. There's a full reception committee waitin' for ya."

"Oh, I'd be nervous to leave it," he said. "Even for a minute. You never know like…"

On reflection, I agreed. There were people in the Daymo who could rob the elastic out of your smalls, and you wouldn't know until you felt the breeze. So we dragged all the stuff indoors, and did the formalities during the process.

"Peggy, this is Mr O'Connor, tha' I was tellin' ya about," I said.

"Oh, PJ please", PJ said. "Call me PJ."

"Hello PJ," Peggy said, one eye on him and the other on the mountain of luggage. "Ya're very welcome."

She didn't sound very welcoming, but at least she wasn't slinging him back out into the street. He also distracted her by pressing a bottle of brandy, and a large bunch of weeds into her hands.

"I got these for you," he said.

I had not told her about his proposed cure, so Peggy and the girls did not know what to make of his odd gift. If he was a local, they would know that he was taking the piss, but who knew what strange customs they had elsewhere. Peggy muttered her thanks.

"And these must be your two lovely daughters," he said. "Although you hardly look old enough to have grown-up children - sure you could be three sisters!"

Jaysus, PJ, I thought, you're laying it on a bit thick. Peggy gave him a two watt smile, and I introduced him to Angela and Marian. By now we had lugged everything in, and we did our best to sit down amongst the jumble. Peggy went into the kitchen to make tea.

"Is that bacon I can smell?" PJ asked. "That's a beautiful aroma. My mother used always to put on a load of bacon and cabbage for the men after a day in the fields. Sure it was like nectar. Nectar!"

"Ya're from the country are ya, PJ?" Marian asked, coming close to breaching the rule that there is no such thing as a stupid question.

"Yerra, I am," PJ said. "A simple son of the soil is all that I am."

"An' I hear tha' you're the man inspirin' me Da to grow veg," Angela said.

"I'm doing little enough – only a smidgeen of advice, that's all. Back home we grew everything – spuds, cabbage, turnips, carrots – you name it. And we had a few cattle and sheep … and pigs of course. There were always pigs in our family."

"I can see tha' right enough," Angela muttered to Marian.

PJ strained to hear.

"I said I believe y'ave only jus' come up to Dublin," Angela said, more loudly.

"That's right," he said. "My poor sister died and left me a little place. I'm trying to fix it up, but it's very slow."

"An' where were ya before tha', PJ?" Angela asked.

"Yerra, sure where wasn't I, would be the better question. There was never a living for us all on the farm, so we had to scatter. I've worked all over the place – London, Birmingham - even beyond in America for a while."

"So this is yer first time livin' in Dublin, is it?" Angela was on his case like Hercule Parrot.

"It is. It is," he confirmed, before changing the subject like a matador.

"You're married with a family yourself, Angela?" he asked.

"Tha's right, PJ. Guilty as charged. I've three children – or four if ya include me husband - an' another one on the way," she said, making a statement of the bleeding obvious, given her dimesions.

"Ah, little blessings!" PJ said, showing that he had not met them.

"Yeah, ya could call them tha' right enough," Angela agreed.

PJ moved on to the next witness.

"And yourself Marian? You're not married, are you?"

I moved to fill him in.

"Not at all, PJ. Sure Marian's a l…"

Peggy must have been lurking within earshot. She shot back into the room like a greased greyhound.

"No, PJ. Marian isn't married. She's no interest in walking up the aisle. Not jus' yet anyway. Have ya, Marian?" Peggy was all smiles, but she had her eyes fixed on Marian, willing her to just nod and shut up.

"Not this week anyway, no," Marian said.

"By God!" PJ seemed stunned by this news. "Well, I'm sure that a good looking young woman like yourself will have plenty of offers."

Marian smiled at him in a way that clearly said 'would ya ever feck off', but PJ seemed to be oblivious. He then astounded the assembly by getting to his feet, clearing his throat, and launching into a verse of the 'Rose of Tralee':

"She was lovely and fair as the rose of the summer ....

Yet 'twas not her beauty alone that won me ...

Oh no,'twas the truth in her eyes ever dawning,

that made me love MARIAN, the Rose of Tralee."

We all applauded - or I should say that me, Peggy an' Angela applauded. Marian looked stunned - like a defendant who had been expecting to be bound over with a small fine, hearing that she had got the death penalty.

I thought that PJ's voice was okay, but boy had he met a big fan in Angela.

"My God, PJ," she said. "Where did ya get tha' beautiful voice? Ya'll have to sing for us again after the tea."

"I am more than happy to sing for my supper," he said. "I certainly am. Is there anything that you would like me to sing, Marian?"

The steering mechanism between Marian's brain and her tongue had developed a fault. She started to babble.

"Wha'? Me? Well I don' mind... I ..."

Marian was now like the defendant, who after getting the death sentence, is asked for a preference between hanging, stoning and firing-squad. Angela stepped in to assist.

"Do ya know any Barry White, PJ?" she asked. "Marian loves tha' kind o' thing, don't ya Marian?"

Marian smiled in a sick kind of way, probably at the happy thought of strangling her sister.

"I don't, Angela," PJ said. "But I know everything that Percy French ever wrote. Or I could have a go at the Mountains of Mourne," he suggested.

"I don't know if tha'd be far enough away," Angela said.

PJ looked confused again.

"I mean Marian prefers more exotic places like Venice, Rome.... Bali Hai", she said.

"Bally where?" PJ asked. "I could do Ballyjamesduff," he offered.

"Yeah, that'd do," Angela said.

Peggy asked me to come into the kitchen to help her with something. This had never happened before, especially not when she had two daughters on hand to lend any assistance that might be needed. I was going to point this out when I caught her eye, and the words froze on my lips. I left PJ and the girls to sort out the details of the postprandial entertainment.

In the kitchen, Peggy shut the door, and quickly had me surrounded against the wall. For a woman in poor health, she was still an impressive force.

"You listen to me, Frank Flynn," she said, as though I had an option. "You make sure that gobshite is gone out o' here in two days flat. Do ya hear me?"

I was going to protest, but she cut me short.

"Don't say anythin'. I'm not interested in yer oul blather. Jus' nod once to show ya understand."

I nodded.

"Good man," she said. "As if it's not bad enough havin' tha' eejit in on top of us, he's got more luggage than the Queen o' England. Wha' the hell is it all, anyway?"

"Well, he said tha' his father left him …" I started to explain.

"Shut up," she said. "I don't give a shite. You jus' make sure tha' him an' it are gone out o' here in two days. Two days, do ya hear me?"

I nodded again.

# 9. Builders

The day after PJ moved in, Peggy was admitted to the Northside. We went to see McCormick, and he said that the only way to tackle the job was through extensive cutting and filleting. Betty Magowan had been right, as usual. To our surprise, rather than sticking Peggy on to the usual waiting list, stretching from a long way off into infinity, McCormick said the job needed to be done immediately, and that he was ready, willing and able to do it. I was sent home to fetch the jim-jams and the slippers, and we were in business.

It turned out that there was quite a bit of sludge to dredge out, along with miscellaneous lumps of rock and gravel. As he explained afterwards, Peggy's insides were like the bed of the Royal Canal, and she had got silted up. I would not have been surprised if he said that he had found a pram, a bike and a couple of dead dogs in there. The operation itself took a few hours, and Peggy was kept in for what turned out to be a fortnight, to allow her - and me - to get over it.

This episode could have seriously disrupted the running of the Flynn household and estate. Previously, in the rare event of Peggy being crocked, normal service would have been maintained by me going around to Angela's for my sustenance. But although I love her dearly, prolonged exposure to Angela, her kids, and the dreaded Tommy, is more than my sensitive nerves can stand. A fortnight would have been way over and above the maximum safe dosage. However, my motto is: 'Trust in the Lord, for He shall provide,' and so He did, in fairness to Him, and Angela's assistance was not required.

When the builders got into PJ's place, they found that the electrics were not the only problem. There was also serious damp, and the sensible thing was to let them tackle it, while they were pulling the place apart doing the rewiring. The job was now going to take over a week. As soon as PJ heard this, he said that he would move out, and find himself a hotel, but I could hardly let him do that. Peggy wasn't there to mind, and we had more space than ever. Anyway, after we had nearly killed ourselves stowing his stuff away, it would have been ridiculous to move it all again.

PJ turned out to be a dab hand at the household stuff – a cross between Monica Sheridan and Man Friday. Every day there were square meals on the table, at breakfast, dinner and tea. He was even able to work out the sacred mysteries of the washing machine, so the shirts, socks and jocks supply was kept up.

Within a few days we had settled into a little routine. We were like the Odd Couple. The day started with the fried breakfast, folllowed by a bit of gardening - PJ did most of that. I have never seen such a man for work. He was like a combine harvester moving across the land. I tried to slow him down a bit, but once he was fired up, there was no stopping him.

In the evening, after the tea, I would go and see Peggy in the hospital. Then I would meet PJ in Magowan's, where we would have a few well-earned scoops. And last thing before beddy-byes, PJ would put up a plate of sandwiches, which we would wash down with a little nip of something - there being nobody there to tell us not to.

The only thing that was casting a cloud over my parade, was the fact that I might have intimated to Peggy that PJ had left, as he had been required to do under the terms of the tenancy agreement dictated by her. It didn't seem worth bothering her, as I figured that he would be long gone by the time she was out. Marian and Angela didn't know the true lie of the land either, as they had no reason to visit me, so there was no chance of them informing.

Unfortunately, as the days went by, the bloody builders were not making the planned progress. In fact, instead of fixing things they seemed to be making them worse. PJ was in an awful state. He said that he was sorry that he had ever let them in, and that he was an awful burden on me. Of course, I told him not to give it another thought, and that he was fine to stay where he was until his place was sorted out. I think I probably added that Peggy was also insistent that he stay. I had several libations sloshing around inside me at the time, which tends to make me deal dismissively with unappealing facts.

Towards the end of the second week, McCormick decided that Peggy was fit to go back into light training, and issued her with a twenty four hour notice to quit. I could have used another week, but McCormick was gone before I could think of a way of mounting an appeal. This was a desperate situation. There was no way that PJ was going to be out of the house in time, and I faced the very painful prospect of breaking the news to Peggy.

She had been getting back into her stride in the past few days, talking about resuming the house clearing operation as soon as she got home, and getting John-Paul back on the case. She was also getting excited about us going out to look at a house in Sunnyside at the coming weekend. The fact that her little nest was still stuffed to the rafters with PJ, and all his worldly goods, would delay her plans a bit. I feared that she would take it badly when the full facts became know to her. Hell hath no fury like a woman who comes home expecting it to be empty, finding it up to the picture rails in culchies and their effects.

As I prepared to give her the bad news, she was still in her hospital bed, fairly well anchored down with blankets and tea trays - in other words, not ideally placed to inflict immediate violence on me. Peggy might have been getting over an operation, but wounded beasts can be even more dangerous than usual. In preparation, I shifted back a few feet, and made sure that I was between her and the door. I thought that adding a bit of smoke to the battlefield might help.

"Ya know tha' dog ornament on the mantelpiece tha' got broke," I said.

She looked pained and nodded.

"Well, ya know tha' other one tha' was beside it - the ballerina?"

She nodded again. I knew that this was a particular favourite of Peggy. She got it as a wedding present, but even so it had sentimental value for her.

"It got broke," I said.

It didn't, but I figured that she would be so relieved when she heard the good news, that she would mind less about PJ. I planned to slip in the PJ news at the right moment, when she was overcome with relief regarding the ballerina's safety.

"Yeah," I said. "I was dustin' this mornin', an' I knocked it over. It's in bits."

"You were dustin'?" she asked.

Shit! I could see immediately that I had allowed the creative juices too far off the leash, and they had started spouting gibberish.

"Well, ya know, kind o' dustin'. Wavin' the duster around a bit."

I was not even convincing myself.

"Ya didn't break it at all, did ya?"

I have no idea how she performs these feats of mindreading. It is a gift, or a curse. Either way, I had to give up on my smokescreen plan, and come out into the open, defenceless.

"Nah!" I said. "I was only messin' with ya."

She looked at me like she was discovering new unimagined depths to my stupidity. I knew that time was running out. Given her powers, it would not be long before she would be looking into my eyes, and seeing PJ sitting in my chair, watching Judge Judy on the Flynn telly. I had nowhere to run. I would have to give her the plain unvarnished truth, and let honesty be my shield. My confidence in this plan was not high. It was like hoping to survive a firing squad, by ducking the bullets.

"Ya remember PJ?" I asked, gritting my teeth and hoping beyond hope that she might not.

"Yeah," she said, like she had bitten into something rancid. "Wha' about him?"

"He's still havin' awful trouble with the feckin' builders," I said. "They're givin' him a right run around. Electrics. Damp. Ya wouldn't believe it."

She did not gush with the required sympathy.

"Ya know wha' they're like," I said. "Bloody builders! They're all the same. Yer heart'd go out to the man."

Peggy's heart was clearly staying where it was. If PJ's problems were gnawing at her vitals, she was masking it well.

"Ya see, the thing is…" I said.

I could not find the words that I was seeking because they probably did not exist. They would have conveyed the message that PJ was still in situ, but would have made Peggy say that that was grand, and even if it was not grand, that it definitely was not Frankie's fault.

She was eyeing me closely now. Her antennae were extended on full alert. All her weapon systems were being armed. She spoke, and cut to the nub of the matter.

"He's still in the house, isn't he?"

A politician would have ducked the question with 'I'll answer that in a moment, but first I want to draw your attention to the improved inflation figures.' But I was not up to speed on the latest inflation figures, and I could not think of any other diversion.

"Ah look," I said. "I couldn't jus'..."

She raised her voice so that everyone in the ward, the adjacent wards, and even the lads down in the morgue, could hear her clearly.

"He's still in the house," she wailed. "I don't believe it. I don't feckin' believe it. Me mother warned me, she did. Even your mother warned me. But would I listen? No. I said ya couldn't be wha' they were makin' ya out to be. Nobody could be tha' thick, tha' useless... Well I was wrong. God help me, I was wrong."

After making that little speech, she took to whimpering softly, or maybe she was praying. Anyway, I was glad that I had got it over with, and that it had not gone as badly as I had feared.

"It'll only be a few more days," I said, hoping that this might cheer her up.

She growled at me malevolently. She was like the young wan in the bed in the Exorcist. If she had swivelled her head around a few times, and puked a pint of green muck at me, I would not have been surprised.

★ ★ ★

The next day, when I got her home in a taxi - as the bloody hospital insisted, even though the bus nearly passed both doors - PJ had a lovely lamb stew on the go. Complete with new potatoes and various veg, it was enough to save him from being fired out on his ear there and then. The smell and PJ met us at the door, luckily in that order. Before Peggy could open her mouth, PJ was all over her like a warm bath.

"How are you, Peggy girl?" he gushed. "Come in. Come in. Sit yourself down here."

He guided her into my chair.

"Sure, God love you," he said. "You've been through the wars, and no mistake. I'll have a nice cup of tea for you in a minute, and there's a little bit of dinner on. Maybe you'll manage a small bit of it. You'll need to eat to build your strength back up. And take it easy. Take it easy. You're not to lift a finger in this house. Myself and himself have everything under control. Isn't that right, Frankie?"

I confirmed that his remarks added up to a true and fair view of the situation as I understood it, at the time and date of reporting.

"Yep," I said.

"Angela and Marian will be in shortly to welcome you home," he said. "I asked Angela not to bring the children, as I thought it might be too much for you yet. I hope that's okay?"

All of this old soap seemed to be having the desired effect. There were signs of a thaw on the parts of Peggy nearest to PJ's warm glow. She cleared her throat, and made a noise like a cat when you scratch under its chin. When PJ went to get the tea I said:

"Ya see? He's handy to have around, isn't he? It's like havin' a butler."

"I'll butler ya," the cat hissed.

Angela and Marian arrived as per the published schedule, and we got stuck into the stew. Thankfully, neither the matter of PJ's residency rights, nor the previously pressing need to get the place stripped and ready for John-Paul's inspection came up in discussions. All focus was on Peggy's recuperation, as PJ and the girls competed for the right to dance attendance on her. Towards the end of the meal, as we did damage to an apple tart – which PJ had baked himself – Marian asked Angela if she would like to go to some play with her later that evening.

"I got tickets weeks ago, but Susan is after textin' me tha' she's stuck at work. Will you come Angela?"

Peggy provided PJ with a quick note on the dramatis personae: "Susan is Marian's friend."

"Ah, I can't Marian", Angela said. "I'd love to, but I can't leave Tommy with the kids for too long, the way he is, ya know."

"Tha's a shame," Marian said. "It's on at the Abbey. It's supposed to be very good. Ah, never mind. I won't bother."

PJ's head came up like a meerkat.

"Marian, is that the Abbey Theatre that you are speaking of? The theatre of Yeats and Lady Gregory? I hope that I'm not being too forward, but I would regard it as a great honour, if you would allow me to accompany you to the performance."

Marian wobbled like she had been whacked around the head with a snooker ball in a sock. She looked dazed, and clearly in need of assistance. Angela was first on the scene, but instead of lending sisterly support, she delivered a further blow just above the neck.

"Ah, tha's great, PJ," she said to him. "Isn't tha' nice o' PJ, Marian?"

Her face registered sudden and severe pain as her shin took the force of Marian's size 6 under the table.

"Ah no, PJ," Marian was saying. "It'd be too much trouble. An' at such short notice - I couldn't. Honest!"

"It's no trouble at all, girl. No trouble at all."

He was a model of chivalryness, chivalrocity or whatever you call it.

"I'm sure that your father will manage in Magowan's on his own without me for one evening."

I nodded that I would indeed soldier on.

"Just give me a few minutes to put on a suit, and I shall be at your service, ready for escort duty."

Marian tried again.

"Bu', it's jus' a romantic oul thing PJ. I doubt tha' ya'd like it…"

PJ wasn't having that.

"Marian, on the outside I may seem to be just a plain simple Irishman, but inside there are hidden depths. Hidden depths, Marian. I have passions, just like any man, and they can be inflamed by art, drama and beauty. They can indeed."

Marian was still reeling, and looked far from convinced, but it sounded to me like PJ was going to the right place. I thought that he would be in his element. The theatre never did anything for me. On the take it or leave it spectrum, I was all for leaving it. I gave PJ the benefit of my views.

"Ya'll prob'ly enjoy it so, PJ. Personally, I can't stand tha' theatre crap. Playwrights are all up their own arses, an' actors are jus' a bunch o' shirtlifters, the lot o' them. I'll go to the Gaiety or the Olympia at a push. At least there's the chance of a laugh or a tune, bu' the Abbey! No way! They only go for pain an' misery in tha' feckin' place. I see the people comin' out o' there after a show. Half o' them charge into the pub in sore need of a drink, an' the other half throw themselves in the Liffey."

Angela, still recovering from the assault on her shin, moved in for revenge.

"Tha's a great idea! Why don't yis go for a little drink after the show? Jus' the two o' yis like?"

"We'll do that. We will," PJ said. "There's a quiet little bar I know not far from the theatre that will be just the thing. Now, if you will all pardon me for a moment, I will go and get that suit on. Then Miss Flynn, the evening is before us."

PJ did a little bow and sloped off upstairs. Angela was grinning like a lunatic, and Marian was looking sicker than her mother.

"You're some bitch," Marian said.

Angela stopped grinning for a second to stick her tongue out at her sister.

"Ya'll prob'ly need a drink right enough, love," Peggy said to Marian.

"Thanks, Ma."

Peggy pressed her hand, like Marian was going off to fight a war.

Of course, I got the blame as per usual. Peggy shot a look at me that would have set fire to a wet towel.

"You!" she said. "Give me strength!"

She took a swipe at me, but was handicapped by still holding Marian's hand, and missed.

"How was I to know tha' he was a ladies man?" I asked.

"Ladies man, how are ya!" she said. "He's like the rest o' yis. He'd climb over ten naked women to get at a drink."

# 10. Sunnyside

A week or two after Peggy got out of the Northside, she was fully back on form, and decreed that we would go to see a show house in Sunnyside. My enthusiasm for the mission was not high, but I lacked the stomach to object. I prepared myself like a refugee about to leave all that I held dear.

In case you do not know the Fair City, let me give you some orientation. Until recent years, Dublin was a neat and manageable place arranged on the banks of the Liffey, and spreading north and south around Dublin Bay. Presumably the founders liked fish, or wanted to be able to take to their boats if the savage natives from surrounding areas became uppity. A few miles inland and you were in amongst fields. Over the years Dublin acquired a number of interesting features like parks, churches and the finest brewery known to man.

In the 1930s they started building house out in the fields – in places like Cabra, Finglas, Kimmage and Ballyfermot. Even so, you could still cycle from one side of the city to the other without breaking sweat. But more recently, house-building had gone mad, with each new estate merging into the last one. The city spread into the west and over the horizon like a fungus. The houses all looked the same, creating an endless featureless maze of brick and concrete. How residents managed to find their way home to their own little box in the evening, was a mystery to me.

Sunnyside was one of many identical developments. It was described in the developer's brochure as 'an exclusive residential development of executive homes in a much sought-after location, close to main arteries and amenities'. In fact, it was rows of houses, just like the ones they built in the development beside it. As for amenities – there were none. The only pub was a concrete and steel bunker, with a car park that would have served a medium-sized airport. An illuminated sign by the road warned that this hellhole welcomed children - obviously not caring a damn who knew this. Certainly I was not attracted to the prospect of sipping pints, up to my oxsters in chicken nuggets, nappies and snot.

Peggy took a different view. Through her rose-tinted blinkers, she saw Sunnyside as an Emerald City, with many delectable attractions. The houses all looked the same to me, but she could give you chapter and verse on the differences between the 'Merrion,' the 'Regal' and the 'Belvedere.' It was something to do with the colour of the bricks, or the shape of the windows. As far as I was concerned, she might as well have been pointing out which sheep was which in a flock.

She had made an appointment for us to visit this urban blight, so that we could ooh and aah at the delights of the Regal. She had acquired a bundle of brochures, and the Regal was the one that she returned to time and again to salivate over.

As the new estates spread, the bus service had to subdivide to keep up. There used to be just the plain old 34 covering the whole western territory. Then they had to create the 34A, 34B, 34C, etc., to get to the new places that the 34 on its own could not have reached in a week.

We got on the 34X, Y or Z in Abbey Street, and headed off into the wilderness. In fairness to Peggy, she knew where she was going. She was as impressive as a treasure hunter, marking off a hundred paces this way, fifty paces that, then digging and finding the loot. As the bus wandered around in the featureless desert, she said: "Right, we get off here," in a place that had no identifying feature that I could spot.

We were met at a sales office by a woman of uncertain age called Moya, who was possibly the friendliest person that I have ever met. She took a great liking to us, and within minutes we were on first name terms, like we had been in school together. Moya's hair was dyed a pinkish purple, and was set into a nest shape that could have housed a couple of large hens, or an extended family of rodents. Her face was caked in a tan-coloured embalming plaster, in some misguided effort to bank up the dying embers of her youth. She wore a light brown suit, topped with a huge scarf or tarpaulin arranged around her neck and shoulders. Dozens of bangles rattled when she moved. The net effect was of an over-done Christmas tree in a strong wind.

Before inspecting the Regal, Moya insisted on giving us tea - an obvious ruse to extract information on our bona fides. There was a wide choice of tea which was further learning for me, as I had thought that Susan's camomile was the only poisonous version available. Moya had potions made from fruit, spices, and probably mashed insects or boot polish. I told her that I only ever drank tea made out of Irish tea leaves, which she thought was hilarious. In fact she thought that everything I said was hilarious. She told Peggy that she must find me a laugh a minute. Peggy said "Yeah, I hardly ever stop."

After she had taken our names, address, religion, inside leg measurements and favourite colours, Moya led us on the grand tour of the Regal. I expected to be underwhelmed and I was not disappointed. We looked into one room which was a rectangle, with a door and a window. There might have been a radiator and a light switch. Luckily Moya was on hand to fill in details that were not obvious to me.

"This is the main reception, ideal for entertaining friends and family - with direct access to the vestibule, and from there to the kitchen-diner, and to the downstairs cloakroom.

Can't you just imagine yourselves in here on a winter's evening, all nice and cosy?"

Moya's imagination was better than mine.

"It's a nice sized room, isn't it Frank?" Peggy said, and I issued a noncommittal grunt.

We traipsed around the rest of the Regal, and I thought that if that was what Royalty had to live with, I was giving up envying them. Their main problem seemed to be incontinence - there were toilets everywhere. When we lived in Mountjoy Square there was only one toilet between two families, and we thought that was luxury. The Regal had three! Three! And there would only be the two of us living there. Mind you there were three bedrooms too, but Moya told me that I could turn one into a study if I preferred. I said that I would have to think about that. She gave me a little shove, and told me to stop, or she would die laughing. A happy prospect, but I thought it unlikely.

At the end of the tour, Moya said that she would leave us to have a little chat. Chat about what, I thought? The state of the nation? United's chances in Europe? It soon became clear.

"Well, wha' d'ya think?" - another trick question from Peggy.

"Ah, yeah – right enough," I offered, hoping that would do.

"It's gorgeous, isn't it?"

"Gorgeous," I replied.

I meant to make it sound like a question, as in 'Gorgeous? Are ya stark raving mad? It's a concrete box in the middle o' nowhere. Get a grip on yerself, an' let's get out o' here quick.' But I didn't actually say that, and somehow she took it for agreement. Peggy seemed content, and after a while Moya dragged her chains back into the room.

"How are you guys gettin' on?" she asked.

"Remarkably well, after bein' married for over thirty years," I said.

My motto is that you have to take every opportunity for a laugh, even if you are in the mood to put your head in the oven, as I then was. Moya nearly wet herself.

"We think we'd like to put our names down for one," Peggy said.

I wanted to cry out and run, but I had lost the power of speech and movement. It was like one of those nightmares where you are trying to run through a swamp in wellingtons full of sand.

"That's great news," Moya said, and she had a twenty one gun rattle in celebration.

"I have the site plan here. Why don't we pick out your plot, and we can go and have a look at it while you're here."

In a trance I found myself agreeing which bit of the field we would prefer. I stood in muck, getting trenchfoot, while Moya pranced around showing us the view from where the kitchen window was going to be, and she and Peggy decided where to put the sofa.

That evening, it was an unusually morose Frankie who put lip to pint in Magowan's. PJ did his best to keep my spirits up, pointing out that the building was not even started yet, so there would be a stay of execution. It would take months, so I would have plenty of time to think of some way to effect an escape - or to say my farewells.

★ ★ ★

The next morning when I came down to greet the world, it was well past ten. I knew this because the early morning pain-in-the-neck on the radio had been replaced by the mid-morning pain-in-the-neck.

Peggy was out on patrol, and I had successfully foraged for bread, marmalade and tea, when she staggered back through the door, laden with bags of groceries.

"Ya're up, are ya?" she asked, obviously not believing the evidence of her own eyes.

I provided confirmation.

"O' course I am," I said. "I've been up for hours."

"An' wha' about tha' other eejit?" she asked. "Is he still above in the bed?"

"I haven't heard a gig out o' him," I said. "I suppose he is."

"Jaysus Frank, when is tha' fecker goin' to leave? He's here nearly a month now."

"I told ya. It's the builders. They keep findin'…"

"Feck the builders! I'm sick to death o' the builders, an' I'm sick to death o' him. How are we goin' to get this house on the market with the place lookin' like Steptoes' yard? We have his rubbish in the bedrooms … in the shed … even in the feckin' toilet!"

Peggy had been steadily raising her voice as she developed her theme.

"Sshh," I said. "Will ya keep yer voice down? He'll hear ya."

This was probably the wrong line to take. Peggy turned the volume up to full.

"I DON'T GIVE A RUNNY SHITE IF HE HEARS ME!"

If the walls of Jericho had been nearby and intact, they would not have stayed that way.

"Do ya know where I've been while you an' him have been sleepin' off the drink? I've been down to Moore Street lookin' for special rashers for him, because he won't eat Tesco's rashers. Am I mad or wha'?"

"Look," I said, trying to be the voice of reason, "if the man can't eat Tesco's rashers, then he can't. He's a guest."

"Guest, me arse!" she said. "He's a bum an' a freeloader. Livin' here like Lord Muck."

Since Peggy had come home from the hospital, she had resumed all catering and household duties. If PJ had any inclination to continue in the role of below-stairs drudge, Peggy made it clear to him - without uttering a word - that he would enter her kitchen again at the risk of his life. However, he was still beavering away out of doors, and I thought I would point this out.

"Look wha' he's done in the garden," I said.

She would have to admit that he had done a fine job. The jungle had been completely cleared. Unheard of varieties of winter vegetables had been planted, and he had even found my old bike, not used since the unfortunate canal incident.

"Feck the garden," she said, clearly not feeling in the mood to admit anything.

"An' he brought Marian to the theatre."

"Marian doesn't want anythin' to do with him. If he goes near her again, she'll up an' emigrate to Australia. Let me make it clear to ya…"

Peggy started poking me in the chest.

"You get tha' fecker an' all his stuff out o' here by the weekend, or I'll sling him, an' it, AN' YOU, out into the street meself. Do ya hear me?"

"I'll see wha' I can do," I offered.

"Frank!"

"I'll talk to him. I'll talk to him," I said, little realising that matters would be taken out of my hands, later that same day.

★ ★ ★

After demolishing a plate of rashers and other pork products, PJ had gone down to the dead sister's house. Angela had come around for a tea break with her mother, and I had retreated to the back yard. I had my arse planted on a plastic garden chair, and was chatting with Bertie. The great thing about talking to pedigree dogs is that they hang on to your every word, and they never disagree. I often thought that if Peggy was more of a pedigree, it would be easier to live with her.

I was complimenting Bertie on what a good dog he was, when our conference was interrupted.

"Frank!" Peggy shouted. "Frank! Come in here! Now!"

As you will have gathered, Peggy's was a voice that needed no amplification. The woman was a great loss to the public address industry. She could have been a great success announcing train departures at Grand Central station, or ensuring the safety of shipping on foggy nights.

"Did you call, my sweet?" I asked, stepping back into the kitchen.

The sarcasm was lost on her.

"Angela, show them to yer father," she ordered.

Angela held out her hand, revealing three or four yellow things. They were three eights of an inch or so long, and about half as wide. There was a line scored across the middle, and a word – 'Wyeth' – was printed on them.

"Yeah, wha'? I asked. "Magic beans are they?"

"Angela found them in one o' PJ's parcels," Peggy explained.

"Wha'? Y'ave no business goin' near the man's personal belongin's ..." I said, trying to defend PJ's property rights, but my objection was over-ruled.

"Shut up, Frank, an' giver yer gob a rest," Peggy said.

"Da, I jus' picked up one o' the parcels, an' gave it a little shake. I was wonderin' wha' was rattlin' inside, an' the curiosity got the better o' me..." Angela explained.

"Well ya'd no right..."

I had another go at setting out the principles of private property, decency and decorum, which are the hallmarks of civilisation, and a central tenet of the ancient code of the Flynns.

"Didn't I tell ya to shut up?" Peggy said. "Angela was dead right to look. There's hundreds – thousands – o' them things, an' others – different ones."

She looked at me like a Christian Brother about to quiz me on my Irish grammar, confident that I would not acquit myself well.

"Ya know wha' they are, don't ya?" she asked.

"I do," I said, taking the wind out of her jib. "I know, because PJ told me."

Peggy waited for me to continue, thinking that she would allow me enough rope to hang myself. But I knew that I was on solid ground, so I carried on fearlessly.

"They're plant seeds. PJ has a huge collection o' rare seeds. An' tha's wha' they are. Plant seeds."

I tried not to look smug, but I am only flesh and blood, so traces of smuggery may have oozed out.

"Why are ya makin' a face like an imbecile?" Peggy asked.

"Ah, Da!" Angela said. "They're not seeds. They don't even look like seeds. They're tablets."

"Don't mind him, Angela. Seeds! How could they be seeds, y'eejit? Seeds are natural things. I was raised with seeds, and these aren't seeds. For a start, seeds don't have brand names stamped on them."

Peggy stated this as irrefutable fact - as though she was Moses explaining the commandments to the lads in the desert.

"Yeah, well eggs are natural, an' they have stamps on them," I pointed out.

Peggy looked exasperated, if that's what you look like when you roll your eyes, wring your hands, and make a noise like boiling water.

"They're drugs, ya feckin' gobshite," she said. "Drugs! Ya're after bringin' a drug dealer into the house. We've got more stuff in here than the Northside hospital. Oh my God, if the Guards come, we'll all be locked up."

"Whatya mean 'we'?" Angela asked. "It's nothin' to do with me."

I was not pleased with Angela's lack of the musketeer spirit, but I let it go as it seemed to me that they were jumping to conclusions.

"Listen, calm down," I said. "Sure wha' would PJ want with drugs?"

"Try and get yer thick head aroun' this," Peggy said. "He's a drug dealer. A drug dealer. An' tha's what they have – drugs!"

"No, he's not," I argued. "Drug dealers don't look like PJ."

At that point, we heard a key turning in the lock. I had given PJ a key so that he could come and go as he wished.

"Quick, put them tablets away," Peggy said.

The yellow tablets that Angela had shown me were on the table, in full view. I was over near the window and Peggy was at the kitchen door. Only Angela was within range, but she had the manoeuvrability and speed of a giant turtle. It was too late.

"God bless all here," PJ said. "There you are Angela. Are you keeping well, girl?"

Angela mumbled that she was grand, thanks.

"There ya're PJ," I said, trying to draw his attention away from the table. "Ya were down in the house?"

"I was. I was. I was," he said. "Trying to get the builders to get a move on, but sure tis like herding chickens."

Peggy and Angela laughed, much more than the joke was worth. PJ sat down at the table.

"Ah, builders. Wha'?" I said.

"Do ya know what, Peggy – I could kill for a cup of tae," he said.

Peggy jumped like she had had forty thousands volts shot through her. "Tae? Tea. Yeah. I was jus' goin' to make a pot. Isn't tha' right Angela? Wasn't I jus' sayin' tha' I was goin' to put the kettle on?"

"Yeah, Ma", Angela agreed. "Ya were. Yeah. We were jus' talkin' about tha'. About makin' tea…" Angela gave the topic all she had.

"Why don't you sit down Frankie," PJ said. "You're jumping around like a cat with a sore paw."

I sat in my chair as Peggy went to put the kettle on. The bloody tablets were right in front of PJ, as obvious as a Las Vegas neon sign on a dark night.

"It's warm out," I said, to break the silence.

"It is that," PJ agreed, and the silence returned.

Peggy came back with the tea, and put it on the table, avoiding the area with the tablets like there was an invisible force field around it.

"Would ya like a biscuit PJ?" she asked.

"Ah, no. Thanks," PJ said.

More silence.

Eventually PJ picked up one of the yellow things, and like he was making idle conversation asked:

"Where did ye get these, lads?"

We looked at one another like we were not sure what it was exactly that he was talking about. Peggy was the first to speak.

"I think they fell out o' somewhere."

"Yeah," Angela said. "When ya were doin' the dustin'."

"Is that right?" PJ asked. "Fell out of somewhere. Fell out of where exactly?"

I didn't like his tone. Angela got to her feet like a whale breaking surface.

"I have to go," she said. "I have to get back an' …"

PJ had put his hand into his jacket pocket, and it emerged holding a black gun. He waved Angela back to her chair with it.

"Sit down," he said. "There's nobody going anywhere for a while yet."

Peggy was jabbering - she might have been talking in tongues. Angela started to cry, and I got to my feet.

"Listen PJ," I said. "We're all friends here…"

"Shut up, and sit down," he said, so I shut up and sat down.

"Frank, will ya do somethin'?" Peggy wailed.

"Wha' do ya want me to do? I'm not feckin' Batman, ya know."

"Other men'd do somethin'."

"Well I'm not other men."

"Ah, Da, can't ya..." Angela threw in.

"For God's sake," PJ shouted. "Will ye stop your endless bickering? Since I arrived in this mad house, ye have me driven demented with it. Do ye ever stop?"

There was a stunned silence.

"There's no need for tha'," I said, feeling aggrieved, after all I had done to show him hospitality.

PJ pointed the gun straight at me, and if he had said "go ahead punk, make my day," I would not have been surprised.

With his free hand he took a mobile phone from another pocket, pressed a couple of buttons and held it up to his ear.

"Hello Danny, it's me," he said. "Listen we have a problem. The safe house is blown. We have to move the stuff right now. Will you call Vinnie and both of you get around here fast?"

He listened for a moment, and then went on.

"I don't know how. The idiots here have been going through my stuff. They might have told someone already. They're not great at keeping their mouths shut."

He listened again, and said: "Yes, we'll deal with it."

My blood ran cold. Peggy and Angela whimpered. PJ hung up.

"Okay, listen to me," he said. "Some friends of mine will be here soon. Until then, we're all going to sit nice and quietly."

"I've got to go home to me kids," Angela wailed.

"You stay right where you are until I tell you, if you ever want to see them again," he said.

Peggy and Angela clutched one another.

"Our Marian'll be very disappointed with ya PJ," I said, and this got his attention.

"What do you mean?" he asked.

"I mean that she's grown very fond o' ya, PJ," I said.

"Tha's right," Peggy agreed, which surprised and pleased me, even in the stress of the moment. "She was jus' sayin' the other day wha' lovely manners ya have."

PJ seemed to welcome this information, and we felt emboldened to spoon him some more.

"Yeah, an' Marian is very choosy when it comes to fellas, isn't she Ma?" Angela threw in.

"Oh, yeah," Peggy said. "I can't even remember the last time she went out with a fella, an' enjoyed herself so much."

"She'll be very annoyed with ya, if ya shoot us," I pointed out, in case this important point might have escaped him. It did seem to give him food for thought.

"What else did she say?" he asked.

"She's says ya've got a lovely singin' voice," Angela said. "She says it makes her go all dreamy."

"Dreamy?" he asked.

"Yeah, I heard her sayin' tha' meself," I said, seconding the motion.

"'PJ makes me dreamy – his voice – singin' like,' were her very words. Jaysus tha' time ya sang the Rose o' Tralee, I could see tears in her eyes," I added.

"Tha's right," Peggy said. "I saw them too."

"Yeah," Angela added, making it unanimous.

"This is a very difficult situation," PJ said.

"Not at all," I said. "Sure these things are always happenin'. I read about it every evenin' in the Herald. We all have our little secrets, an' you're entitled to yours. We'll forget the whole thing, no bother. Isn't tha' right?" I appealed to the ladies.

"O' course," said Peggy. "Sure half the people aroun' here are up to somethin' hooky. The drug dealin' tha' you're at is no different."

I winced. There was an obvious difference between a man having a little sideline in stolen electrical goods, and PJ's status as a major gun-toting drugs baron. PJ would have understood the nuance. Weighing up the pros and cons of committing mass murder, Peggy had just added to the pros.

"Look, we don't know tha'," I said. "We don't know nothin'."

"Ye know too much," PJ said. "And if you managed to keep your mouths shut, it would be a first - and a miracle!"

"Not at all," I said. "The Flynns were never informers. 'Hear nothin', see nothin', say nothin'' – tha's our motto. Isn't tha' right?"

I looked to Peggy and Angela for agreement, and they nodded so much, that their brains must have rattled.

"I'm probably a fool, but ... the boys will be here in a minute," he said. "Get ye all into the kitchen now, shut the door, and don't come out for an hour. If the Guards ask questions, ye know nothing, d'ye hear? If ye say anything, it'll be the worse for ye. I've plenty of friends, and they're not as nice as me."

Needless to say I was up and squeezing Angela through the kitchen door as fast as I could.

"Good man, PJ," I said. "Sure maybe we'll go for a pint the next time ya're aroun'?"

Peggy pushed me past Angela, so that I flew across the kitchen, and collided with a white appliance.

"'Maybe we'll go for a pint!" she said. "Did ya ever hear the like of it, Angela?"

"I was jus' tryin' to keep on his right side," I said, checking myself for damage.

PJ had banged the door shut behind us, and a short while afterwards, there was the sound of others in the living room and up the stairs. They kept their voices down, but I did hear PJ saying: "No. Leave them. It'll be alright." Presumably one of the others was of the 'dead men tell no tales' persuasion. After another ten minutes or so, there was silence.

"They're gone," I said. "Come on."

"No, Da!" Angela said, alarmed. "He said that we were to wait for an hour."

"Ah, relax, they're gone," I said, but Peggy was not having it either.

"How do ya know, ya eejit? There could be one o' them sat out there with a bazooka aimed at the door. I've a good mind to let ya stick yer fat head out. A bullet through it might do ya some good."

On reflection, I decided that there was no great rush.

"Okay then," I said. "We'll wait. Ya might as well put the kettle on while we're sat here. An' did ya say there were biscuits?"

Peggy gave me one of her dirty looks, but she went and filled the kettle.

# 11. Deegan

Deep down, I always had a sense that PJ was not all that he was making himself out to be. Call it instinct. The Flynns always had good instinct. It was me who first suspected that Tony Cascarino wasn't Irish. His name never seemed right to me.

Needless to say, we went nowhere near the constabulary with our suspicions – about PJ, not Cascarino. But they found their way to us. One day, a week after PJ had left, there was banging on the front door, and when I went out, I found a whole posse of flatfoots crowded into the front garden. It transpired that the law had caught up with PJ and his associates, all of whom were now residing in the Bridewell, assisting police with their enquiries. In doing so, one of them made casual mention of PJ's recent residence with us, hence the force on our doorstep, complete with fingerprint powder, sniffer dogs and size twelve boots.

Instead of fighting to defend the home from these interlopers, Bertie wagged his tail and took to sniffing the police dogs' arses, the dirty little collaborator.

I demanded to see a warrant, like I've seen done in the pictures, but a big lug - obviously not a fan of the movies - pushed past me, telling me to eff off unless I wanted to be arrested for obstruction, aiding and abetting. I took an instant dislike to this lug, a plain clothes Inspector called Jim Deegan. Having mixed with the criminal classes for most of his life, Deegan's view of humanity tended towards the cynical end of the spectrum. Introduce him to a passing stranger, and his attitude would be 'and what has he been up to then?'

Deegan was about fifty five, over six foot three, and weighed in at eighteen to twenty stone, bone dry. He wore shiny grey trousers, and a brown check jacket. He had red and grey bristles growing out of his ears and nose, but there was hardly any hair on his head, other than a few untended clumps over his ears. It didn't add up to a great look, but I decided not to comment. People can be touchy about personal criticism, even when it is honest and kindly-meant. I could have honestly told him that he looked like shite, but out of kindness, I let it pass.

I suspected that he was a policeman of the old-school. He looked like a man who pined for the halcyon days of his youth, when the administration of justice was largely left to his personal discretion – those bygone days before politicians and other busybodies tied him in knots, with pettifogging rules about evidence and the rights of suspects.

Apart from the quisling Bertie, I was alone when they arrived. While the foot soldiers invaded every nook and cranny of the happy home, Deegan sat me down for a little chat.

"I understand that you are a close friend of Mr P J O'Connor," he stated.

Before I could even draw breath to reply, he was scribbling a suitable answer on his pad.

"Wha'? Me? Friend? Not at all," I said, with as much conviction as I could drum up.

Deegan glanced up from the pad. He looked like he was already bored with me, but not surprised, as he had seen my type before. He sighed in an irritated kind of way.

"Really?" he said. "Then why were you in his company nearly every night for weeks until recently? And why was he living here?"

From a certain angle, I could see that the facts could be twisted to give a very wrong impression. I moved to correct this.

"Ah no, it wasn't like tha', no," I said. "Ya see he used to be in the pub, an' he had a house tha' was bein' done up, an' he had to move in here – jus' for a few days like - while the builders …"

"Where was this house?" Deegan interrupted. "What was the address?"

I said that I did not know - which was the honest truth.

"A stranger appears out of nowhere, tells you a yarn about a house that probably doesn't exist, and you invite him to stay with you? You're a very trusting man, Mr Flynn."

I doubt that he meant it as a compliment. He went on to ask me several more questions about PJ, his habits, his friends, and about all his parcels and packages. I was not able to tell him very much.

"Have you ever heard of benzodiazepine, Mr Flynn?" he asked.

"Benjy who?" I asked back.

"Or methamphetamine? Or pcp?"

I guess that the blank look on my face suggested that I had not.

"So, let me get this straight," he said. "You never met this fellow before, and within weeks he is using your home as his own private hotel and drugs warehouse - and you didn't notice?"

I resented Deegan's implied slur on my observational skills, but in dealing with the boys in blue, my motto is to stick to 'Yes Officer / No Officer / Anything you say Officer' replies, whatever the provocation.

I remember once being caught having a slash up against the gates of the Garden of Remembrance by a man-mountain in blue. I foolishly attempted to lighten the moment with a bit of Daymo humour. It was curtailed by a sudden shortness of breath, as he grabbed me by the throat, and lifted me off the ground. He shared with me his strong negative views of people who piss on national monuments, before releasing me to go and sin no more, with an encouraging kick up the arse.

Therefore, I kept my replies to Deegan to yeas and nays, and the odd non-committal shrug.

While we were chatting away like this, the platoon was getting on with its business. This seemed to involve a clog dance in the upstairs rooms, while they opened and emptied every cupboard, drawer and box that they could find. Meanwhile another gang, deemed too rough for indoor work, were in the garden uprooting every living thing, while burrowing to a depth of several feet.

Of course, they found nothing. PJ and his friends were not in such a panic as to leave any of the stuff behind. We had checked.

When Peggy came back, the posse had already ridden off, and I was putting things into what I thought were their usual places. She came in and stared about her. Eventually she managed a spluttered 'Mother o' God!'

"Yeah," I said.

"I heard that PJ an' the rest o' them are after bein' arrested," she said.

"So it seems," I said.

"An' the Guards came here?"

"Indeed they did. Complete with motor-cycle outriders, scuba divers, an' the Garda band."

"They gave it a right goin' over," she said.

I complained that they had given me a right going over too, but she regarded that as only poor consolation for having her home turned upside down. Of sympathy for Frankie, there was none.

"Wha's after happenin' to the garden?" she asked. "It looks like someone's been through it with a plough. Everythin's dug up. Ya'll have to start plantin' yer veg all over again."

"I will an' me arse," I said. "I'm done mullickin' out there like a feckin' horse. Ya can get yer veg from Tesco's. They've loads of it."

Peggy stared at me.

"Bu' wha' abou' the savin's? The exercise? The fresh air?"

"Never mind tha'," I said. "If God had meant Dubliners to grow veg, he wouldn't have invented culchies. An' I'm not goin' to come between a bogtrotter an' his livelihood. If every Dubliner grew his own veg, where would they be? I'll tell ya where. The feckers'd be up here, takin' the few jobs tha' they haven't taken already. Tha's where."

The more I thought about it, the more sense it made, and I resolved never to lift a spade or a fork again.

Although our worldly goods had been rearranged, there was no serious damage done to the fabric of the premises. Peggy put everything back on its allotted station, and told me to sit down out of the way, when my helpfulness was judged to be counterproductive. It was all soon back to normal. My fear was that she would regard the destruction of her nest as the final straw, and that it would harden her resolve to move to Sunnyside. But the outrage did more to bring out the old protective maternal instincts, and I stayed hopeful. She would have skinned Deegan if he came back again, and found her at home.

I was concerned that PJ and his little troupe might blame me for putting the police on to them, but I need not have worried. For a start, they were remanded as guests of the nation until the trial, which would not be for ages. Then, according to the Herald's crime correspondent, PJ had more to worry about than me.

It seems that the cops had been keeping an eye on one of PJ's confederates – a known outlaw, and a significant previous customer of the justice system. When they saw him and others humping suspicious looking parcels around the city, they decided to haul them in for a heart to heart.

The stuff had come from a gang in London on the strength of a cash deposit, and a convincing marketing plan. Full payment was due as soon as the merchandise had been sold to Dublin's large and enthusiastic junkie community. Now, with the product confiscated, PJ was not in a position to pay. The London suppliers would not take this setback in an understanding and philosophical way. It was unlikely that PJ would have insurance to cover this setback. Rancour, angry words and shootings were the usual results of such business disappointments in the drugs trade.

Therefore, I reasoned that PJ was probably hoping for a long stay behind stout walls, and my worries faded.

★   ★   ★

One evening in Magowan's, shortly after the police raid, Betty and several interested citizens were hanging on my every word, as I regaled them with the inside story.

"So tell us, Frankie," Joe Horgan said. "Wha' first made ya suspicious?"

"Ah, it wasn't any one thing," I said. "It was jus' a feelin' I had, ya know?"

They all nodded.

"When ya've been knockin' aroun', as long as I have, ya develop a nose for these things," I said. "I knew tha' there was somethin' fishy about yer man."

"Did ya?" Betty asked.

"I did," I said. "There were things in his story tha' jus' didn't stack up. Like, he came in here out o' the blue, with some half-baked yarn about his sister leavin' him a house. Did any o' yis ever set foot in the house, or even know where it was?"

They admitted that they had not.

"I never believed a word of it," I said. "Not a word."

"So why did ya invite him to come an' stay with ya, Frankie?" Paddy Mulhall asked.

I looked at the others, and slowly shook my head, to suggest that I had never heard such an elementally dumb question.

"I had to lure him in, didn't I?" I explained. "Win his trust, like. To find out wha' his game was. An' I did. Sure I had him eatin' out o' me hand." I laughed. "I even had him out diggin' the feckin' garden for me."

This got a cheer.

"Ya're a gas man, Frankie," Joe said.

"But ya never told the Guards?" Paddy asked, beginning to annoy me now.

"No," I said. "I didn't tell them exactly. Did ya ever hear o' subtlety, Paddy? I jus' led the horses to the water, an' I let them lap it up for themselves. D'ya folley me? I made it so plain tha' even a gobshite like Deegan could work it out. I knocked the ball up, an' all he had to do was nod it into the net."

"Yeah, bu' wha' I don't understand is why your Marian was goin' out with him."

Paddy was now being a serious p in the a.

"Who told ya tha?" I asked.

"You did," Paddy said. "Ya told us weeks ago. Ya thought it was a great laugh."

"Oh," I said. "Tha' was all part o' the plan. Cod him tha' everythin' was grand, kind o' thing."

"Jaysus, Frankie," Joe said. "Ya've nerves o' steel all the same. Sendin' yer young wan out with an armed criminal."

The way he put that did not strike the perfect note, but Paddy saved me.

"I wouldn't mind sendin' my missus out with an armed criminal. He'd want to be feckin' armed. I often think a gun'd be handy."

"Ah no, Paddy", Joe said. "Not a gun. A tazer maybe? That'd do ya. Jus' to stun her like."

"Or a hypodermic," I said, "like they use on big cats. That'd be more humane."

"Yis're all very brave when ya're in here," Betty said. "But I see yis out with yer missuses, trottin' along behind them, like butter wouldn't melt in yer mouths."

It was a fair point, and it stopped a discussion developing on the best way to bring a rampaging Dublin housewife to her knees.

"Betty, put up another few pints, will ya," I said.

# 12. Babby

With Peggy back to full fitness, and PJ gone, there was nothing now in the way of getting on with the move. I did my best to throw spanners into the machinery, but Peggy knew my game, and she watched me like I was a suicide risk.

Every day, we had either John-Paul or the lovely Moya on the phone. He was chivvying us to get ready for sale, and she was keeping Peggy excited with talk of kitchen units and bathroom suites. Peggy was on the point of getting us under starters orders, when Angela's waters broke, bless them.

It was a Tuesday afternoon, if I remember correctly. Peggy had gone into town for something vital for the smooth running of the home. Angela and the kids had come around. As usual, some part of Tommy was malfunctioning, and she wanted to give him a rest. I kept my feelings to myself, other than maybe mentioning that I thought that it was a bit rich him watching the afternoon telly in peace, while I was trapped with his screaming kids.

"Ah Da, bu' the kids love to see ya," Angela said.

At this point, little Christian (or 'Christ Almighty' as I usually called him) was demonstrating his affection for me by wiping snot into my trouser leg. Chandler was charging around in circles like he was on something he had acquired from PJ. And the toddler, little Daphne was sitting on the floor eating something out of the dog's bowl, that Bertie had turned his snout up at.

"I know Angela, an' I love to see them too," I lied. "It's jus' tha' right now I was busy with somethin', tha's all."

The something was a planned visit to J P Twomey's to get a market update on the 3.10 at Cheltenham, where I saw the possibility of a transaction on favourable terms. This might have been combined with a little libation in Burke's, especially if the gods looked favourably on my investment. But now I was like a rat in a trap, with three lunatic terriers, intent on tearing me to bits.

"Up, Ganda! Up! Up!" Christian required to be picked up, presumably so that he could apply snot to my upper reaches also.

I picked him up, and held him at arms length. Daphne crawled over and attached herself to the leg which Christian had vacated. A stink rose up off her that nearly choked me. She smelled like the pigman that all the other pigmen avoided. I started to gag, and would have run away, only for the hold she had on me, and the awkward position I was holding her brother in.

"Jaysus Angela, will ya take tha' child an' change her, before we're all asphyxiated," I said.

But Angela was not listening to me. She had slumped down onto the sofa, with a glassy look in her eyes. Her face was scrunched up into a knot, so that she looked like a badly constipated barrage balloon.

"Are ya alrigh'?" I asked.

She took a deep breath, and sort of shook herself.

"No Da, I ..." She stopped talking, and started to whimper.

"Oh Da! The baby..." She started to cry.

"Don't cry love," I said. "She's only after shittin' herself. She'll be alrigh'."

"Not Daphne, Da," she said. "The baby! This one!"

She prodded her stomach.

"Wha'?" I asked, wanting to get full clarity on the situation.

I read a thing once about dealing with emergencies, and I remembered that the first thing you have to do is establish the facts. Unfortunately I could not remember anything else, other than it was about getting people out of burning buildings. So it would not have been of much use to me anyway, unless I set fire to the place first.

"The baby, Da," Angela elaborated. "It's comin'."

"But it's not due yet," I pointed out.

"Da, they come when they're ready," she said.

I felt that this was unreasonable, and I was going to make a comment about babies and youth in general. She cut me off by letting out a little squeal, and sliding off the sofa down onto the floor. Daphne thought that she would join in this new game. She let go of my leg and shuffled her shitty little arse over, to sit on Angela's foot. I noted a fine brown streak across the floor, marking her route.

"Down, Ganda! Down!" commanded Christian, turning himself into a rod shape to assist the process. I set him free, and he went and attached himself to Angela's neck.

Chandler was not interested in any of these developments, and continued his frantic circuits of the room.

"Ma, can I go out an' play with Bertie? Can I? Can I?"

Angela mumbled something, and I threw the door open. Releasing him was like setting an angry wasp loose.

"Oh God," Angela pulled a face. "Where's me Ma? When will she be back?"

This was a topic on which I had much knowledge and experience.

"Ha," I said. "Where an' when indeed? When she goes out tha' door, God alone knows where she might end up, or wha' time she might be back. If she goes into town, she won't leave until after she's tried on every feckin' shoe in the place. Then she'll be stuck in somewhere drinkin' tea an' eatin' buns. She went out las' week, an' I was nearly goin' to report her missin', she was gone tha' long, only I was enjoyin' the peace. Do ya know wha' I'm goin' to tell ya, Angela?"

"Da", Angela said. "Will ya shut the fuck up!"

"Right," I said.

I untangled Christian from around Angela's neck, and likewise removed Daphne, the human sewage farm. I dropped them in front of the telly, and switched on a programme about DIY. When I was able to give my attention back to Angela, she was a writhing heap on the floor. I got some cushions off the sofa and put them behind her.

I realised that my chances of getting a bet on to the 3.10 were now twelve to one at best, and drifting.

"Will I ring the hospital?" I asked.

In answer she just shuddered, and gave a little scream. I thought of calling Tommy, but dismissed that as an obviously ludicrous idea. I got down on my knees, and gave her neck a rub. She grabbed my arm with both hands, and stuck her fingers into me like she was trying to shred the flesh off the bone. Then she let out a noise somewhere between a scream and a roar, and really went for the arm-shredding in a big way. Out of solidarity, I joined in the screaming.

Angela was out of breath and panting now. She flung the remains of my arm away from her. I examined it and was amazed to find it more or less recognisable, in spite of the mangling it was after getting. I wiggled my fingers to check that they were still functioning. Although it was not my drinking arm, it was the important first reserve.

"So, will I?" I asked.

"Will ya wha'? she asked, irritated.

"Will I ring the hospital?"

"No, ring up RTE an' ask them to play somethin' that I can dance to," she said. "O' course ring the hospital!"

I thought that the sarcasm was not called for, but I rose above it. The problem was that I had no idea where to get the hospital's number, but being ever resourceful, I dialed 999.

"Dublin Fire and Emergency. Which service?" asked a bored male voice, almost before I had hit the third nine.

"It's me daughter, Angela," I said. Then realising that he probably did not know Angela, I rushed to fill in further details, which I will admit might have been a bit garbled.

"She's on the floor. I'm mindin' the kids – at least until the wife gets back. It'll be her fourth. Angela's. Not the wife's. Can ya put me through to the Rotunda?"

"Can you give me the address please?" he asked.

"It's in Parnell Square," I said. I thought that everyone knew where the Rotunda was.

"No, sir. Your address. Where you are right now? At this moment, sir?"

"Oh right," I said, and gave him the details.

"She's a female Caucasian – Angela is," I added, remembering that these things are usually important to the emergency services.

"Thank you, sir. And what seems to be the problem with the lady?"

At this stage Angela gave a splendid impression of a moose impaled on a spear. Daphne glanced over her shoulder, and turned up the volume on the telly to full whack. I shouted down the phone.

"The problem seems to be that the lady is lyin' on the floor about to have a babby. Tha's the feckin' problem. So if ya'd send an ambulance, or a fire engine or whatever ya have handy, an' send it fast, like a good man, that'd be grand."

"Okay sir. I'll send an ambulance to you right away. It will be there very soon. In the meantime, try to keep the lady comfortable."

"Thanks very much," I said, and hung up. What did he think I was going to do? Get her to do hand-stands and juggle fruit?

Angela was screaming like a Formula One racing car, the DIY man on the telly was drilling through concrete, and Daphne's arse was making the air deadlier than Chernobyl. Other than that, I felt that I had things pretty much under control. Angela became calmer, when I told her that the cavalry were coming.

"Make us a cup o' tea, will ya Da?" she asked.

"Comin' right up," I said, and dived into assembling the necessary tea bag, water, milk and sugar. I beat my personal best for tea production by a distance.

"Thanks, Da," she said, taking the tea from me. "Sorry for what I said earlier."

"Not at all," I said. "Perfectly understandable in the circumstances."

"Will ya ring Marian an' tell her? Maybe she'd meet me at the Rotunda, if she's not too busy."

"O' course she won't be too busy."

"An' me Ma, when she comes in."

"She'll be down after ya like a scalded cat."

"An' Tommy," she added.

"Yeah," I said without enthusiasm. "I'll tell Tommy too. Don't worry about it. Don't worry about nothin'. It'll all be grand. An' the kids'll be grand with me."

I thought grimly about the prospects awaiting me in Daphne's nappy, and hoped to God that Peggy would come back, and tackle it. Women have no sense of smell, and are fearless when it comes to sticking their noses even into the most appalling places.

"Thanks, Da. I don't know wha' I'd do without ya. Without you an' me Ma. Yis're great."

She started to cry. I sat on the floor beside her and put my arm around her. Not all the way around obviously – I'm not an orang-utan - but as far as it would go.

"Tha's wha' we're here for love. Tha's wha' we're here for."

"If it's a boy, I'm goin' to call him after you. An' if it's a girl, after me Ma."

"Lovely," I said. "Little Peggy or little Frankie. Great."

Angela gave me a poke in the ribs.

"No! Francis or Margaret. I think that'll be nice. Francis Doyle or Margaret Doyle."

"Yeah," I said, putting on my newsreader voice. "And here is the news, read by Margaret Doyle: 'The defendant, Francis Doyle of Connolly Street in the Daymo, pleaded guilty to all the charges'."

"Feck off," Angela smiled and winced at the same time.

A blue light was flashing outside. Using my powers of deduction, I surmised that the emergency services had arrived. I got up from the floor and had a look through the curtains. A gang of kids had gathered around an ambulance, as the two operatives hauled a stretcher out of the back, and came through our gate. Chandler could hardly believe his luck that they were coming his way. He and Bertie provided an advance guard up to the front door.

"Grandad! Grandad!" he yelled, like he was announcing the second coming.

As well as yelling, he was banging the knocker, and kicking the door to get attention. As I opened up, he and Bertie knocked me back onto the stairs, as they came charging through.

"Right," said one of the bright yellow ambulance men. "So where are we then?"

I led them to Angela and they set to doing their stuff. I offered them tea, just to be civil, but they declined.

"We were hopin' they'd send a helicopter, weren't we Angela?" I said to lighten the moment, but they ignored me.

"I'm sorry abou' the smell o' tha' child. I don't know wha' they feed her. Have yis got any oxygen with yis?" I asked, but they ignored that too.

"Are yis busy these days?" I asked. "I suppose yis mus' be with one thing an' another. I hope yis locked yer van up out there. Or the next time yis see it, some chancer'll be sellin' ice cream out o' the back of it."

Nothing. I thought these people were supposed to have good communication skills. They strapped Angela on to the gurney. She seemed to be having another surge as they were leaving, and was flapping around like a beached walrus. I rubbed her shoulder, but kept my arm well away from her grip. I told her again that she would be grand, and that I would send Marian and her Ma up to meet her, and that I would tell Tommy.

I will admit that I shed a little tear after she had gone. It might have been the emotion, and the miracle of birth and creation. More likely it was the ammonia and the other noxious gasses coming out of Daphne's nappy.

★ ★ ★

The way some people go on about childbirth these days, you would think that it had just been invented. Humans have been doing it forever, so what all the fuss is about beats me. Cats manage litters of kittens without going to prenatal classes, or having epidurals. Out pop the kittens, and after a quick lick of the bum, the cat is back on the prowl. Elephants are pregnant for years, and they just carry on with their business. Have you ever heard of an elephant looking for maternity leave?

Anyway, following the tried and trusted procedure in the Rotunda, Angela had no bother producing nine pounds seven ounces of Margaret Adele Doyle. MAD looked twice as big as any other kid on the ward, and half the size of the little Filipino nurses. I suggested to Angela that she skip the milk stage, and put this kid straight onto something needing a knife and a fork.

Calling her after Peggy was an inspiration, as they had so much in common. There was the angry red face, and the boxer's nose, but it was the voice that really did it. Both of them could let a roar that would loosen teeth. And when either of them demanded attention, there was no reasoning with them. Every decibel screamed: 'I want it, and I want it now.' You would need to be made of stone to ignore them.

The day after Margaret was born, we assembled at the Rotunda for the formal introductions and the official photographs. According to a sign by the hospital door, it was a strict rule that patients could only have two visitors at any one time. We had Peggy and me, Marian, Susan and Tommy. We thought that any more would have been taking the piss.

The women were talking shite about what a little dote Margaret was, and who she most looked like. I thought Danny deVito or ET, but I was out-voted.

"Aah, will ya look at her little chin! Tha's a Flynn chin." Marian said.

I looked as instructed, but I was damned if I could see anything remarkable about it. It was a chin, located at the southern tip of the face, as per the manufacturer's specifications.

"She's definitely got Angela's eyes," Susan said, but again, apart from the unremarkable fact that they had two each, I could not see what she was on about. I was glad that nobody was saying that she had anything of Tommy's, because there were few parts of that gobdaw that had not malfunctioned at some point.

Far from doing the proud new parent thing, he was on tip-top moaning form. He seemed disorientated by the fact that it was Angela who was in the bed, being attended to, and not him. The fact that she had just produced a contender for the middleweight championship of Ireland, seemed to pass him by. Two minutes after getting there, he was talking about some swelling he had on his knee. He even had the cheek to ask one of the nurses if she would take a look at it for him. She told him in no uncertain terms, that unless he was about to sprout a sprog, he was outside her jurisdiction.

The conversation moved on to the mechanics of Margaret's delivery. I could see that Tommy had a serious interest, so that he could check things off against his own symptoms, but I knew that it was likely to contain details that I definitely did not want to hear. It was time to make an exit.

"Tommy, how about us slippin' out an' wettin' the babby's head? I'm so dry, I'm fartin' dust."

Peggy fixed me with the laser look.

"Don't you go turnin' this into a piss-up," she instructed.

"An' you be careful Tommy," Angela chipped in. "Don't forget yer stomach."

As though the fecker would be likely to forget his stomach! Anyway, she need not have worried, as he was unlikely to be enthusiastic. Tommy was never one of life's bon vivants. You could send him out on the lash with Oliver Reed, Peter O'Toole and the Emperor Nero, and they would all be back home and in their beds by nine o'clock.

"Well, I suppose we could go for one," he said, stunning me with this gush of mad good fellowship.

"Right ya're," I said, striking while the iron was warmish. "Come on then. You're buyin', Daddy."

We went up to Kinsella's in Dorset Street, where I knew the pint would be of a satisfactory quality.

"Now, we're jus' havin' the one, Frankie," Tommy said as we entered – keen to kill off the party before it had even started.

"Don't be ridiculous, Tommy," I said. "A bird never flew on one wing, an' there wouldn't be enough in one pint to wet a gnat's head, never mind tha' babby o' yours. So go on now, get up there an' order, before I die o' thirst."

I was careful to make sure that the miserable little bastard bought the first round, so that I could make a move on getting the second. I knew that if I got the first one, wild horses would not drag him up to get another one.

Reluctantly, he called for the pints. It was like watching a nun being forced to do the can-can.

"An' give us two large Jemmies as well, while ya're at it," I added over his shoulder to the barman.

"Jaysus Frankie…" he started whining.

"Good man, Tommy. In for a penny, in for a pound, wha'?"

He let it go, and paid up like a martyr.

We picked up the drinks and stationed ourselves at a table, backs to the wall, ready to repel boarders.

"Slainte, Tommy," I said, raising my pint to him. "Here's to you an' Angela, an' o' course to little Baby Margaret. God bless her."

He raised his pint, and took a suspicious sip.

"Fair do's to ya," I said. "Ya're doin' more than yer fair share to protect the nation's future. It might stop the yellow hordes takin' over the world."

Tommy looked confused, so I explained.

"The yellow hordes, Tommy. The Chinese. There's gazillions o' them."

He still looked like he was struggling to keep up with the programme.

"An' ya're balancin' things out a bit, producin' little Paddies .... an' Margarets."

"Oh," he said.

He was hard work.

"Anyway, here's to ya! Ya're a patriot. Let no man impede the birth of a nation, as Parnell or O'Connell or one o' them lads had it."

I raised my whiskey glass, and held it in the air, until he raised his too.

"Bottoms up," I said, and surprise, surprise, he downed his in one. I know that he did not like it, and that he wanted to get rid of it as soon as he could. But that was not likely to work, as I knew where we could get more.

"Four chisslers, Tommy," I said. "Ya won't know wha' to do with all the children's allowance money. They'll be bringing it to ya in a security van."

He smiled. I thought we might be having a breakthrough.

"So when are ya off to Sunnyside, Frankie?" he asked, the smile broadening into a grin.

The whiskey must have been making him brave.

"Never, I hope," I said. "An' you better hope so too."

"Why?" he asked "Whassit got to do wi' me?"

"Think about it, Tommy. Think about it. Where's Angela goin' to go with the four nippers, if her Ma is livin' a hundred miles out past Timbuktu? I'll tell ya where. No feckin' where. Ya'll have the whole gang o' them all over ya, mornin', noon an' night. Put tha' in yer pipe!"

This gave him something to think about. He furrowed his brow, and took a man-size swig out of his pint.

"An' the next thing will be tha' Angela will want to folley her Ma out to bleedin' Sunnyside. Then ya'll have tha' to contend with. Bu' sure maybe ya'd enjoy bein' out there with all tha' space. It'd prob'ly be a great place to raise the family right enough. I could see Angela goin' for it, if she thinks about it enough."

I knew that just breathing wore Tommy out, and the thought of a house move could cause him to seize up altogether. He was sucking up his pint now like a camel at a watering hole. It was draining away nicely, like a lock on the canal.

Using the sign language known to all Dublin barmen, I issued an order for further supplies, by catching the barman's eye, and moving my head slightly. This had two nice fresh creamy pints with side orders of malt - in the go-large measures - appearing at the table a few minutes later. I waited for Tommy to protest, but he was still contemplating life in the Sunnyside gulag.

"Here's to yer good health," I said, but the sarcasm was wasted on him. "Ya're not such a bad bastard. I take back all them things I said about ya."

"Ah yeah, thanks," he responded, diving into the new pint.

This was more like the spirit of the old brigade. I looked on him with a new fondness.

The thing about drinking that you need to remember – and I have spent years researching this – is that you have to get used to it. I can mop up a couple of buckets of the black stuff, without there being much of a bother on me, but it has taken years of training. I had to start off on a few pints of cider, graduating to beer, then stout, with the odd drop of electric juice thrown in now and again, just to explore the limits of what was possible. There was many a mishap and spillage along the way, before I felt that I had the measure of the thing.

Tommy had not put in the necessary groundwork, and without the right training and assimilation, he was looking for trouble. If he had asked me, I could have predicted a problem. If you go from the paddling pool, straight off the high diving board, you end up splat on your kisser.

He was okay in Kinsella's, apart from dribbling a bit, and falling over once on his way to the jacks. But when we got outside, the air hit him, and it was like he had been filleted. I was in the middle of telling him a story about two lepers playing tennis, when he dropped like he had been taken out by a sniper. His hat flew off and landed in a puddle. I went after it, shook the worst of the muck off, and brought it back to him.

"Tommy! Tommy! Here's yer hat," I said, but he wasn't interested, and seemed to be having a snooze.

"Are y'all right, Tommy," I asked, jamming the hat back onto his head.

He was making a noise like a cat with a fur ball, and experience told me that this was not good. There was going to be an eruption, and he was not in a good position to manage the process. If you are going to throw up, the recommended technique is to adopt a standing or kneeling position, and to poke your head as far forward as possible, thus avoiding contamination to clothing and shoes. If Tommy was aware of this, he was either in too relaxed a condition to care, or he was not capable of executing the manoeuvre.

I will not describe the next moments in all their grisly details. It is enough to say that within moments, Tommy was transformed. One second he was a respectable member of the community, out enjoying a quiet celebration with a close family member. The next he was a sodden, sticky, smelly mess, that the above-mentioned close family member very much wished to disown.

When he had ejected everything that he had consumed in the previous day, week and month, he continued going at it, like he was trying to turn himself inside out.

"Good man," I encouraged from a safe distance. "Ya'll feel better when ya have it all up off yer stomach."

In fairness to his civic mindedness, he had managed to protect the footpath by personally absorbing most of what he had thrown up. It was like, having paid for it, he was intent on bringing every drop of it home on his person. He rolled over onto his side, and spoke.

"Disisflabubable."

"Ya're prob'ly right there, Tommy," I agreed. "Bu' could ya say tha' again, an' speak clearly into the microphone, so tha' the audience can hear ya?"

"Isedisisflabubable."

I was no wiser.

"Sorry, oul son," I said. "Y'ave lost me there."

"Fuck off, Frankie."

I understood that well enough. I might have been peeved at this growing tendency of him and his wife to tell me to eff off. However, I could see that the man was tired and stressed, and he might be forgiven for forgetting the normal social graces owed to a senior family member. These require, amongst other things, that you do not tell them, in the course of a sociable night out, to eff off - especially if their only crime is to try to assist you in your hour of need. Anyway, the effort exhausted him, and he went back to sleep, so there was no point in remonstrations.

The problem now was deciding what to do with the bugger. The last time I had had a proper skinful, I had fallen off my bike into the canal. Or to put it more accurately, a rat had run out in front of me, and in trying to avoid the little shite, I had changed direction, and ended up in the deep end. The thing to note is that it had a remarkably refreshing effect on me. The Frankie who dragged his bike back onto terra firma was a more sober Frankie, than the one who had executed a perfect closed pike moments before.

Remembering this, I pondered how I could get Tommy as far as the canal, and feck him in. It was not far, and if I could get him on to his feet, he might stagger there. The idea had much to commend it, but I feared that he might not be able to get out again. Knowing my luck, if he was drowned, I would be blamed. Reluctantly I shelved the idea.

Another option was to leave him resting where he was, giving him time to contemplate the stars, and to take himself home whenever he felt up to it. Luckily for him, Angela and the babby were still in the hospital, and the other junior

Doyles were staying with Tommy's mother. But it was late in the year, and if he got his death from pneumonia, I would get blamed for that too.

Having considered and abandoned Plans A and B, Plan C arrived around the corner in the form of Joe Horgan and Paddy Mulhall.

"There ya're Frankie - a fine clear evenin'," Joe said.

"Yeah," I agreed. "Bu' cold enough."

"Well yeah, bu' it won't be long before it's Christmas, so why wouldn't it be cold?" Paddy said.

"Were yis in Kinsella's?" Joe asked, nodding in the direction of that establishment.

I confirmed that that was indeed the place where we had taken refreshments.

"Always a good pint in there," Joe said.

I agreed, and said that this was the very feature that had drawn us there, like pigeons to their roost.

"Is tha' barman still there? Yer man with the little tache. He's an awful bollix."

This enquiry came from Paddy.

"Yeah. He was there tonight. Wha's wrong with him? He never did me any harm," I replied.

The barman in question had a notable cantankerousness, but was a skilled operator in pint creation, and in my book that got him a certain artistic leeway.

"Oh, I dunno," Paddy said. "He jus' gives me a pain in me hole, tha's all."

"Is tha' your Tommy?" Joe enquired, pointing at the remains of my son-in-law with his foot.

"Yeah," I confirmed. "Angela had the baby – a girl it was – yesterday, an' we dropped in to have a little drop, on the strength of it."

"Good man, Frankie. Congratulations. How many grandchildren is tha' ya have now? Four is it?" asked Paddy.

"Yeah, two boys an' two children," I said.

Joe added his congratulations.

"Tommy's after makin' a right mess out o' himself," Joe said, after briefly surveying the scene. "What're ya goin' to do with him?"

"I suppose I'll have to try an' get him home to his place. Will yis give us a hand?"

One thing I will say for the good citizens of the Daymo. When a neighbour is lying in the gutter covered in vomit, they won't just leave him there and pass quietly by. No, they gather round and laugh. But after they have had a good laugh, they might try to get him home.

Manhandling Tommy was not easy. He could not bear his own weight, or even stand up, so we pretty much had to carry him. Paddy and Joe took an arm each, and I led the way, yoked between his legs, with an ankle in each hand. This process was not much fun. Touching any part of him was vile, as the puke coverage was total and comprehensive. The combination of weight and slime made it hard for the lads to keep a firm grip. Every now and again one of them would let go, and Tommy's head would hop off the pavement like a ping pong ball. Also, breathing in his vicinity was best avoided, and with the exertion, we were gasping for breath after a hundred yards.

The lads called for a break, and without ceremony, we dropped him to the ground.

"Where does he live anyway?" Paddy asked, and I told him.

"Feck tha'," he replied. "Your gaff is nearer. Tha's where we're goin'."

"Ah Jaysus, lads", I said. "Herself will do her nut if she sees the state o' him."

I am a proud man, but a touch of pleading may have entered my voice.

"Tough titty, Dolores," Joe said. "It's either your place, or we leave him here, an' ya can pickle him, or do wha' ya like with him."

I feared that my evening was not going to end well. Hope rested on the fact that the hour was late, and Peggy would probably be in bed. With luck, we might be able to slip Tommy in, without bringing immediate fire and brimstone down upon me. I would just have to explain his presence in the morning. Right then I could not imagine how I would pull that off, but I was sure that something would come to me. As Scarlett O'Hara would have said, if she had been there (and she wasn't): "I can't think about that right now. If I do, I'll go crazy. I'll think about that tomorrow."

# 13. Santy

I was not expecting a medal for looking after Tommy, and for getting him safely home, but if you heard the things that Peggy and Angela said to me, you would think that I had murdered him, and scattered his body parts. In fact, with the lads' assistance, and in spite of their strong objections, we had hauled him upstairs and thoughtfully deposited him in the bath. I reasoned that he would be adjacent to all the facilities that he might be likely to need. I even threw an old coat of Peggy's over him. The Good Samaritan would not have done more if he had found Tommy lying pissed on the road to Damascus.

Unfortunately, in the wee small hours of the morning, when the whole wide world was fast asleep, Peggy needed to go to make her bladder gladder. Being only two percent awake, and as she didn't bother to turn on the light, she didn't notice the recumbent Tommy in the bath. Somewhere midstream, he moved, grunted or farted - his exact action is not recorded. Whatever it was, Peggy discerned that she was not alone, as she would have preferred and expected. Women are fastidious about their privacy in such situations.

At the time, I was fast asleep myself. In my dream, I was MU assistant manager, on the bench beside Alex Ferguson. It was nil-all, with twenty minutes to play. Alex was asking me whether we should stay with just the one up front, or throw on another striker. Before I could give him my considered view, my ears were assaulted by the sound of Peggy screaming. I had to tell Alex that I would get back to him. When I opened my eyes, Peggy was charging into the room, with an item of clothing flapping around her foot, looking like she was being pursued by a pack of wolves.

"Eh? Wasswrong?" I enquired, feigning interest.

My mind was still largely on the match. Peggy slammed the door and threw her weight against it.

"There's someone in the bathroom," she hissed.

"Eh? Wha'?"

For a second I forgot that that was where we had billeted Tommy. Then it came back to me, and I laughed.

"Wha' are ya laughin' at?" she asked.

"You!" I laughed again to show that my view on the subject had not changed. "There's no need for the mad panic. It's only Tommy."

She moved from anxious to accusatory, like a leopard going from defence to attack - all in a heart beat.

"Tommy? Wha's Tommy doin' in the bathroom? Is tha' wha' the smell was? Did you go an' get him pissed?"

I had to hand it to the woman. She had done it again. All I said was 'it's only Tommy,' and like Sherlock Holmes at his best, she had the case solved. In fact she was better than him. He would have been arsing around looking for footprints, bloodstains and cigar ash. But not Peggy! The faintest sliver of a clue, and she had me handcuffed, charged, and asking for other offences to be taken into consideration.

"I didn't get him anythin'," I offered for the defence. "He's a grown man, isn't he?"

She growled like a leopard saying: "I'll rip you to pieces later," and went back to the bathroom.

When Tommy woke up in the bath, soaked in puke, with Peggy staring down at him, and shouting at him, he probably was not feeling like a million dollars. In fairness, Tommy has never felt like a million dollars, but this will have been a low point for him. He must have thought that he had died and gone to hell and damnation. I heard Peggy organising him to have a shower. This involved her shouting a lot, and him mumbling continuously that he was very sorry. Then she had the cheek to come and swipe various items from my wardrobe for him. After a while, I thought I could hear him singing in the shower, but it was possibly weeping. He spent the rest of the night more comfortably in a bed, and I got back to the match. We won two-nil.

★　★　★

The following morning I was downstairs drinking tea, when he presented himself for inspection. Peggy had gone to harass the local grocers and victuallers. Tommy looked like a dead fish gone past its sell-by date, but at least he didn't smell like one any more. There was a bruise on his forehead the size of a small fist, and various scratches, marks and contusions on his face. One of his eyes was half closed, and the other one was the colour of a London bus.

"There ya're Tommy," I said. "Good man. Did ya sleep well? Ya're lookin' well anyway," I lied.

He replied with a noise like a death rattle.

"Sit down there," I said, and he collapsed onto a chair.

"Will ya have a cup o' tea?" I asked.

Without waiting for an answer, I poured him some, and shoved it in front of him. I thought that a little coaching talk was in order.

"Listen Tommy," I said. "Ya can't be goin' out an' lashin' into the gargle when ya're not used to it. Ya need to build up yer tolerance. 'A little sip here an' a little sip there,' - tha's my motto. Wha' we'll do this lunchtime, is we'll go down to Magowan's an' have a little hair o' the dog. I'm not talkin' about a session – jus' a couple o' nice creamy pints to settle ourselves. Have ya me?"

He was looking at me like I was casting a spell in a strange tongue. Anxious, worried and confused, I would have called it. His hands shook, and his skin emitted a shiny damp glow, like you might get if you put a bright light behind a prawn.

"Bu' before tha', wha' ya need is a good feed. When Peggy comes back, I'll get her to put on the sausages an' rashers, an' maybe a nice fried egg or two, wha'?"

This idea seemed to buck him up, and put a bit of life back into him. Before I could suggest a side order of beans, and maybe some nice buttery toast, he had shot up and was headed back upstairs at speed. I guessed he had forgotten something. Anyway it was the last I saw of him that morning.

On her return, Peggy resumed his care, and I left her to it. After she had done the necessary - burning his clothes, dosing him with painkillers, and putting him back to bed - she turned her attention to me. Needless to say, I got the blame for the fact that the eejit can't hold his drink. Most days she can find reasons to tear into me for doing nothing, and now that she felt she actually had something to complain about, her vitriol hit new heights. I let her get it out of her system, and when I thought she had run out of steam, I pointed myself at the great outdoors.

"Where do ya think ya're goin'?" she asked, and not in friendly interest.

"Out," I said, feeling that that provided her with all the details she needed.

"Ya're an' yer arse," she said. "Now tha' ya're after destroyin' Tommy, y'ave a job to do."

"Wha'?" I enquired. "Wha' job? Wha' are ya on abou'?"

I feared that the task, whatever it was, would be unlikely to be suitable, or in my interests - and I feared correctly.

"Tommy was due to play Santy Claus at the school Christmas Fair this afternoon. He can't go in the state tha' he's in. You'll have to do it."

"Ya can feck off," I said, after giving the proposal the microsecond's consideration that it merited.

Apart from the fact that I had other plans, Frankie Flynn does not voluntarily and knowingly put himself into enclosed spaces with large numbers of small children.

"The suit is around in Angela's," Peggy said, ignoring me. "The only place ya're goin' is with me aroun' there right now, to try it on."

I felt that I had not made myself clear enough on the subject.

"I'm not doin' it," I said. "No feckin' way! If ya seriously think tha' I'm goin' to dress up an' go yo-ho-hoin' into tha' school with hundreds o' feckin' kids, ya need to have yer head examined."

"Now you listen to me," Peggy said. "Poor Angela is lyin' up in the hospital exhausted after havin' little Margaret. Tommy is lyin' up on the bed lookin' like he's after givin' birth himself, after wha' ya did to him. I've got to go an' get the kids from the Doyles an' bring them back here for their dinner. So you can do wha' yer told. An' wha' I'm tellin' ya is tha' ya're goin' to put on a Santy suit, an' a cotton wool beard, an' give out presents to the little children in the school. Ya can yo-ho-ho if ya like. Then ya can feck off back to Lapland!"

As she spoke, she edged closer to me, so that by the end, we were nose to nose. On balance, I felt that a continuation of my policy of intransigence might be dangerous.

"How long will it take?" I asked, running up the white flag.

"A half an hour," she said. "Maybe an hour. Tha's all."

I thought that I would have to suffer it, and offer it up for the holy souls in purgatory, or wherever they are these days.

"Okay, come on then," I said, putting on the brave face.

We left Tommy quietly decomposing, and went around to Angela's.

Although I say so myself, I made a fairly convincing Santy. Tommy would have made Santy look like he had contracted an eating disorder, but I filled out the costume in the way that the Lord intended. Peggy supervised the fitting, and satisfied herself that I would do.

"The spirit o' Christmas," she said. "God help us."

"Come over here an' sit on me knee, an' see what Santy has in his trouser pocket for ya," I invited.

"Feck off," she replied. "Ya're expected at the school at two o'clock. Make sure tha' ya're on time. An' please, jus' for once, don't make a pig's ear out of it."

After she had revved up her broomstick and flown away, I took the costume off and stuffed it into its bag. I had the best part of an hour to kill, which I thought I could put to good use in Magowan's. As well as needing the previously-mentioned canine hair, I wanted something to support me through the ordeal ahead.

As it was Saturday lunchtime, there was a big turnout of the Daymo's prominent citizens gathered in the bar. I was hardly through the door, when Joe Horgan had caught a glimpse of the red outfit, and before I even had a pint ordered, he had the full details of my mission wrung out of me. Big mouth Joe soon had the attention and interest of the assembly. Naturally, once they had the full facts, nothing would do them other than I put the thing on. I was obliged to trot off to the jacks, and to do just that.

When I made my re-entry, I was greeted with a roar that would have pleased the team emerging from the tunnel at Lansdowne Road.

"Wey, hey! Will ya look wha's after fallin' down the chimney?" Larry Edwards was as excited as a five-year-old.

We had an impromptu medley of 'Santa Claus is coming to Town', 'I Saw Mommy Kissing Santa Claus' and 'Jingle Bells'. Then the requests came pouring in. Joe asked in a baby voice if he could have an Action Man, as he had been a very good boy - which seemed unlikely. Larry wanted a train set, and Paddy Mulhern asked if a ride would be out of the question. "In the sleigh, I mean", he added, thinking that he was hilarious.

Betty refused to take money for my pint, and I had hardly started into it when someone put another one up for me.

Clearly this was the most exciting thing to hit Magowan's since a double decker with steering problems came through the side wall in 1978. Some of the lads were on their mobiles passing the word about Santy's visit, and within fifteen minutes of me getting there, the place was jammered.

"Eh Santy, can I sit on yer lap?" asked a man known as 'Two Dinners', for very good reasons.

"Ya can feck off," I replied, leaping out of the way, as he tried to do it anyway.

They were lining up to have their photos taken with me. If I had been better organised, I could have levied a charge, and made a few bob.

"Eh, Santy, will ya do us a big favour?" Iggie Farrell was drunker than it was respectable to be at that stage of the day.

"Will ya tell Marie tha' I love her, an' tha' she's as beautiful as the day I met her?" he slurred.

"Ya'll have to tell her yerself. Santy doesn't tell lies," I said.

He didn't seem to understand, so Paddy lent a hand with explaining.

"Santy says tha' ya're to go home an' tell her yerself. If ya set off now, ya might make it in time for Christmas."

To great applause, he actually finished his drink, put on his coat, and tottered off.

And so the merry banter went on, as the beer flowed. It seemed like a shame to break up the party, we were having so much fun, and with the free pints coming at me like water out of a fire hose. But duty called, and the time had come for me to go up to St Patrick's, and entertain the Daymo's munchkins. I had been dreading the task, but after the good reception me and the Santy outfit had in Magowan's, I set out full of beer and optimism. If Frankie was not a wow, these kids would not know a wow if it came up and bit them on their arses.

Some of you may have memories of bringing little children to see Father Christmas, maybe in a department store. The kids stare at the great man in wide-eyed wonder, as you nudge them forward. He opens proceedings with a bit of 'ho-ho-ho-who-have-we-here-then', interrogates the child re his or her behaviour during the year, and dispenses a small gift (blue packaging for boys and pink for girls). He then moves smoothly on to the next customer, repeating the process. That is the time-honoured routine, but it did not work out quite like that at St Patrick's.

The school was no more than half a mile from Magowan's, so I walked there, already kitted out in the Santy regalia. I had gone most of the way, when I excited the interest and animosity of a large black dog. He was distinctly lacking in the Christmas spirit, a fact I could tell immediately from the tone of his growl, and his exhibition of large yellow teeth.

This was a dog who did not beat about the bush. After only the briefest growling and teeth-bearing formalities, he launched into attack, going straight for my lower slopes. My focus was on his ranks of teeth, like razorwire, which seemed to go back for miles. If he opened his mouth wide enough, he could hardly miss me. He was like one of those whales that open their mouths, and can scoop up half the ocean. If it was not for the generously proportioned trouserings with which I had been provided, he would have made a meal of the Flynn ankles. But while he was lost in the folds, I managed to administer a juicy boot to the side of his head. This gave him pause for reflection, and gave me a few seconds head start up the road. He caught me as I turned in at the school gates, and we had a tug of war over possession of the festive trousers. I won on points, in that he only managed to rip away about half a leg's worth.

St Patrick's school hall is one of those multi-purpose sheds which serves the school and the community in a range of ways. It is basically a rectangular box, about half the size of a small football pitch, with a stage at one end. It is the venue for school assemblies and concerts, and also functions as the school lunch room. It has mass said in it on feast days. Various community groups including alcoholics, junkies and gamblers hold their merry little soirees there. Its walls echo with the grunts and cheers of karate and basketball enthusiasts - not together probably, but I would pay money to see a match between them. The place gives off a fruity smell combining old lunches, sweat and damp.

On the day in question, it had been turned into a kind of grand bazaar. There were rows of stalls made of fold-up tables, dressed in crepe paper. Teachers, parents and volunteers were manning these enterprises, selling a variety of junk, including broken toys, dog-eared books, unwanted cans, jars, bottles and other detritus. There were various games of chance, including guessing the number of sweets in a jar, and the weight of a cake that looked like it was made of coloured concrete. There was also an area set aside for tea, buns and other so-called 'refreshments'. The Summer Fete provided a beer tent, but the Christmas Fair did not - which explained why this was Frankie's first visit.

I had slipped in a side-door to avoid making a grand entrance, and because that was where I was driven to by the rabid dingo. I could see that most of the women and children of the Daymo were jammed into the hall, engaged in a series of fairly good-natured scrums around the stalls. Everyone was shouting, babies were bawling, and there was some dreadful Christmassy jingle being played. The combined decibel level might well have drawn complaints from the airport, ten miles away.

Adding to the din was a woman standing on the stage beside me. She was armed with a microphone, and was engaged in highlighting the many delights on offer. I subsequently discovered that she was Mrs Garvey, the headteacher.

"Ladies and gentlemen, boys and girls! Don't forget to visit our excellent tombola stall. Five tickets for a euro," she advised anyone who cared to listen, which would have been approximately nobody.

Faced with this mayhem, I thought of turning and giving the gig a miss. I was prevented by the thoughts of the Hound of the Baskervilles outside, and of Peggy, who would be displeased if I failed to carry out the mission as stipulated. While I was musing on this and other injustices in my life, Mrs Garvey spotted me.

"Ladeees and gentlemen," she bellowed. "Boooys and girls. It's the time we have all been waiting for. Guess who has come to see us? It's Santa Claus!"

The sound level doubled as the mob launched into cheering, whistling and hooting. They turned as one in my direction – it was one of the most bowel-loosening moments in my life.

Someone told me that I had to make my way to Santa's grotto, which turned out to be a storage cupboard in a corridor outside the hall. Luckily it was close-by, and I didn't have to run the gauntlet of the rabble to get there.

A couple of 'elves', in the form of two snotty sixth class kids, were on hand to assist me. One of these I recognised as Miley Magee's grandson, one Master Madser Magee, a well-known apprentice lawbreaker in the district. How anyone can have put him in a position of high responsibility, such as elf, beat me.

The storage cupboard smelled of dust and old socks. Madser and his lieutenant welcomed me to Santa HQ, and gave me a briefing on the drill. As expected it was straightforward: child enters stage right – yohoho – whosbeenagoodboy/girlthen – heresyerpresent – child exits stage left - repeat.

"Jaysus Frankie, ya look like gick on a stick," Madser said. "But ya needn't worry, the little feckers don't know wha' Santy is supposed to look like, so ya'll be grand."

"Less o' the 'Frankie'," I instructed. "It's 'Father Christmas' or 'Santa Claus' to you."

Elf 2 started to laugh.

"This is great, Madser," he said. "He's feckin' pissed."

I resented the accusation.

"Excuse me, young man. I am nothin' o' the sort. I may have had somethin' festive, but Santy is allowed a little drop o' sherry. Everyone knows tha'."

They looked at me and grinned. I slumped into the armchair that had been provided, and asked for a reminder of the process, just to be sure.

"The kids come in with their Ma's, so tha' ya can't be touchin' them up or anythin'," Madser said. "We take their tickets. You talk to them, and give them a present outta tha' box, and then they feck off. Tha's all."

I had to hand it to him. He had the gift of clear and succinct communication. I could see that he had a great future in his likely chosen profession of armed robbery. There could be no misunderstanding him, when he might say "stick 'em up."

"Right," I said. "Throw open the portals. We are open for business."

Trade was indeed brisk, and the process was largely as set out by my able young assistants. I have long fancied myself as having the elements of acting skills. If fate had dealt the cards differently, Jack Nicholson might have been painting skirting boards in Dublin, and I would have my name engraved on the Hollywood sidewalk.

I got well into the part, and developed a good line in impromptu dialogue with the customers. Every one of them left as a satisfied client. Every one, that is, until Madser ushered in a woman with a sullen little thug, aged about five. I suspect that this latter was a close blood relative of the hound who had done recent damage to my trousers.

"Yo ho ho," I said civilly. Even though I did not like the look of him, professional standards had to be upheld.

"And what's your name?" I enquired, expecting the answer to be Caligula or Rasputin. In fact, he never got around to telling me.

"You're not Santy," he said instead.

This took me aback, as I was not expecting a frontal attack on my authenticity. I looked to the elves for guidance, but help from that source came there none.

"So have you been a good little boy?" I asked, getting back to the script. "I'll bet you have," I said, giving him more than the benefit of the doubt.

My frank opinion, based on what I will admit was only a brief acquaintance, was that he was a little shit, and that the chances of him qualifying for good little boy status, were as of a camel getting into heaven through the arsehole of a flea. He confirmed my low opinion by stepping forward and kicking me soundly on the shin.

I don't know if you have ever been kicked soundly on the shin - especially if the kicking was administered by a little ball of muscle and fury, who appeared to have been equipped with steel toe caps. It affects your mood and outlook. One second you are full of goodwill to all men, even children, and the next you want to kill somebody – especially your assailant, if he happens to be to hand, as mine was.

Without considering the legal niceties, I jumped up, grabbed him by the scruff of the neck, and proceeded to whack him. The elves stood well back, and left me to it. I detected not only approval, but a new respect for their leader.

The kid's mother took a different view, mothers lacking objectivity when it comes to seeing their little darlings being duffed up. Any fair-minded person would have seen the squirt for the pestilence that he was, and would have judged my reaction to be reasonable and proportionate in all the circumstances. But not his Ma. She started to scream at a pitch likely to break wine glasses, and came charging at me like an open-side flanker getting a glimpse of a loose ball. Her attentions caused me to lose my balance, so that she, me and the kid ended in a heap on the floor, flailing for mastery of the contest.

Her screaming was soon joined by the screaming of other mothers in the Santa queue. Before I knew which end of me was up, a large man in a black suit was dragging me to my feet. This annoyed me, as I felt that I had not yet administered sufficient justice to the young perpetrator. To free myself, I took a swing at the black suit, and caught him nicely under the left eye. This caused him to lose his grip, and I was once again free to pursue the child rodent. But again I was foiled, this time by the mother who was on the floor holding my knees together. This caused me to keel over like a felled tree.

I was tangled in the Santy suit as well as the arms and legs of my opponents, and I had swallowed a chunk of my beard. Opposition reinforcements were arriving in numbers. The game was now well and truly up. I was grabbed, sat upon by several large arses, and deprived of all movement.

When calm had been restored, and the gang felt sure that I was not going to run amok, the arses were removed one by one. I was hauled to an office where I was joined by Mrs Garvey, and by the man in black. The latter turned out to be our Parish Priest, the very reverend Monsignor Jim Collins, last seen by me officiating at Matty Maguire's funeral.

I have to confess that I am not the most religious person in the parish. 'Lapsed' might loosely describe my general stance. Collapsed would be an even closer description. When the priest intones 'The Lord be with you' at mass, I often think that He might indeed, but that I had never seen much of a sign of Him. The height of my religious fervour was when I made my communion at the age of seven, when I collected nearly eight quid from relatives and neighbours. When I realised that this was the final dividend, and from there on it would be all paying in, my enthusiasm waned.

The Rev Collins was a priest of the old school. He was from a wholesome mountainside somewhere, and he doubtless thanked the Lord through gritted teeth, when he was called to come amongst the Daymo's scruffy sinners to save our souls. He will have realised after a year or two of virtuous endeavour, that he was wasting his time. Apart from the infirm and the ancient - those sans teeth, sans eyes, sans taste, sans everything - the citizenry did not wish to bother God much. Not that they were against Him or anything like that. They were just busy doing other things that were more fun or remunerative.

Therefore, Father Collins took a simplified approach to his job. He didn't waste theology on us, having discovered that there was no market for it. His main focus was on his role as tithe collector, which he applied himself to with enthusiasm. I feel sure that he will have had a deep understanding of the mysteries of life, faith and eternity, but he kept them to himself. His sermons were always about money, and the endless need to collect more of it. He regularly spoke passionately about his disappointment at our puny efforts in supporting the main collection, the Share collection, the fund for retired priests, the missions, the roof, the boiler, etc. I can see him in the pulpit now, red-faced, with arms and spittle flying:

"I see children over in the shop with five and ten euro notes," he would say. "They're buying sweets and crispies. And I see their parents coming in here to mass, and putting coppers on the plate."

He would pause, and stare in accusation up and down the pews, implying that the guilty knew who they were. It took firm resolve to clatter a fistful of shrapnel onto the plate after that!

If he had not been called to the priesthood, he would have made a good policeman. He had the build of Jim Deegan, and he employed the same strained politeness with members of his congregation, that suggested that he might administer a clip around the earhole, if annoyed. Without saying it, he made you know that he thought you were a gobshite, but that he would nevertheless deal with you, because it was his job, and he had to do it.

I am telling you all this, so that you understand what was now before me. This was the man whose eye had just received a meaty right hook from me. It was already swelling nicely, and would excite much interest at mass the next day. We were both breathing heavily after our exertions. I sat on a chair, and he stood in front of me, clenching and unclenching his fists. He fixed me with a rictus smile that spoke neither of forgiveness nor charity. Smiting the wicked was clearly what he had in mind. Luckily, Mrs Garvey was present to ensure that the requirements of the Geneva Convention were observed. She opened proceedings by inviting me to plead to the charge.

"Mr Flynn, what in the name of goodness were you doing? Did you strike that little child?"

I thought that 'little child' was hardly an apt description of the lout. She was making him sound like Tiny Tim.

"He started it," I said, employing the self-defence defence.

"Don't be ridiculous," growled Father C., looking like he was about to blow a rivet. "You are a grown man. And as well as the child, you attacked his poor mother – a defenceless woman."

This was too much for me.

"Ah Father, are ya jokin' me, or wha'?" I said. "Tha' one - defenceless? Sure she has me battered black an' blue."

"Be quiet," he roared. "And you hit ME!" he added, seeming to find this hard to believe.

"I'm sorry about tha', Father," I said. "I didn't know it was you."

"Did you not?"

There was a sneer in his voice.

"And who did you think it was, dressed like this? Is it a fancy dress dance you think you're at? I've a good mind to give you a piece of your own medicine."

He was still doing the fist clenching stuff, and looking like he meant it. I shrank back into the chair.

"Ah Father, hold on now. Relax. Anyway, aren't you fellas supposed to turn the other cheek?" I asked.

A few more of his rivets were seriously stress tested.

"I'll turn the other cheek for you, you blackguard!"

I am sure that he would have matched action to sentiment, only for Mrs Garvey's intervention.

"Please Father," she said. "Perhaps you will leave this to me?"

With some difficulty, like a snake swallowing a buffalo, he forced himself to do what she suggested. He went and sat on a chair by the door, making it clear by his body language, that he was still available for rough stuff if called upon.

"Mr Flynn," Mrs Garvey edged closer to me. "May I ask you a question?"

"Ask away," I said.

"Mr Flynn, have you been drinking?"

I felt that a sharing of the undiluted truth might not serve me well.

"Drinking?" I asked.

"Yes drinking," she said, clarifying what she meant.

"No," I said. My philosophy is to plead not guilty to all accusations, until evidence is produced.

"Mr Flynn, there is a very strong smell of alcohol off you."

"Oh tha'," I said, smiling at my forgetfulness. "Tha' mus' be from lunchtime. Yeah. I had a pint then. Tha' mus' be it. I thought when ya said 'drinkin'' ya meant like now. Here in the school like. Out in the grotto. But I wasn't. No. I wouldn't do tha'. Anyway, ya don't have a beer tent, except for the summer fete, do ya?" I asked, checking in case I had missed something.

"No, Mr Flynn, we don't have a beer tent at the Christmas Fair. Mr Flynn, this is a very serious matter. I don't know if the parent involved, or indeed Father Collins here, might wish to involve the Guards, and to press charges."

The Rev impatiently waved away his right to legal redress. He still looked like he would favour sorting it out mano a mano in the playground.

"Well, I will have to discuss it with the parent, and let you know," she said. "Can I suggest that you take off that outfit, or what is left of it, and let yourself out the side door? And go straight home, Mr Flynn," she advised.

"Ya don't want me to do the other kids?" I asked. "There was still a queue. They'll be disappointed."

"They won't be disappointed, Mr Flynn," she said. "They are all quite traumatised, and may be terrified of Father Christmas for the rest of their lives. Now please."

She gestured towards the door.

Under the watchful eyes of the venerable Monsignor, I removed Santy's hat, jacket, and the tattered remained of the trousers and beard. I held my head high and made as dignified an exit as I could manage.

As I stepped out from the bright lights of the school, the door sprang shut behind me. I paused to acclimatise to the dark. It was also surprisingly quiet after the racket inside. All I could hear was a light wind in the trees, a car some streets away, and a low growling.

The bloody dog! The bastard had been sitting outside, waiting for me all this time. The fact that I had changed into civvies didn't throw him off the scent. He recognised his old enemy immediately. From the tenor of his growl, I guessed that he had not decided to forgive and forget the kick I had given him. He had started with a low opinion of me, and his experience had only served to confirm and deepen this first impression. He increased the volume of growl, and added a few threatening yips and yaps.

I considered administering a further kick to the head, but I figured that he would not fall for that trick a second time. I decided on a policy of peace and reconciliation.

"Nice doggie," I said.

This didn't appease him at all. In fact it only annoyed him. He made a lunge at my ankles, and I leapt into the air, pirhouetting like Nureyev in his prime.

The direct route to the school gate was straight across the playground, but I thought this would be too exposed. Having something solid behind me was a key part of my defence strategy. The school hall abutted the boundary wall, so I set a course along the edge of the building, and then along the wall, heading for the gate. This could only be accomplished in short stages. The process was as follows. The hell hound would make a lunge at me, and I would leap, pirhouette and move a few feet in the desired direction. Then we would stare at each other for a little while like prize-fighters, until he made another lunge. I would do the leap and pirouette routine again, and we would settle down to a bit more staring.

My motto is to live and let live, but this mutt was getting on my wick. By the time we got to the gate, I was fed up with him. I decided that the time had come for a change in tactics. There was a bush or similar vegetation, consisting of branches and leaves growing beside the gate. Without taking my eyes away from him, I managed to rip a lump off it. This turned out to be a piece about three feet long. It was more like a fan than a stick, and not really my weapon of choice. But in life, you have to make do with whatever the Lord provides, and what He had provided was something a desert tribesman might use to sweep the floor.

I summoned up my courage, and released the battle cry of the warrior Flynns - "YAAAAA, YA LITTLE BOLLIX," was the essence of it. As I did so, I charged at the animal, swiping at him with the foliage.

The results were gratifying. It was as though I had been losing a boxing bout on points, going into the fifteenth round, and some noble soul had slipped a lump of lead into my glove.

The cur quickly withdrew to a distance of about ten yards, and contented himself with yapping about what he intended to do to me. I could see that this was mere bluster, and that from here on, he would be all talk and no action. I gave him another dose of the charge plus war cry, and that settled it for him. After a few more yaps, just to have the last word, he turned and toddled off into the night.

# 14. Motor

Christmas came and went with the usual excesses, and exchanges of socks, ties and bathroom accessories. Peggy had the whole gang around for Christmas dinner, with the additions this year of Marian's pal Susan, and little Margaret. It was uneventful, apart from Tommy breaking into a rash, after forgetting that he is allergic to sprouts.

The Christmas season also gave respite from the migration to Sunnyside malarkey. Moya and John-Paul seemed to have gone into hibernation, jail or wherever estate agents feck off to in the depths of winter. But I knew that I was not safe. There would be a Spring offensive, and I needed to use this time to hatch a plan that would kibosh the scheme for good.

I was reading the Herald one evening, when I had a brainwave. The used car section is a bit of the paper that I normally flick past. My motto has always been that the oul bike is your only man, being well capable of bringing me anywhere that I have ever wanted to go. As far as I am concerned, (at its furthest only a few miles from here), the civilised world ends at Cabra. What goes on beyond there is no business of mine. The call of the open road is a call which falls on deaf ears, when it comes to me. I have never understood man's alleged need to find out what is over the horizon. If Christopher Columbus had tried to involve me in his plans, I would have laughed in his face, and told him that I would see him when he got back.

As I skimmed the Herald's motoring section, I temporarily set that policy on hold. My brainwave was that if I had a car outside the door, and could bring her nibs for occasional forays into the country, it might satisfy her hankering for wide open spaces. With a bit of luck, after a few Sunday afternoons in the wilderness, she would grow sick and tired of it, and realise that there is no place like home and the Daymo.

An enterprise called Des Swan Motors always advertised in the Herald. It claimed to have hundreds of vehicles in stock – 'a car to suit every family, and every budget'. The ad said that they were open for business seven days a week, and could be found in some place out near the airport. I decided to pay them a visit as soon as matters allowed.

Around about the same time, we had our annual visit from Peggy's nephew Mick, from London. Mick was Peggy's older sister Eileen's son. Eileen had gone to London as a nurse, even before I met Peggy. She married a builder called Paddy Carney, and they lived in a place called Cricklewood. Mick was their youngest. He was single, and lived at home with his Ma and Da.

Every few years, since he was a teenager, he would come and stay with us for a week or so, sometimes in the summer, and sometimes around Christmas. Mick was one of those second generation 'plastic paddies' - more Irish than anything born and resident on the Emerald Isle was ever likely to be. He loved Ireland and everything in it. For him, coming to Dublin was like a priest coming on retreat - a form of spiritual renewal. He was an authority on Irish history, and there was hardly a bar of Irish music that was not nectar to his earholes. He even claimed to like the diddly-eye fiddle stuff that sounds like a cat being stretched on a rack. 'Whatever floats your boat' is my motto, and although I would personally rather eat Agnelli's chips than listen to the ceili music, I respected his right to do it.

Having said all that, I liked Mick a lot. He was good company, and he could swallow pints like Dublin Bay taking in the rising tide.

If Dublin was his Mecca, then Magowan's was his Kaaba. For him, it was the source of all that was great and wonderful in the world. As you know, I yield to no man in my admiration for Betty's establishment, but even I thought that Mick pitched it a bit strong.

You may be wondering what Mick had to do with the car thing that I started to tell you about. Bear with me, and all will become clear.

The week before Mick showed up - which would have been the first week in the new year - I made my way out to Des Swan Motors, and I was fortunate enough to deal with the proprietor himself.

You have probably already got a picture in your mind of what Des was like: shifty, fast-talking, Arthur Daley with a Dublin accent. Well you should be ashamed of your prejudices, because you could not be more wrong. Des looked more like a bank manager, than a car salesman. He wore a suit and tie, was clean shaven, and his hair was neatly cut and combed. He was medium height, quite slim and fit-looking. If you crossed Liam Brady - before he went to seed - with a greyhound, you would have Des.

I was mooching around amongst the acres of stock, all present and correct as per the advert, when Des came out of his office to say hello. It was freezing cold, and there was a northerly wind blowing, that would have frozen a horse's piss mid-stream. I touched the bonnet of a car with my bare hand and it nearly stuck to it. I thought that I would lose a finger.

"Come in, will ya? Come in out o' the cold, an' have a cup o' tea," Des said.

I did not need to be asked twice. I was through the door, and in front of a little electric fire, almost before he had finished asking me. There was tea as promised, and into it went a little drop of something that Des pulled out of a drawer.

Irish men have ways of identifying each other, without asking dumb questions. It is a bit like dogs sniffing bottoms, but faster. The giving of information is invited only. The length and breadth of answers are left to the other's discretion. Most will freely cough up the necessary details, with bells and ribbons attached.

You don't ask: "Who are you, and where do you live?" You ask - as Des did: "Did ya have far to come?" And the answer won't be: "Five miles." It will be (as it was with me): "Ah, no. I came out on the bus from the Daymo. It's only a hop, skip an' a jump."

The other guy will then do a brain search, and download all the info he has on the area, providing connections in order of likely importance. He might know the pubs, or that his wife's sister lives there, or that he bought a dog off a man there once.

Des's databank on the Daymo was vast. He knew every stone in the place, as well as every man, woman, child and all their seeding and breeding. Even more importantly, it transpired that not only was he a dedicated Man U man like myself, but he went to school with Miley Magee - in the very same class! Are we living in a small world or what?

I never came across a man like Des for stories. For every one I told him, he had a better one. He told me an excellent one, which he swore was true, about two Kerrymen fighting over a skateboard, but I can't remember it now.

In the course of our chat, I filled him in on various details regarding Peggy, Sunnyside, Tommy, Susan and PJ. I even mentioned the time when I fell into the canal, and the Santy Claus episode. In all honesty, I can't remember meeting a more decent person than Des. When I told the lads in Magowan's about what had happened to me in the school and with that bloody dog, they nearly laughed themselves sick. But Des didn't. He could not have been more sympathetic.

"Ya could have taken an action against tha' school," he said. "Ya went there as a good citizen, to help them out, an' ya get assaulted. Ya're thrown out, and you still traumatised. An' they allow uncontrolled dogs on their land. Tha's against the law. If I let the dogs here loose to attack the customers, where would I be?"

I could see his point, and I was impressed at how outraged he was on my behalf. I did my best to share his strong feelings, but to tell you the truth I was struggling to keep up.

"So, ya're lookin' for some wheels?" he asked.

"Eh?" I asked him back, as the purpose of my visit had slipped my mind. "Oh yeah," I said, as it swam back into focus.

He asked me a pile of questions about what I wanted a car for, where I was going, how much I wanted to spend, my favourite colour, and God knows what else. He wrote every syllable down, like a policeman, until he had more information about my motoring needs than I knew I had in me.

"Right," he said, at last putting down his pen. "Ya're in luck. I have the very car for ya. We don't see many o' these, and I only got this one in this mornin'. Whoever ya pray to is looking after ya. An' I might be able to do somethin' for ya on the price - as ya're a buddy o' Miley's."

Cars are not really my forte. I wouldn't know a Ford from a fart, so it was great to be looked after like this by a man who knew what he was talking about.

"Button yer coat up," he said. "Come out here, an' feast yer eyes on wha' I'm goin' to show ya."

Out we went, and he led me over to what I can only call a tank of a car. It was a great big black thing. If you parked it on a tennis court, there wouldn't be room left for a bicycle.

"It's a Volga," he said. "One o' the finest cars ever made in Russia. I got it off a Polish fella. He had to go back home in a hurry, if ya know wha' I mean."

He winked. I did not know what he meant, but I nodded that I did anyway. He opened the door, and ushered me into the driver's seat. I had never actually sat in the driver's seat of a car before, so I was not altogether sure what to make of it. The steering wheel seemed to be bigger than usual.

"Best quality Soviet engineering," Des said. "An' all mechanical. None o' yer modern computerised rubbish."

"Tha's great," I said, for I have no time for computers.

"Wha's tha' mean?" I asked, pointing at a very large number on the dashboard.

"Tha's the mileage,' he said. "Impressive isn't it? There's not many cars could do tha', I can tell ya."

It was impressive. Space ships hardly go that far. I also noticed that the upholstery did not match. The driver's seat, passenger seat and back seat were all done in different cloth. I pointed this out.

"Tha's wha' ya call character," he said. "When these things were made, people paid extra to have them done like tha'. Obviously it's cheaper to upholster the seats in the same oul stuff. Tha's why today's cars are all done like tha'. Cheap, mass produced rubbish - with no more character than a crisp packet."

He pulled a face in disgust at the lack of taste of the world's main auto manufacturers.

The more I considered the Volga, the more I liked it. I got out and had a look around the outside. There were four wheels – one at each corner – and they looked okay to me, being round, as they were. I was a bit worried about what looked like a lot of rust on the bodywork, but Des assured me that it was not a problem.

"Tha's jus' weatherin'," he said. "Ya get tha'. These things are so solid, tha' ya don't worry abou' a little bit o' weatherin'. Sure aren't they made for the Russian winters?"

I agreed that they were.

"So a bit o' Irish drizzle isn't goin' to be a problem, is it?"

I agreed that it seemed unlikely.

"Compare this, to tha' little thing," he invited, pointing at a small blue Fiat. According to the figures in the cars' windshields, both were at the same price. The Fiat would have fitted onto the Volga's parcel shelf.

"Ya're gettin' a hellofa lot more car for yer money," Des said, pointing out the obvious. "Listen, come back into the office out o' this, and ya can think about it," he invited.

We went back into the warm, had another cup of fortified tea, and exchanged a few more yarns. At some point, I seem to have agreed to buy the Volga, and I became a motorist for the first time in my life. I had to tell Des that my driving experience was such that I would be a bit nervous about bringing the car straight out onto the M50, and fair do's to him, he agreed to deliver it. To keep it a surprise for Peggy, we agreed that we would meet at an appointed hour, around the corner from the old abode, and would do the necessary exchange of spondoolicks and car keys.

★ ★ ★

Mick Carney and the car arrived on the same day. I figured this was either divine providence doing its stuff, or Frankie's usual excellent planning. Mick could drive, and I figured that he could show me the basics during his visit.

As I mentioned earlier, Mick felt about his visits to Dublin pretty much like Moses felt about the Promised Land. I was watching the news on the telly, when Peggy let him in. He was like a dog with several tails, that had just won a sack of Bonzo's Supreme Jellymeat Sensations in a raffle. I was afraid that he might jump up and lick my face.

"'ow are you Aunty Peggy? You alwight? An' you Uncle Frank?" he babbled, as he pranced about, like he needed the jacks.

He produced a carton of fags for Peggy, and a nice bottle of Jameson twelve year-old for me. I put this into safe-keeping in the press.

"Only for emergency purposes, eh Uncle Frank?" he asked with a panto wink.

"Yeah," I said.

"Yeah," Peggy agreed. "An' we have an awful lot o' emergencies aroun' here."

Mick laughed. I didn't. There's no point in encouraging her to think that she's a great wit.

"So ya got over alrigh'?" I asked. "The usual Ryanair job was it?"

"It was okay," he said.

"Ya'd be better off sendin' yerself by parcel post," I said. "Climb into a box, an' get someone to stick a few stamps on it."

"I might give it a go next time," he said. "'ere, Uncle Frank, you finking o' goin' downa pub later on?"

He seemed keen, and I didn't want to disappoint him. Peggy looked like a cat who has just heard that a foolhardy mouse was about to poke its nose out.

"I dunno," I said. "I haven't thought about it."

This was too much for Peggy. She addressed Mick.

"Did ya hear tha'? Hasn't thought about it? Since when does he need to think about anythin'? Ya could cut his head off, an' the rest of him would still get up an' go to Magowan's. He'd pour the pints down his neck, same as usual. Automatic pilot how are ya - he's like a homin' pigeon."

"Or an 'omin' pigeon wiff 'is 'ead cut off," Mick corrected.

"Well, I wasn't goin' to go," I said. "But as ya're over on yer holliers..."

"Any excuse!" Peggy said. "There's always somebody goin' on holidays somewhere, and tha's good enough for you."

She had had her say, and probably felt better for it.

They say that some visitors are like fish - that they go off after few days. Peggy's mother was definitely like that. Others, like Mick, are welcome to stay as long as they like. I regarded him as the son I never had. The only other candidate for the role was Tommy, and he had failed the medical, the practical and the many interviews.

I always had great banter with Mick. He would go on endlessly about how proud he was to be Irish. In my own view, this was a dubious honour at best - indiscriminately bestowed on some of the greatest liars, lunatics and layabouts on God's earth. There was also the small detail that Mick had been born in London, had lived all his life there, and had an accent like Del Boy. When he would start eulogising 'our boys', meaning the Republic of Ireland soccer team, it was more temptation than I could resist.

"Would ya ever feck off," I said, and not for the first time, that evening down in Magowans. "Sure aren't ya as English as the Royal family."

"They're German actually," Paddy Mulhall said, butting in. "Apart from Prince Phillip – he's Greek. An' Prince Harry. We're not sure about him."

"Thanks very much Paddy, for the lecture on the Royal blood line," I said. "Bu' tha's not the point. The point is me bucko here, goin' on like he's Eamon DeValera..."

"He was American," Paddy said. "Tha's why they didn't shoot him."

"I wish someone'd shoot you," I said. "Will ya shut up, an' stop doin' the talkin' encyclopedia. Yer man here is English, an' tha's tha'."

"Leave it aht," Mick said. "Just because Oi live there doan make me English. Me Mum is Oirish. Me Dad is Oirish. Oi'm Oirish!"

The debate was joined by other regulars, and I knew that deep down, the strong consensus was that they didn't give a shite. However, their instinct told them that this was important to Mick, so there would be great scope for slagging him. No red-blooded Dub was going to turn his nose up at an opportunity like that. An impromptu citizenship test emerged, with questions being created and fired at Mick from every angle.

"Wha' year did Dublin last win the All Ireland? Who's the Minister for Finance? Where would ya get a train out to Howth?"

"Where would ya get a ride for a tenner?" Larry Edwards asked.

"Wha' kind of a question is tha'?" Paddy asked him.

"I don't know," Larry said. "I was hopin' tha' someone'd be able to tell me."

There was a good roar at that one.

Ginger Celtic had been on the outskirts of the conversation, saying nothing. Ginger had known strong Republican leanings. In Dublin this meant no more than that he knew all the words of the 'Foggy Dew' and 'Kevin Barry'. But it was enough for him to be regarded in the Daymo as the rightful bearer of the flame, and defender of the cause. At last he piped up.

"Who do ya folley?" he asked Mick.

"Ireland. The Republic," Mick said.

"No. I mean yer team. Who's yer club?"

"The Arsenal, mate," Mick said.

"Why?"

"Cos of O'Leary an' Stapleton an' Quinn an' Brady."

"An' who do ya like in Scotland?" Ginger asked.

A silence descended. This was the jackpot question. It could turn very ugly if Mick got this one wrong.

"Celtic," Mick said. "Who else would it be?"

"Good man," Ginger said, clapping him on the back. "He's alright lads. Leave him alone, will yis?"

The matter was regarded as settled – for the moment at least – and Mick and I were left in peace with our pints.

"Can I tell ya somethin' on the QT?" I asked him.

He confirmed that his policy was to protect confidential information like a lioness would her cubs, and that he would not break even under the vilest torture.

"I'm after buyin' a little car," I said. "Well, when I say a little car, I mean a big car. A huge big car, in fact. 'In for a penny, in for a pound,' is my motto."

Mick sucked a few inches off the top of his pint, and eyed me like he was seeing me anew.

"You?" he said. "You've got a motor? Cor blimey, mate!" He seemed impressed. "Where is it?"

"The dealer left it around the corner from the house," I told him. "It's parked in a side street. I have the keys an' all."

"What do you want a motor for?" he asked.

I explained my plan for giving Peggy access to the hills and valleys, without actually going and living amongst the bloody things. He seemed dubious.

"She seems very keen," he said. "She told me that you've already picked the 'ouse an' all."

"Tha's only a technicality," I said. "Until we're there, we're here, an' possession is nine points o' the law."

He looked confused.

"If you say so, Uncle Frank." He lifted his glass to toast me. "Good luck! 'appy motorin', mate!"

"There's jus' one problem," I said.

"What's that?" he asked.

"I can't drive," I told him. "I never needed to bother. I thought you might show me, while ya're over."

"Show you?" He seemed perplexed by the concept. "Have you never driven at all?"

"Not so much as a horse an' cart," I said.

"Well, I don't know," he said. "You'd be better off with proper driving lessons. At least until you've got the 'ang of it. Then maybe..."

"Drivin' lessons, me arse," I said. "Any fool can drive. Sure every gobshite in Dublin IS at it, an' if they can, I can. I jus' need ya to point things out to me, an' tell me wha' they're for. I'll soon get the hang of it. It can't be much more complex than the remote on the telly. There's more buttons on tha', an' it's no bother to me."

★  ★  ★

Mick was not very keen on the plan, but blood is thicker than muck, and he was not going to let a favourite uncle down. The next morning, after we had got ourselves outside the rashers and sausages, we told Peggy that we were going out for a walk. Once we were sure that she wasn't following us – you can never underestimate a woman with a suspicious nature - we slipped around to where the car was parked. Mick was immediately impressed.

"Flaming Nora!" he said. "What the 'ell is that?"

"It's a Vodka," I said. "No, not a Vodka. A Volga. It's Russian."

"Bloody 'eck!" he said. "It's left 'and drive."

"Wha'?" I asked.

"Left 'and drive. The steering wheel is on the left. Not on the right. In Ireland and England, they're on the right."

I hadn't noticed this.

"So wha'?" I said. "Who cares? It's in the front, isn't it? Ya can see where ya're goin' jus' as well from either side."

Mick made a noise like he was coughing up a bit of rasher. I think he was saying 'streuth'. I had a fumble with the key, and we got in, Mick in the driver's seat and me riding shotgun. We sat there for a while looking at the buttons and switches. I opened a little pigeon-hole in front of me, and pulled out a booklet.

"Here ya're Mick. Instructions."

He took the booklet from me, had a flick through and handed it back.

"Thanks," he said. "It's in Russian."

"It's a shame me Da isn't here," I said.

"Yer what, mate?" he asked.

"Never mind," I said. "Come on. Stoke her up, an' let's go." I did my Captain Bligh impression: "Cast off forrard! Cast off aft! Mr Chistian, if you please sir!"

"What about insurance and tax?" Mick asked.

"Would ya ever feck off," I said. "Ya're in Ireland now. There's plenty o' time for all tha' nonsense. Ya're not a subject o' Her Majesty here. Men fought an' died for our right to travel the nation's highways as we damn well like. So come on. I'm gettin' old sittin' here."

The appeal to Mick's love for the land of saints, scholars and law breakers won him over. He stuck the key into the ignition and gave it a twist. A noise rang out somewhere in front of us that was like sustained artillery fire. It spread through the car, until I was not sure where it was coming from. I could feel it, as well as hear it. It was like being shut in a food mixer. I looked at Mick and gave him a grin. He grinned back.

"Not bad, eh?" I shouted.

"No," he shouted back.

"Well, come on then cowboy," I said. "Let's moo them out."

Mick pulled up the anchor, and off we went. Heads turned in amazement as we made our way in stately fashion through the Daymo. This was what it was all about, and no mistake.

"Roll 'em roll 'em roll 'em," I sang.

"Though the streams are frozen.

Keep them doggies movin' Rawhide."

Mick joined in with me:

"Through rain and wind and weather,

hell bent for leather,

wishin' my girl was by my side.

All the things I'm missin':

good vittles, love and kissin',

are waitin' at the end of my ride."

Where are we going?" Mick asked.

"Take us up to the Phoeno, an' I'll have a go," I said.

"You'll 'ave a go?" Mick laughed. "If you say so, guv. You're the boss."

We drove to the back of the Phoenix Park. At that time of year, there was hardly a soul there. Even the nutters in the elastic running outfits had decided to stay at home by their fires. Mick pulled in by a grassy bank, and stopped the engine. I thought that I had gone deaf. We swapped seats by getting out and walking around, but there was so much space inside, we probably could have managed an internal seat change.

I took the steering wheel, and asked: "Right, wha's the drill?"

Mick explained lots of stuff about indicators, windscreen wipers, lights and mirrors, all of which were surplus to my immediate requirements.

"Too much information for now, Mick," I said. "Jus' tell me how to drive the feckin' thing."

He showed me how to start it, and I did that. I sat there for a minute pressing my foot on and off the accelerator thing, just feeling the power.

"Right," I said, feeling that I was doing well. "Got that. Now, wha' next? How do I make it go?"

Mick told me about the clutch and the gears. It's funny, but in all my years sitting next to drivers, I never noticed them doing all that farting around.

I gave the accelerator a good prod, pressed down the clutch, and put the gear stick into first. As I took my foot off the clutch, the car took off like shit out of a goose. I yelled in exhultation, and Mick yelled in something else. He grabbed the steering wheel to help me keep the thing between the ditches.

"Second! Second!" he shouted.

"Second wha'?" I shouted back.

"Gear! Put your foot down on the clutch again."

I did, and Mick whacked the gear stick down somewhere.

"Up clutch! Let the clutch up," he shouted.

I took my foot off the clutch again. The car leapt a few inches off the road, and charged forward like a one-car stampede.

"YEE HAAA!" I roared. "Ride 'em cowboy!"

We were approaching the main road that goes down the middle of the Park. There was quite a bit of traffic on it, as people use it as a short cut between the City Centre and the suburbs. Mick said something about slowing down, but he had not covered the brakes in his tuition to date, so I was not able to assist him.

There was a side road directly opposite the one we were on, and I reckoned that we would just pop across the main road, and continue along that. This is exactly what we did, and it worked just fine. Drivers on the main road, being familiar with the braking process, had the good sense to do so, as we shot across their bows. Mick screamed like a girl.

"Olé!" I cried.

"Brake! Brake! Take your foot off the accelerator and put it on the brake. It's the next pedal along. The one in the middle."

I had to take my eyes off the road for a bit, while I searched the floor for the item of which Mick spoke. He took control of the steering, while I was thus occupied.

"Ah yeah," I said. "I see it now."

I moved my foot over, and gave the brake a bit of a jab. The car stopped like it had hit a wall. We were nearly cut in half by the seatbelts, and the engine conked out. Mick vented a string of words which I believe to be Anglo-Saxon in origin.

"Not bad for a beginner," I said. "Eh?"

Mick was breathing heavily. Then he laughed, low at first, but then louder and louder. There were tears and other fluids pouring out of him. He couldn't speak. He was just waving his hands at me. Every now and then, he would get calmer, and then say 'not bad for a beginner' to himself, and would start all over again.

"Come on, Mick," I said. "Get a grip on yerself. I need a bit more practice."

This tickled him too, and off he went again. It was quite a while before he had full control of himself, but through deep breating, and me giving him a couple of thumps, he got there eventually.

He then applied himself to filling in the gaps in my motoring education. This included chapter and verse on brakes, so that the next time we crossed the main road, I paused for a few seconds, before cutting across the selfish bastards who seemed to think that they owned the road.

At the end of an hour in the Park, I felt sufficiently confident to drive back to the Daymo. Bearing in mind that I was a novice, I felt that it went very well indeed. Mick had to park the car, as the subtleties of the more minor manoeuvres were beyond my novice skills.

To reward his teaching, I brought Mick straight up to Magowan's, and set the finest pint money could buy in front of him.

"Thanks Mick," I said. "Tha' was great. I might bring Peggy out for a run in it tomorrow."

He didn't think that was altogether a great idea.

"I dunno, Uncle Frank," he said. "Maybe leave it for a bit. After you've 'ad another few lessons, eh?"

This seemed a bit English to me. I was hardly planning to fly a Jumbo Jet. It was only a car.

"For feck's sake, Mick," I said. "Stop bein' such an oul woman. Wha' else is there to know? Accelerator, brake, gears an' the other thing..."

"The clutch," he reminded me.

"Yeah. The clutch," I agreed. "We've done the lot. I am ready. I have seen the Promised Land."

I rubbed my hands together.

"Jaysus Mick, I can't wait to see Peggy's face."

"No," he said. "Me neither."

★ ★ ★

The plan was to unveil the car to Peggy the following morning, and we would have the whole day before us to go exploring. But mornings are not great for me, and it was nearly lunchtime before all the necessary parties were on parade.

Me and Mick were laying into the full Irish, and Peggy was doing something with the iron, when Angela arrived with her gaggle. Instantly the peace of the happy home was replaced by all the fun and colour of the circus, when the animals have been let loose.

"Come out an' play football, Granda," Chandler urged.

I cried off, telling him that my fifth metatarsal was banjaxed. He accepted this, being aware that this is a regular weakness amongst fellow professionals, and he called Bertie up to the squad as a late replacement.

Daphne jumped up on my lap and ate the rest of my breakfast. Little Christian thumped the baby, and she started bawling. Angela thumped Christian which set him bawling, and Peggy thumped Angela for thumping Christian. I thought of thumping Peggy just for a laugh, but not seriously.

It was a while before the bawling had reduced to whimpering, and we could discuss the news of the day. There were the usual standing items regarding Tommy's health, and the part of the world Marian was currently infesting. Then we moved on to deaths. Some old codger had finally relinquished his grip on life. He was so vaguely known to me, that I could not recall anything about him, but I thought I might make a guest appearance at his send-off anyway, as a mark of respect.

Moving on to lesser items, Angela had news of a dead cat.

"Mrs Keegan's cat – ya know the little white one – was killed yesterday," she said.

"Ah no," Peggy said. "She loved tha' oul cat."

"Some fecker in a car flattened it," Angela said. "Didn't even stop. Came flyin' aroun' the corner. The poor thing had no chance. No chance at all."

I gave Mick a look to warn him to keep his trap shut.

"Well it shouldn't a bin out on the road," I said. "What do ya expect?"

"It wasn't on the road," she said. "It was on the pavement. Jus' sittin' there. Mindin' its own business."

"Mother o' God," Peggy said.

"Yeah," Angela said. "The car was goin' so fast tha' it cut the corner, an' came up on the path. It only jus' swerved back onto the road before the bus stop. An' there was a load o' people standin' there, waitin' to go into Town."

"It was lucky then tha' only the cat was killed," Peggy said, blessing herself. "It'll be some young tearaway. Prob'ly in a robbed car. Prob'ly on drugs."

"Yeah", Angela said, and I nodded in agreement.

"Anyway," she said, "the Guards are after whoever it was, and they should have no bother findin' him. Apparently the car is very odd lookin'. A huge big black thing it was. The people at the bus stop all got a good look at it."

"When they catch him, they should lock him up, an' throw away the key," Peggy said.

Mick cleared his throat as if to speak, but I cut him off with a root under the table.

"Come on, Mick," I said. "We'd better go. You were wantin' to go to the Museum down in Collins Barracks. We'll go an' have a look."

Peggy was dumfounded, or suspicious, or both.

"Wha? You're goin' to a museum? Is there a bar in it?" - her usual witty cocktail of bile and acid.

"It's me heritage," I said. "I'm as entitled to go an' look at a museum, as any feckin' tourist. No offence, Mick."

"Da, maybe ya'd bring Chandler with ya," Angela suggested. "He'd love tha'. He loves geography."

I parried.

"I'll bring him another time Angela, jus' me an him. He'd only get bored with me an' Mick. Mick are ya comin' or wha'?"

"They're goin' to the pub, Angela," Peggy concluded.

I often think that woman has a one-track mind. When we were outside, Mick laughed.

"Wha' are ya titterin' at? I asked.

I did not regard the prospect of further dealings with the cops as a laughing matter. My tone was curt, and if Mick discerned that I was irritated, then he discerned correctly.

"I thought you went over somefing, right enough," he said.

"Ya never said nothin'," I pointed out.

"I was worried about my own neck. I 'adn't time to fink about moggies!"

"I never went up on the path."

"You did - a few times - once on the right."

"Wha'? Where was tha'?"

"I'm not sure. I 'ad me eyes closed most o' the time."

"Jaysus," I said. "Wha' am I goin' to do? If tha' bastard Deegan gets wind tha' I might be involved, I'm for the high jump."

Mick asked who Deegan was, and I explained my previous dealings with Inspector Clouseau in the great Daymo Drugs Mystery. I feared that Deegan might still harbour doubts about me being as white as the driven snow in the matter.

"Jaysus," I said, a nasty thought occurring to me. "They'll lock me up with feckin' PJ."

Mick raised a quizzical eyebrow, and I had to explain that it was my expert sleuthing that had put PJ and his gang behind bars.

"I can imagine that they'd be 'appy to see you alright," Mick said. "There'd be a right ol' knees-up on the wing to welcome you."

I did not like Mick's flippancy in this matter of life and death, and I told him so crisply, in terms chosen to make my meaning unambiguous. He apologised.

"We'll have to get rid o' tha' bloody car before the Guards find it," I said. "Even them eejits can hardly miss it. It's like an oil tanker siittin' on the beach among the feckin' pedaloes."

I had a brain-wave.

"I know! We can drive it into the canal."

Mick vetoed the idea, pointing out that the canal would hardly come up to the Volga's wheel arches. The Flynn brain – normally such a prolific generator of wily schemes – had gone blank. I could see me barricading myself into the house like Jimmy Cagney, shouting: "Come an' get me coppers. Ya'll never take me alive." Athough there was a swashbuckling element to that scenario that appealed to me, I was not keen on the full implications.

"Why don't I just take it away, Uncle Frank?" asked Mick.

I was not following him.

"Wha'?" I asked. "You? Where? Wha' are ya talkin' abou'?"

"I could just take it down to the Norf Wall, on to the Ferry, and before the Old Bill know what's what, I'll be 'alfway across the Irish Sea."

I put a coin into the Flynn super-computer, and ran the scheme through it looking for flaws. I could find none. The evidence would be removed from the scene and from the jurisdiction, and Frankie would be free to resume life as a highly esteemed member of the community.

"Ya'd do tha'?" I asked.

"No bother," Mick said.

I grabbed his hand, and tried to convey the appreciation that words could not match.

"Ya're a daecent man," I said, and by God I meant it.

"Don't worry about it," he said.

My conscience felt a pang of guilt shooting through it.

"I'm sorry for pullin' yer leg, abou' bein' English an' all tha'."

"It's alwight, Uncle Frank", he said. "It's only 'avin' a laugh, init? Well, best be getting on wiff it, eh? Let's get back to the 'ouse. Oi'll pack my bag, and Oi'm out of here in two shakes."

I was never happier to see the back of anyone I was so fond of. He was as good as his word. Within half an hour, he and several tons of Russian iron-mongery were gone. We told Peggy and Angela that he was after getting a call on his mobile that he had to be back in work, because someone had gone sick. I drew on my knowledge of Tommy's litany of ailments for something suitable.

Mick phoned a few days later, and told me that the car had had a massive stroke, two miles outside Holyhead. The poor thing had never recovered consciousness. He did a deal with a local garage, that they would not charge him for bringing out a tow truck big enough to get it off the road, in return for them keeping the scrap value. He had to take a train back to London. I thought of trying to get my money back from Des Swan, but I figured that even an honest dealer like Des would expect the faulty goods to be brought back. Altogether I was just happy to have escaped a miserable future, sewing mailbags with PJ up in the Joy.

# 15. Sold

In spite of me employing sabotage tactics that a resistance fighter would have approved, Peggy managed to get the house presentable, and ready for sale. John-Paul was wetting himself at the excitement of bringing this 'much sought after character residence' in 'one of Dublin's up-and-coming areas' to market. I hoped that the city's house-buyers would give it the two fingers - but I hoped in vain.

John-Paul started dropping in at all times of the day, bringing the interested, the curious and the brave on guided tours of the premises. It didn't matter what I might be doing - in they would come. On one occasion, I was sitting on the end of the bed in my vest and drawers, cutting my toenails. A woman came into the room, took a good look around, and remarked that she thought that the curtains were nice.

On another morning, Peggy was out foraging for vittels, and me and Bertie had been left in charge. I had just emerged from trap one, where I had been conducting serious business – it was at least a three flush job. I had been in there for a while, due to having had one or ten the night before, on top of a good steak dinner. It would not be safe for half an hour or so, without a gas mask and protective suit. But long before the all-clear was sounded, John-Paul arrived, steering a young couple in front of him. A 'professional couple' I think you would call them. They didn't look like they did anything useful for a living.

The guy wore a snazzy suit that had not come from Dunnes' sale. He was tieless and his shirt was open at the neck, as is the mode amongst the movers and shakers. Only defendants, undertakers and bank clerks bother with ties these days. Our prospective purchaser sported a couple of days' worth of fashionable stubble, and hair spiked with the assistance of an unguent. The bimbette with him was the colour of a kipper. She was dressed like she was going to a party somewhere sunny, and she had enough bling on board to restore sight to the blind. Jim Deegan would have classed her stilettos as offensive weapons. They spoke in an accent drawn from somewhere between Dalkey and Dallas.

I was sitting in my chair sipping tea, reviewing the previous day's Herald in case I had missed anything. John-Paul fired a 'howsitgoin' at me, and informed me that he was conducting a viewing of the premises. He did not make introductions. I nodded to them, but they ignored me, like I was a fixture that would be heading for the skip if they decided to buy. They stood in front of me looking around.

"It's quaint, isn't it?" she said.

"Very retro," he replied. "We'd have to rip all that out," he added, looking into the kitchen.

"Oh yes," she agreed, wrinkling her nose. "It would all need replacing."

They went through the kitchen door so that they were out of my line of sight. He said something that I could not hear, and she giggled. John-Paul looked at me and shrugged. I shrugged back.

"Upstairs we have three bedrooms and the bathroom," John-Paul informed them, leading the way.

"Not en suite," I shouted after them, trying to be helpful.

I heard John-Paul say: "This is the bathroom," followed by the noise of its door opening, and then the three of them gasping like they had found a decomposing body lying in the bath. The smell would not have been dissimilar in its effect.

"Oh my God!" she said.

"Jesus!" the snazzy suit wheezed.

John-Paul did not join in the supplications to the deity. Someone quickly closed the door, before they lost consciousness.

"Very retro, isn't it?" I called up the stairs, rubbing my hands together, fairly delighted with myself.

They came back down, looking like bystanders caught up in a tear gas attack. If they had not been such pains in the arse, I would have offered them a strong drink, and counselling. But again they walked around me, like I was an occasional table.

"I suppose it might fit into the portfolio," yer man said.

"Maybe," she said. "But would we get the yield? What would be the p.c.m. rental Mr O'Driscoll?"

John-Paul put on a thoughtful face, which didn't suit him. He looked like a horse trying to do algebra.

"Well, it would depend on whether it would be as the property is currently presented," ... he glanced at me, looking like a horse having to choose his words carefully ... "or if freshened up a little."

"It's a great house this," I said. "Brilliant neighbours. Party, party, party, every feckin' night. They're great gas."

I am sure that I was speaking - and in English – I could definitely hear the noise of it. But I got no more response from them than if I had been the wallpaper.

"Thanks very much, Mr Flynn," John-Paul said, as he steered the tour party towards the exit. "I'm very sorry to have barged in on ya like this, but Mrs Flynn said I could come any time. I'll be in touch."

"No bother," I said to him.

"All the best now," I said to the pair. "It was lovely chattin' with yis." Then, when the door was shut behind them: "Yis can feck off the three o' yis. If I never hear from yis again, it'll be soon enough for me."

★ ★ ★

But it was not to be. The buggers made an offer, in spite of being gassed, and warned about the party-mad neighbours. Peggy took the call with the joyful news, and without even referring to me, she accepted. Legal matters were put in train with Messrs Stafford, Proudfoot and Associates, solicitors and commissioners for oaths. When Peggy deigned to bring me up to speed with developments, I committed a few oaths myself, but outwardly I maintained the old sang froid. I even managed a watery smile as sentence was pronounced.

She was straight on to Moya out in Sunnyside. As luck would have it, the builders were just applying the last few bits of chewing gum and string that would hold our new home together.

"This is great," Peggy said, delighted. "At last, things are working out for us. Isn't it fantastic?"

I agreed that it was indeed something along those lines.

"Do ya know wha' we'll do?" she said.

I thought of suggesting a suicide pact, but it might have dampened the mood, so I kept it to myself.

"We'll have a celebration. A little party. It can be like a going away do. We can have the family, an' a few friends an' neighbours."

"Is it not a house warmin' tha' ya're supposed to have?" I asked.

"Ya mus' be jokin'," she said. "I'm not havin' a shower o' knackers from the Daymo anywhere near Sunnyside, wreckin' the place, an' makin' a show of us."

So much for our much-loved friends an' neighbours, I thought.

"So wha's the plan then?" I asked. "Are we goin' to leave no forwardin' address? Tell them tha' we're goin' off to the Congo?"

She ignored me, which was becoming the standard approach to Frankie. I was beginning to wonder if I even existed.

"I'll ring Marian an' Angela," she said. "They can help wi' the food."

"Yeah," I said. "Marian can get Susan to make up a banana an' onion cassarole."

The sarcasm was wasted on her, but something percolated through, to make her worry about the possible delivery of dishes containing artichoke, asparagus or aubergines.

"We don't want anythin' too fancy," she said. "I'll tell her wha' to do."

"Crisps an' peanuts are all ya need for a party," I said. "As long as there's plenty o' drink, ya're away in a hack."

"Listen you!" she said. "This is goin' to be a nice party for family an' friends. Not a piss up. Do ya hear me? Ya're not to go invitin' anyone without my say so. I don't want ya bringin' the dregs o' Magowan's in here."

"Bu' I don't know anyone else," I protested. "If I don't invite people from Magowan's, who the hell am I goin' to invite? Bono? The Dally Lammy?"

"I know plenty o' respectable people," she said.

"Who?" I asked, genuinely curious.

"Never you mind," she said.

"So let me get this straight," I said. "We're goin' to have a hooley to say goodbye to people I don't know, even though I've lived here for over thirty years."

"It will not be a hooley," she corrected, and she may have stamped her foot to emphasise the point. "It will be a proper party. There will be nice people, nice food, an' nice drink. Maybe a few bottles o' wine."

"My Jaysus," I said, disgusted. "Well, it'll be finished in an hour, an' we can go up to the pub. There is tha', I suppose."

"There'll be no goin' near any pub," she said.

"Ah look, Peggy", I said trying - without much hope - to appeal to her reason. "We'll have to show people proper hospitality. We'll need a few bottles o' beer, and a drop o' the craythur. People will expect it. It's tradition."

She seemed to be thinking about it - if scowling and biting your lip are signs of thinking.

"Okay," she said. "Bu' we're not goin' mad, d'ya hear me? I want it kep' respectable."

"Anyway, wha' do we care?" I asked. "If we're movin', they can think wha' they like. We may as well go out with a bang as a whimper, eh?"

"We're not goin' out with any bang. This is goin' to be the start of our new life. We'll have a nice evenin' here, and when we're out in Sunnyside, ya can give up yer traipsin' up to the pub every night. We'll meet new people - respectable people. We can have them aroun' for drinks now an' again. Maybe even dinner, like Marian an' Susan do."

My jaw descended to basement level, as I listened to this industrial-grade drivel. This was worse than in my darkest nightmares after a supper of cheese and pickle sandwiches. The woman was trying to turn us into Margo and Gerry.

I knew that there was no pub worth going to in Sunnyside, but I had sketched out a little plan, which would keep something like normal service intact. This involved the re-creation of Frankie as commuter, using buses to bring me back to civilisation for regular oiling and refreshment. It would mean me legging it out of Magowan's by half eleven every night to catch the last bus. But needs must, and my motto is 'a man's gotta do what a man's gotta do.'

But now this – curfewed, and confined to barracks. All she was short of was getting me elocution lessons, and having people around to play bridge. I was looking into the abyss - if that's where you look when you feel that the game is up – and what I saw was Frankie up against the wall, with his hands tied behind his back. The blindfold was in position. The firing squad of Moya, John-Paul, Stafford, Proudfoot and Associates had weapons cocked and aimed, and were just waiting for Peggy's order to fire.

But it is in adversity that you find Frankie Flynn at his best. Like when the baddie has James Bond by the short and curlies, and says 'Goodbye Mr Bond,' leaving 007 to drop into a vat of boiling acid. Escape seems impossible, but you know that he will get out of it somehow. That is exactly the way it is with me. Desperate situations stimulate the production of adrenalin and other essential juices. Unconsciously, the machinery goes into overdrive and a solution is found. In fact, much of my best work is done when I am unconscious, and when my mind is blank. Like the time I fell into the canal - I was back out and on the path, before I even realised that I had fallen in.

The answer came to me like the Holy Ghost descending on the apostles when they were gathered in the room playing cards or whatever. In my case I was walking down Capel Street, thinking of nothing in particular when it hit me, like a piano falling off a roof. I realised that I had got the psychology all wrong. The more I tried to thwart Peggy in her plan to decamp to Sunnyside, the more she would be hell bent on doing it. In all our years together she could never bring herself to go along with anything I wanted. So it was obvious. All I had to do was to become a zealous convert to the Sunnyside cause, and she would go off the idea faster than fish on a radiator.

Also, I figured that she might be less keen on escaping the Daymo and its proletarian occupants, if she thought that said proletariat were also intent on moving to Sunnyside.

I felt like a right eejit that I had not thought of this strategy before. Now that I had finally come up with the goods, I needed to work quickly. The sand was disappearing through the little hole so fast, that I could count the few grains that were left.

I immediately did an about-face and headed straight home - via Magowan's. My plan needed allies and confederates, and I knew that Magowan's was where I would find them in numbers.

★ ★ ★

Later that day, when I arrived back at the Ponderosa, Peggy and Angela were watching Judge Judy, while the kids were entertaining themselves. Chandler was doing something to an electricity socket with a biro, and little Margaret was red in the face, concentrating on nappy business. Christian was under the table - in his mind a military vehicle – firing shells at an unseen enemy.

Daphne was feeding bits of an apple to Bertie. He was very keen on fruit, although I always advised him against it. It gave him the squits, which I assumed to be a pedigree thing. Daphne was not producing the goods fast enough for his liking, and I could see that he was getting narky. She was nibbling little bits off the apple, and handing these micro-morsels to him. She was in serious danger of losing a finger, or the end of her snoot, if she did not speed up production. As an act of kindness to them both, I took the apple off her, and lobbed it to Bertie. He disposed of it in a matter of seconds, then initiated a search for it, looking mystified at its disappearance, in that way that dogs do. Daphne was neither pleased nor grateful that I had saved her skin, and started howling in outrage.

After greeting the ladies, and feigning interest in whatever ailment Tommy was featuring that day, I dived straight in.

"It won't be long now," I said, rubbing my hands together, like a farmer before his dinner.

Wha' won't?" Angela asked.

"The move out to Sunnyside," I said. "Won't be long now at all. I can't wait."

The two of them looked at me, like they were waiting for a punchline.

"I'm lookin' forward to it," I said, to be clear.

Peggy was not even close to buying this tripe, but I was only laying down a foundation. 'Softly, softly, catchee donkey' is my motto.

"I thought ya weren't keen," Angela said. "Ya said to Tommy tha' ya weren't. Leave her alone," she yelled taking a swipe at Chandler, who had got bored trying to electrocute himself, and had moved on to kicking Daphne.

I filed a note in the back of my mind to inflict some new medical misfortune on Tommy when I next encountered him. In my considered opinion, the only difference between him and a bucket of shit, was the bucket.

"Ah, yeah," I said. "I wasn't tha' mad abou' it at the start. Tha's true enough. Bu' the idea grows on ya, so it does. Ah, it'll be great. New house an' all, wha'?"

"Bu' I thought ya wanted to stay in the Daymo?" Angela said.

"I did, yeah, but there'll be no livin' here in a couple o' years wi' all the tossers tha' there'll be aroun' here."

"Wha's a tosser, Gandad?" Christian asked.

"Here yis are kids," Peggy said, getting out the crisps, and changing the channel to Mickaloadian. When this was sorted out, we got back to the agenda.

"Wha' are ya talkin' abou'? Who's goin' to be livin' aroun' here?" Peggy wanted to know.

"Wha' I mean is tha' all the ordinary people will be gone. The Daymo's bein' bought up lock, stock an' barrel by feckin' yuppies, like tha' pair tha's buyin' this place. Jus' wait an' see. Another few years an' the corner shop'll be a delicatessen, and Magowan's will be one o' them gastric pubs."

Peggy still wasn't quite in the market for this bullshit.

"Fat chance," she said.

"You mark my words," I said. "Sure half the lads in Magowan's are lookin' at movin' to Sunnyside. They think it's the only thing to do. Especially when they heard tha' we were goin'. It'll be great out there - with all the lads like."

"Wha' lads? Who are ya talkin' abou'?"

Peggy sounded irritated. She was still far from hooked, but she was giving the worm her full attention.

"Joe Horgan. Paddy Mulhall. Larry Edwards."

"I don't believe ya," she said. "Paddy Mulhall wouldn't stir himself to breathe. He'd be dead long ago if it didn't happen automatically. There's no way tha' he's goin' to organise a house move."

"Maybe not, but Mary would. He says she's mad to get goin'."

I could see that this point had made it through to the target. Mary Mulhall was one of nature's leaders. If Hitler had had her at his side, things might have turned out better for him.

"Even Betty Magowan is thinkin' about it. She says there's no point in stayin' here if all her customers are out in Sunnyside. She says she might look at wha' she could organise out there. She should have no bother findin' a place. The County Council is obliged to provide amenities for people."

"It'll be like years ago, when all the people moved out o' Sean McDermott Street an' the Diamond to Ballymun," I said.

Peggy pulled a face. Ballymun had not turned out to be heaven on earth. The picture I was painting was not to Peggy's liking. Sunnyside's allure for her depended to a large extent on the absence of Daymoites. Adding a few tablespoons of Horgans and Mulhalls was like putting salt and vinegar in the cake mix.

I had her rattled, but there was still work to be done.

★ ★ ★

A few days later, I scored another bulls-eye. Peggy had phoned Moya to check on progress, or to get toilet seat measurements or something. While they were chatting, Moya thanked her for introducing that nice Mr Horgan to the scheme. Good man, Joe! As requested, he had gone out and feigned enthusiasm for the Merrion or the Belvedere. Moya was even able to describe the particular plot that Joe allegedly had his eye on - which happened to be right in front of ours. Ha!

Peggy looked stunned as she told me this. Her eyes had lost their normal Medusa intensity. She was having the kind of crisis of faith that Father Collins told us afflicted the saints from time to time. Apparently it was good for them -

character building or something – but it was not doing Peggy much good.

"Ya see," I said. "I told ya. It'll be great. Joe an' Teresa jus' across the road from us. Fantastic!"

Peggy could not stand Teresa Horgan. She would rather have lived across from a leaky nuclear power station, where the staff played loud jazz music all day. She didn't like jazz either.

"We'll be able to have them over for one o' them dinner parties tha' ya were talkin' abou'," I said, rubbing the salt in mercilessly. "An' they could invite us back. We could be backwards an' forwards every week."

Peggy looked like she was swallowing gravel.

★ ★ ★

The following Saturday afternoon, Marian and Susan came over. They wanted to drive us out to Sunnyside, so that they could join in the fun of watching the builders botch the finishing touches to Chateau Flynn. I displayed keenness, but oddly Peggy seemed, if not indifferent to the adventure, at least somewhere well short of different.

On the way out, I was laying it on thick and heavy about how great it was that so many dear and close friends would be joining us in Sunnyside - like the lads following Moses into the desert.

"It's a trend ya see all over the world," Marian said. "Developers are smartenin' up run-down areas, with remodelled houses an' new apartments. I see it happenin' everywhere I go - London, Brooklyn - so why not the Daymo as well? In London all the real east-enders moved out to Essex, an' the yuppy bankers took over in Docklands. Even a small apartment there now would cost ya a fortune, but the people who lived there for years never saw a penny o' tha'. It was the smart developers who made the killin'."

Marian's exposé of the evils of capitalism was just the medicine I would have prescribed for Peggy. I had not even tried to recruit Marian to the cause, and here she was, coming up with this top grade stuff, unprompted, unbriefed – unbelievable! Peggy would not wish to be considered part of the great unwashed, being hoodwinked by carpetbaggers.

Susan butted in: "It could take generations before the Daymo would be gentrified, Marian."

I was sitting beside her in the back seat, and I considered reaching over, opening the door, and pushing her out on to the road. With commendable self-control, I didn't do it.

"Ya might be surprised, Susan," Marian said. "It's extraordinary how quickly things can move, once the trend starts. Areas tha' ya couldn't give away, start to be worth a fortune."

Peggy was adding nothing to the debate, but I could detect the whiff of brain cells smouldering away, like damp socks over a brazier. She was taking it all in, sure enough.

"Is tha' right, Marian?" I asked. "Jaysus, maybe we're mad to be sellin' now? Maybe we're jumpin' the gun."

Peggy glanced over her shoulder at me, and I changed my tune immediately.

"But no! We're the trailblazers - boldly goin' where angels fear to tread, eh Peggy?"

There was no reply.

"I can't wait. No sirree jimbobadee. California here we come."

"Ya're not committed until y'ave signed, Da," Marian said. "Until then, ya can do wha' ya like."

I knew this very well.

"Is tha' a fact?" I asked. "Tha's good to know. Just in case, like. Knowledge is power, wha'?"

"Feck off," Peggy said – maybe not the most thought-provoking contribution to the conversation, but it was good enough for me.

Happy that matters were simmering away nicely, I let them rest, and settled down to humming a selection of tunes from MGM musicals for the rest of the journey.

★   ★   ★

Moya jangled up to us as we got out of the car. As usual she was dressed as though Arnotts had told her she could have all the clothes and jewellery she wanted, as long as she wore them all together. I marvelled that she was able to raise her arm to shake hands, with all the shackles she was carrying.

"Frank! Peggy!" she gushed. "How lovely it is to see yis both again! An' these must be yer two daughters. Now, let me guess which is the one with the family."

In her track suit, Susan looked about as much like mammy material as I did. By a process of elimination, Moya decided that it must be Marian.

"It's you!" she said. "Am I right?"

She sounded confident, and that the steward's decision could only be a formality. Marian didn't look too pleased.

"No," she said. "Ya're thinkin' o' me sister. This is not me sister. This is a friend."

"Yes," Peggy said. "A friend."

Moya didn't seem remotely put out that she had stuck her size seven firmly into the brown stuff. Obviously estate agents are not easily reduced to blushes and tears. She guffawed like this was a hilarious misunderstanding that she would be telling people about for weeks.

"Will yis listen to me? Sure wha' am I like at all? Don't mind me. Have ya come out to see where yer Mammy an' Daddy are runnin' off to? In case they won't tell ya?"

She thought that this was comedy gold, and she nearly laughed her loaf off. I didn't think it was much of a gag, but I joined in as best as I could. Now that I was in the Sunnyside fan club, I felt that I had to sing up for the team.

"Come on. Come on," Moya said. "I'll bet yis can't wait to see the house."

She led the way to the little bit of paradise that would soon be ours. Ridiculously, we were issued with hard hats before we were allowed 'on site', even though the house was all but finished. Our place in the Daymo had lots more hazards in it. Susan didn't mind wearing hers, but Peggy and Marian were not keen on having to stuff their hair-dos into the little plastic buckets.

The nearly-built Regal exceeded all my worst fears. It looked like a doll's house, without the attention to detail and build quality that even an undiscerning child would demand. An elderly wolf with chronic emphysema would have had no trouble blowing it down. It had all the character, the charm and individuality of a dead pigeon. I would rather have lived in a hole in the ground.

"Jaysus Moya, it's gorgeous," I said. "I could move into it this minute, I could. Tha's a fact."

"Hasn't the kitchen come out nice?" Moya asked. "We're very pleased with it."

"It's lovely," I said. "Beautiful, gorgeous," I added, just to be on the safe side.

"I can see meself sittin' here, eatin' me dinner. Wha' do yis think girls?" I asked Susan and Marian.

"It's very nice, Mr Flynn. Very nice. I'm sure ya'll be very happy here," Susan said, oozing politeness. They were not the words you would use, if you really liked something, and we all knew it.

Peggy was staring out the window across at where the House of Horgan was rising from the ground like the undead. She seemed transfixed by a horrible dread.

Right on cue, Moya chipped in: "And yis won't be lonely out here – not with yer friends only across from yis. It'll be home from home."

"Tha's great," I said. "Tell us Moya – I suppose there mus' be loads like us comin' out o' town - for the fresh air - an' the en suites?"

"Absolutely," she said, supporting the motion. "Ya needn't worry. Yis'll soon be right at home out here. After a while, it'll feel like yis never moved at all!"

This was hardly balm to sooth Peggy's frazzled nerves. She had been aiming to escape from the Daymo, not to help establish a bloody colony.

Moya and I tried to get Peggy excited about choosing a colour to paint the living room walls. Personally I couldn't have given a hoarse hoot – they could have painted them purple with yellow stripes for all I cared – but encouragingly, Peggy was not that interested either. Without too much debate we settled on something called Dove Grey - or Pigeon Shit - that was probably surplus from painting prison cells.

At this stage, I felt that my work was done. I had set a light to Peggy's touchpaper, and now the thing was to remove myself to a safe distance. 'Don't over-egg the broth' is my motto. There was a risk that I might overdo it, and to avoid that danger, it was safer for me to exclude myself from Peggy's society. So, for the next few days, I almost took up residence in Magowan's, and when I wasn't there, I was in Burke's or Kinsella's.

# 16. Help

By now, Peggy had met our prospective buyers, and she had not taken much of a shine to them. This suited my purposes very well.

"They have great ideas abou' rearrangin' the place," I said. "There won't be a wall left standin' by the time they're finished."

"They can do wha' they like," she barked back at me. "It makes no odds to me."

"The two o' them had a great laugh abou' the kitchen. I don't know wha' it was tha' tickled them so much," I added, knowing that a woman's kitchen is her castle, and insulting it, is like telling her that her kids are ugly.

"Is tha' a fact?" Peggy asked, but only rhetorically, if that's what I mean. Anyway, she was not looking for an answer, but I gave her one anyway.

"It is," I said. "A great laugh! The two o' them were rollin' aroun' on the floor."

"As long as they're happy, I'm happy," she said.

She didn't sound happy, but it was not the high dudgeon and indignation that I was aiming for. I wanted to hear an impassioned speech ending in: "... an' if she thinks she's rearrangin' MY kitchen, she can think again!"

I gave it another go.

"An' the bathroom! They're goin' to rip tha' out. It's the wrong colour apparently."

"Look Frank, I don't care if they turn the bathroom into a voodoo temple, an' go an' shit in the fireplace. They can do whatever they like. If they pay the money, it's theirs. They can paint it pink an' throw sugar at it. I DON'T GIVE A FIDDLER'S FART!"

This was more like it.

"There's no need to shout," I said.

Peggy glared at me while she manoeuvred some dirt around the floor with the sweeping brush. She weighed the brush in her hand, obviously considering whether to hit me with it. Her grip tightened, but she was too close to me to swing it properly, and we both realised that. I guess the benefit of being married for so long, is that you get to share these unspoken thoughts.

★ ★ ★

Stafford, Proudfoot and the lads came through with the news that everything was tickety-boo on the legal front. After much scholarly analysis, they had concluded that the party of the first part (the buyers), were ready to produce the do-re-mi, and the party of the second part (us) were ready to hand over the keys. Moya also informed us that the builders had put away their tools, and that our little bit of Shangri-La was ready and fit for habitation. A date was set for the following Monday for us to show up at Stafford's (and Proudfoot's) place of business, to sign on the dotted line, and say goodbye to life in the Daymo.

But it isn't over until the fat lady sings, or in this case, signs, and my fat lady was only going to sign, after taking the pen out of my cold dead hand. Hopefully that would not be necessary, as it would have defeated the object of the exercise. I still hoped for a satisfactory outcome, with a little help from my friends.

Peggy decided to throw the party the Saturday night before the signing. Her reasoning was that there would not be enough time afterwards, as we would be tied up, putting precious things into boxes, reading meters, etc. The good news was that she had given up on her notion of making it a respectable tea and crumpet gathering. I think she had discovered that there was not much of a market for that class of thing in the Daymo, and that if she persisted, she would be on her own. I told the lads in Magowan's to come and enjoy the send-off, but to bet their last bob with J P Twomey that the Flynns would be going nowhere.

Peggy wanted to get wine, and she said that I wouldn't know the difference between Pinot and paintstripper - which was true. Therefore she had taken it upon herself to go to the off licence to order the booze. Fearing the worst, I had gone in after her and increased her miserable beer order by several multiples.

★ ★ ★

On the Saturday lunchtime, Peggy had summoned Angela, Marian and Susan to make sandwiches, and to cook chickens' legs. As usual Angela had brought the kids, as Tommy was not up to looking after them. There was no place for Frankie in such a forum, so I de-camped to Magowan's. Such was the pandemonium in the household that Bertie jumped up to come with me. This was unusual, as he had by then decided to avoid strolls with the Master, following some doggy health and safety assessment he had done in his head. Therefore, it was no great surprise that, when I had found his lead, he changed his mind and backed off.

"Ya can feck off then," I told him.

He had a further change of mind, when Daphne waddled over and sat on him, and Margaret started screaming for something – a particular trial for a dog with sensitive earholes. He signalled this change of mind, by an increase in the rate of tail wagging, and plaintive yipping, but I had made my mind up.

"No – ya had yer chance, ya little bollix," I said. "There is a tide in the affairs o' dogs, and unfortunately for you Bertie oul son, the tide is goin' out without ya."

I thought that this would be a valuable dog training lesson. The next time that I called the bugger to heel, he would come running.

Peggy was marshalling her catering corps, and a visit to Magowan's would give me an opportunity to marshall mine. By the time the evening was over, I wanted Peggy to believe that every gurrier in the Daymo would be sleeping in the bed with us in Sunnyside.

When I came through Magowan's portal, Paddy Mulhall was sitting on a stool at the bar studying the Herald. He looked up when he saw me.

"There ya're Frankie," he said, stating an indisputable fact. "Have ya not moved down the country yet?"

"No, I haven't, an' I'm not goin' to either," I said.

"Well, ya're goin' about it the wrong way then," he said. "If ya're stayin' put, ya don't put yer house on the market. Do ya folley me? I thought tha' even you'd know tha', an' ya know eff all."

"Would ya ever feck off an' leave me alone," I said. "Do ya want a pint?"

He nodded that he did, and I nodded the nod on to Betty, who had materialised in front of us looking for instructions.

"There's a story here about a fella up in court for murderin' his missus," Paddy said. "They found bits o' her under a patio he laid - a nice job apparently."

"Is killin' yer wife against the law?" I asked. "I'll have to try to remember tha'."

"As yer man Dickens said: 'the law is a feckin' eejit'," Paddy agreed.

"I've got Peggy on the edge," I told him. "It'll only take a little nudge or two, an' the Sunnyside file can be consigned to the archives."

"She's goin' off the idea, is she?" he asked.

"She is indeed," I said.

"Wha' made her do tha'?" he asked.

"She thinks tha' you're movin' out there," I said.

I realised that this may have lacked tact. Although Paddy has the skin of an armadillo, that has been treated with extra insult repellant, he could do sensitivity when it suited him. He certainly looked like a man about to take offense. He sucked in air like a surfacing whale, and set himself to give me an earful. Luckily, at that moment, Betty arrived bearing pints, and it's hard for a man to take umbrage with someone whose pint he is about to swallow. So he released his lungful of air harmlessly, stuck a top lip onto his glass, and gave it a good pull. While he was thus distracted, I rushed to elaborate, and to make amends.

"I don't mean you, specifically, Paddy," I said. "I mean the whole kit an' caboodle. Peggy is lookin' to get out o' the Daymo, so if she thinks tha' the Daymo is movin' with her like the great Sioux Migration, there'll be no bleedin' point, will there?"

"Why would she think tha'?" he wanted to know. "Nobody'd want to move out to tha' kip."

"Well Paddy, tha' might be the way you see it," I said. "An' it's the way tha' I see it. But it sure as hell isn't the way tha' Peggy sees it. So if she thinks tha' Sunnyside is the new

Garden o' Eden, she prob'ly thinks tha' you might think so too. If ya folley me."

It was all a bit much for Paddy to take in, but he was willing to give me the benefit of the doubt.

"Whatever ya're havin' yerself," he said. "So ya want me an' Mary to come up to your gaff this evenin', an' let on tha' we're movin' to Sunnyside?"

I looked for flaws in his summary of the mission, and I could find none.

"Yeah," I said. "Well – jus' tha' yis're thinkin' about it. Don't overdo it. Throw in stuff about fresh air, an' kitchen diners."

"Eh?"

"Say tha' ya think they're great. Tha' only a gobshite wouldn't go mad for them."

Paddy rubbed his chin like a man who had now heard it all. I was satisfied that he had enough information to carry the job off. Any more would risk shortcircuiting his brain.

I could see Ginger Celtic over in a corner, in earnest conversation with a man in a moleskin coat, unknown to me (both the man, and the coat). I surmised that he had been directed to Magowan's and to Ginger, because he was in need of satellite television. The man finished his drink, got up and shook Ginger's hand, indicating that the business was being concluded.

"So I'll see ya then – ya have the address alright," the man said.

"Yeah," Ginger said. "No bother. I'll look after tha' for ya."

"Good man," the man said, and left.

I made my apologies to Paddy, and slid across in Ginger's direction. My aim was to get him to come to the party, and to declare himself as one of the Sunnyside elect. As you will have gathered, Peggy had a low tolerance for much of the Daymo's population. Competition would have been fierce for her nomination of excrescence-in-chief, and Ginger would have been a strong contender. The thought of sharing the same bit of suburbia with him would not have pleased her. In her book, Ginger's presence would automatically knock twenty five per cent off property values. I figured that the prospect would not just nudge her over the edge back to where I wanted her - it would catapult her over it. It should have her and her descendants glued to the Daymo for generations.

"How's it goin', Ginger?" I enquired.

He gave me a grunt in reply, indicating that everything with his family and business were as good as could be expected in the prevailing economic conditions.

"Tha's great," I said, grinning like a fool, to show that I was pleased to hear it.

"Ya gettin' the football okay?" he asked.

"Oh yeah," I reassured him. "Fantastic. Not a bother."

Satisfied that in Frankie he had a contented customer, he turned away to give his time and talents to anyone who might be suffering fuzzy reception. I moved in his way.

"I was wonderin' – are ya doin' anythin' later this evenin'?" I asked.

Given the nature of Ginger's business, he had to be careful with information regarding his movements. He looked cagey.

"I don't know," he said. "Why?"

"It was jus' tha' me an' the missus are havin' a little get-together in the house, an' I was wonderin' if ya'd like to come," I said. "It'll jus' be family, friends an' people from here. Nothin' fancy."

"A party?" he asked. "Ya're havin' a party?"

I nodded to confirm that his personal reception was working perfectly, and that he had received the signal loud, clear, and in HD.

"An' ya're askin' me to come?"

I nodded again, and added "yeah" just for the hell of it. If I'd had flags, I would have done him a bit of semaphore.

"An' it's this evenin'?"

I nodded some more. I was beginning to get motion sickness.

"Yeah, maybe," he said. "I'll have to see."

"It'd be great if ya could, Ginger." I said. "I'd really appreciate it."

I hadn't felt like this since I was a teenager, trying to persuade Bernie Rooney to indulge in a bit of fandango with me in the laneway behind the Pro Cathedral.

"An' if ya do, could ya do me a big favour?" I added.

Ginger looked like a huge red-headed mouse in cat country - wary, you might call it.

"Wha' kind o' favour?" he asked. "The telly's workin' okay?"

Ginger's experience of dispensing favours was obviously limited to fiddling with valves, tubes and satellite dishes.

"No, not tha'," I said. "The telly's grand. Wha' it is, is tha' the missus wants to move out to Sunnyside..."

"Tha's no bother," he said. "Let me know when ya're goin', an' I'll come an' sort it out for ya."

He tried to escape again. Without thinking, I caught his arm to hold him back. I realised that this was a dangerous thing to do. Ginger could interpret even a wave in his direction as a preliminary to GBH, and take pre-emptive steps. I have seen him put people on their arses over less. I let him loose, and cowered slightly, hoping that this would be accepted as a submissive stance in the baboon society with which he would be familiar.

"It's nothin' to do with the telly," I said. "I'm not movin'..."

"Ya just said tha' ya were..."

"No," I said. "The missus wants to ... but I don't. Tha's where ya might be able to do me the favour."

Ginger was looking at me like I had lost the grip on my horizontal hold.

"If ya could jus' come this evenin' – even for half an hour – an' tell Peggy tha' ya're thinkin' o' movin' out to Sunnyside yerself... that'd be great," I said.

"Tell her tha' I'm movin' out to Sunnyside? Wha' would I be doin' out in a shite hole like Sunnyside?"

"Only tha' ya're thinkin' about it..."

"But I'm not."

This was beyond exasperating. You would think that a man, whose whole life was based on dishonesty and deceit, would be quicker on the uptake in a matter requiring the subtle use of facts.

"Jus' let on," I said.

"Ya want me to lie to her?"

Eureka! At last he recognised the familiar concept.

"Yeah," I said. "Exactly!"

Ginger sniggered. I was glad to find that he had a sense of humour. It oils the wheels, and creates bonds in the common cause. I joined him, and had a snigger myself.

"Yeah, alright then," he said. "Sunnyside! For feck's sake."

I let him go this time, and sauntered back to the bar. Paddy was talking with Betty. He had bought me a pint, and I fell on it like a lion on a sick wildebeest. I needed it after Ginger.

"So have ya signed him up as well?" Betty asked.

"Yep," I confirmed. "He is willin' to attend an' testify."

"Ya're a gas man, an' no mistake," Betty said.

"It's psychology, Betty," I said. "Tha's all. Ya have to study yer opponent's strengths and weaknesses, and work accordingly. Like in chess."

"Or judo," Paddy said.

"Wha'?" I asked.

"In judo, ya use the other fella's weight an' momentum to land him on his arse," he explained. "So even a little squirt can take on a big fella. Tha's why the Japanese are keen on it. They're only little feckers."

"No, they're not," I objected. "Wha' about the wrestlers? The big fellas in the nappies. Whatyacall them?"

"Sumos," Betty said.

"No, it's not tha'," I said. "It's Soonamy or somethin'. Anyway, they're huge big buggers. Bu' anyway', ya're right Paddy. Know thine enemy. Tha's the thing."

"The poor woman," Betty said. "If I was her, I wouldn't waste me time with chess or judo. Wha' ya need is a good belt o' the poker, so ya do."

I winced, as that was very much in line with Peggy's favoured approach. I realised that if I did not play my cards right, I could find myself in A&E explaining how that poker came to be stuck where it was.

# 17. Hooley

I got back to the house in what I thought would be good time to greet our guests, but already half a dozen oul wans were there, getting stuck into the chicken legs and the bottles of Harp. The next door neighbour was prominent amongst those present. She was never a woman to enjoy life in all its joy and beauty. If you brought her into the Sistine Chapel, she would only see the dust behind the radiators. She was appraising our front room with a disdainful look. She was like a valuer from Sotheby's who had been misinformed that the place was full of objets d'arts.

"There ya're," I said civilly to her.

She gave me a nod, and a look that would curdle petrol. I figured that at some time in her life, she must have seen something that she approved of, but it must have been a long time ago.

Peggy gave me a bright smile, and said something kind and welcoming, which worried me, until I realised that it was for the benefit of the assembly. I still steered well clear of her, as she would be well capable of giving me a sneaky kick if I got within range.

"Ya were out?" the next door harridan enquired.

I was going to say that I wasn't – that I had been there all the time, and that I was practicing my special invisibility powers. But I did not. I settled for "yeah," without providing the details that she so clearly craved.

"It's well for ya," she said.

"Wha' d'ya mean?" I asked, genuinely stumped.

"Tha' ya can go off divartin' yerself whenever ya want. I wish I could. Tha's a fact."

I could not imagine where she might go for amusement, but I could not see what might be stopping her either. I made the enquiry.

"Wha's stoppin' ya?"

Parts of her face shot off in different directions. The eyebrows flew up and the jaw flew down, like they were trying to get away from each other – which would have been very understandable. The eyes bulged. She was like a bad actor trying to do incredulity.

"Are ya jokin' me or wha'?" she asked.

I wanted to assure her that I would not dream of wasting comedy on a sourpuss like her, but I just shook my head.

"Sure I don't have a minute to meself," she said. "Tha' house doesn't clean itself, ya know."

She lived on her own since her husband went to his eternal peace. I thought of pointing out that the sole cause of dirt and disease on her premises could only be herself, and herself alone. Maybe if she gave up making a pig's mess of it, she could cut back on her sanitation duties. But my internal censor cut me short. Seeing that her glass was empty, I thought that I would steer the conversation on to more familiar ground.

"Let me get ya another drink," I said.

She pulled a face, like I was offering her poison, but accepted it when I poured her a can.

"Ya can get too fond of it," she said, and I detected an accusatory tone. "I was never bothered about it meself. Christmas and christenin's, and maybe a drop to keep the cold out."

"Ya're dead right," I agreed. "Sure, it's the ruination o' the country."

Her ugly mug started doing the incredulity thing again. Before she could give me the benefit of her further views, I was saved by the cavalry. Through the door came Joe and Larry and their misuses, followed by most of the dramatis personae that makes up Magowan's Bar. It looked like the coach tour from hell. I could hear Peggy grinding her teeth from the far side of the room.

"Here yis are lads," I said. "Come in. Come in. There's drink for the men and tay for the women. Help yerselves."

I pulled Joe aside.

"Yis got here jus' in time. Another minute o' tha' oul' wan, an' I'd a bin dug out o' her."

Joe peered in her direction. She was eating two chicken legs at once.

"I wouldn't ha' thought she'd be yer type, but the best o' luck to ya, Frankie."

"Feck off," I said. "I don't mean tha'. I wouldn't touch her if ya gave me a lend o' yours. She's like a black hole in the cosmos. Any bit o' craic tha' goes near her, gets sucked in an' disappears."

"Ya're not coddin' me," Joe said. "Ya fancy the knickers off her. Ya're jus' puttin' on a front."

"Feck off," I said again, with feeling.

Larry came over, with a glass of Harp fizzing over onto the carpet. Peggy was watching him, and it was not fondly.

"How are the men? Wha's goin' on?" he asked.

"Frankie wants to get the ride off yer wan over there," Joe said, nodding towards the lady in question.

Larry gave her an appraising once-over.

"It'd be different anyway," he said. "Wha' is it? Animal, mineral or vegetable?"

"Don't you be slaggin' Frankie's bit o' stuff," Joe said. "Can't ya see the man's in love?"

"Feck off," I said again, largely for the benefit of Larry, who had not heard my views on the subject earlier.

"Ya want to get her a box o' chocolates or somethin'," Larry said. "The way she's gettin' stuck into tha' grub, I'd say she hasn't eaten for a while. God knows wha' she'd do for a bag o' sweets."

"Although ya might have to chew them for her," Joe said.

While the two of them laughed at their great wit, Angela had arrived with her brood, and came over, greeting Joe and Larry. She had the baby under her arm.

"I don't know wha' yis're laughin' at, an' I don't want to either," she said.

"Jus' as well," Joe said.

"No Tommy with ya?" I asked.

"He said tha' he might come later, but he has his tinnitus, so he's havin' a rest."

Joe, Larry and I exchanged glances. The lads knew well what a malingering little hypochondriac Tommy was.

"He's better off not bein' here then," Joe said. "With all the racket, he'd hardly be able to hear the ringin' in his ears."

"Yeah," Larry said. "It'd be wasted."

"I would have come back earlier to help me Ma, but I jus' couldn't get away 'til now," Angela said.

"Don't worry about it," I said. "We had everythin' under control."

Little Margaret was looking out from Angela's oxster up at me. She gave me a big smile showing off a full set of shiny gums.

"Come here to me," I said, taking her from Angela, and holding her in the air over my head.

"Who's a great girl? Gah, gah, gah, babababababa", I added, giving her a roller coaster swoop through the air.

Margaret made appreciative gurgly noises.

"Da, go easy ...." Angela said.

"Gah, gah, gah, babababababa, booboooboo," I said, developing my theme, and lifting Margaret high and fast like a launching rocket.

Angela tried to take the child back, but she was a second too late. I took my eye off the ball for the blink of an eye, so that I could locate the maternal docking station, and Margaret exploded like a tin of beans in a micro. An extraordinary amount of warm, lumpy sick shot out of her, and came down on me like a custard waterfall.

Angela and the lads dived for cover, but all I could do was hold on to the source of my misery. When she had finished dousing me with vomit, she started bawling, as though it was me that had committed the offence. I shoved her back at her mother.

"I don't know wha' she's cryin' for," I said. "It's me tha' should be cryin'."

The puke was warm and sticky when it hit me, but it was rapidly cooling down and setting. To say that I was not happy would not do justice to the strength of my feelings. The stuff was on my face, in my hair, up my arms, down the back of my neck, and all over the front of my shirt.

There was a tiny trickle dripping off my chin. Joe wiped it off with a serviette.

"Now ya're grand," he said.

"Are ya lookin' for a kick up the arse?" I said.

I enjoy a bit of banter, but my appetite for witty comments was at a low point. Peggy came over like a policeman to sort out a disturbance.

"What are ya after doin' on the poor child?" she asked - note that there was no word of sympathy for the state that I was in.

"Go upstairs and get yerself cleaned up," she ordered, in a tone that would have been familiar to Stalin 's attendants.

I did as I was bid, and made the best job I could with a face-cloth and a spongey thing I found in the bath. When I rejoined the merry throng, the place was heaving, like sales day in Arnotts. Somebody started singing a dirge about a little brown road winding over a hill to a little white house by the sea. It went down fairly well, but I thought it was a pile of shite. I launched into my Elvis repertoire, to add some zip to the party atmosphere. I gave them 'Blue Suede Shoes', 'Love Me Tender', and before they even had a chance to call for more, I dived into 'Can't Help Falling in Love'.

"Put a sock in it Da, an' give someone else a chance to murder somethin'.."

This came from our Marian. You raise them and give them everything you have, and this is what you get back. But it would take more than a barb like that to stop Frankie the entertainer.

"Wise men say, only fooools rush in," I sang.

"They certainly do," Marian said.

"...but I can't help falling in love with you," I soldiered on in spite of the flak.

Joe dived into the crowd and emerged clutching her from next door. She looked resentful. Lucky for him she had a glass in one hand and a ham sandwich in the other, and couldn't belt him. He manoeuvred her so that she was planted right in front of me.

'In for a penny, in for a euro' is my motto. I got down on one knee and sang straight up into her mug, as she chewed on her sandwich. There were drops of lager hanging off her moustache.

The lads in the room cottoned on, and there was much whistling, hooting and cries of "Get in there Frankie, ya boy ya!"

When I got to "take my hand, take my whole life through," I grabbed her paw, sandwich and all, and clasped it to my bosom. She had been fairly cooperative up to that point, but I had crossed some invisible line. She started to struggle like she was drowning, and I was trying to separate her from her lifebelt. I hung on like a barnacle.

"Lemme go," she said, through a gobful of ham and sliced loaf. "Will yis get him off me? He smells o' sick. Get off me, ya fecker."

I held on for the craic, and she stabbed me with an elbow under the ribs. That knocked most of the air out of me, but I spluttered on: "...cos I can't stop falling in love with you."

She gave me another jab with the elbow, and stamped on my foot. This was too much for me. There was a lurch as I lost my grip, and a tidal wave of her lager hit me the face. I can confirm that it was at the manufacturer's correct chilled temperature of minus something. I yelped in the middle of the final bar, and the song came to an abrupt halt.

"Now look wha' ya done," she said, fighting free and staring at her empty glass. She checked that the sandwich was still in working order, with a ratty little nibble. Policewoman Peggy arrived at the scene of the incident, fully intent on making a bad situation worse.

"Wha's tha' eejit after doin' on ya?" she asked, and I thought that such a leading and prejudiced line of questioning would not stand up in a kangaroo court.

"He's after makin' me spill me drink," the oul wan whinged, which I thought was rich, given that I had paid for it, I was soaked in it, and she had only spilled in because she had attacked me.

"Go an' get another drink for the poor woman," Peggy ordered me. "An' wha' are you grinnin' at?"

This question was aimed at Joe, who I remembered was the cause of all the trouble. I hoped that he was going to reap something like his just deserts. A lorry load of shit dumped on him would have cheered me up considerably. His smirk disappeared like snow in bright sunshine – not that there was much in the nature of sunshine coming from Peggy.

"Nothin'," he said. "I was jus' thinkin' ... tha's all."

"Well don't," Peggy barked. "Ya'll only hurt yerself. Joe shrivelled back into the crowd like a salted snail.

I got the woman another glass of Harpic, which she took from me with the best of bad grace. It was like giving a steak to a starving dog. Before Peggy could give me another lecture, and send me off to change again, Paddy Mulhall called for silence.

"Ladies an' gentlemen! A bit o' hush please. I have been asked to say a few words to mark this sad – an' indeed happy occasion."

There was a loud groan. The only person likely to have asked Paddy to speak, would have been Paddy. The common view was that Paddy could bore for Ireland. If he was going to tell his very long and crap story about a priest and a rabbi, there was a fair chance of him being lynched. However, he was not put off by the groan.

"I say sad, because two very dear friends an' neighbours are leavin' us."

This got a little cheer, but people were already looking at their watches.

"Who's tha' Paddy?" shouted Miley from the kitchen.

This brightened the rabble. It mightn't be so bad if there was to be heckling. You never know, somebody might even throw something. Paddy growled.

"I've known Frankie Flynn since he was in short trousers, covered in spots an' snot."

"Ah Jaysus Paddy, ya're not goin' to give us Frankie's life story are ya?" asked Joe. "I saw the fillum an' it was shite."

The mob liked that.

"No, I am not," Paddy said, drawing himself up to his full height. "All I'm goin' to say is tha' if there's a more decent, harmless poor fecker aroun' here, then I haven't met him."

I was not sure if I welcomed being referred to as harmless. I liked to think of myself as a bit of an outlaw – out there on the edge kind of thing. But I let it go.

"Frankie Flynn would give ya his last make," Paddy continued. "He's always there for a friend in need, with a kind word an' a helpin' hand."

I thought that this was true, but only up to a point. It depended on which friend, how much need, and the mood that I might be in.

"I'm goin' to be sick." Angela had come around and was standing beside me.

"But I like to think that we are not so much losin' friends, as gainin' a holiday destination," Paddy said.

This also went down well.

"We'll all be out to stay with yis, won't we lads?" he continued. "Put me an' Mary down for the first two weeks in August."

"Yis can feck off," Peggy said, to a great cheer.

I could see that Mary Mulhall was torn between laughing, and coming over and decking Peggy. It was one of those awkward social dilemmas that people write to magazines about. Paddy held up his arms for hush.

"Shurrup!" he shouted. "Will yis shurrup? I'm not finished."

Here we go, I thought - the priest and rabbi story – I hope they tear him to shreds. The noise went down like the easing off on a motorbike throttle, but the engine was still throbbing away.

"In fact, ladies an' gentlemen," Paddy said, "as yis know Joe an' Teresa Horgan are also movin' out to Sunnyside, an' after much reflection, meself an' Mary are after decidin' to do the same ourselves."

A couple of thousand volts seemed to shoot through Peggy. She gripped the back of a chair, and went the colour of marrowfat peas.

"Tha's great news," Miley roared. "More hooleys!"

Paddy was not giving up the floor yet. The peril of the priest and rabbi story was still with us.

"We all have to move with the times, ladies an' gentlemen," he said, although you would never think it, if you saw his clothes. "Progress – tha's wha' it's all about. The Daymo was a great place in its day, but like a good shepherd, when all the grass is gone, ya have to head off to pastures new."

He raised his arms like the statue of Jim Larkin in O'Connell Street. The mob responded by making loud sheep noises. For some reason, known only to him, Miley did an impression of a dog howling. Maybe he was being the sheepdog.

"We'll leave this place to bankers an' chancers," Paddy said. "We will rebuild our community in Sunnyside!"

I think that this was meant to be a big crescendo. Paddy probably expected to be carried shoulder high around the room, but it didn't happen. After a pause, he continued.

"So, Frankie an' Peggy, we'll be with yis not just in spirit – we'll jus' be aroun' the corner, jus' like now. This is au revoir, an' not goodbye. Ladies an' gentlemen, I give yis Frankie and Peggy Flynn."

There was a great cheer – mostly due to the relief that there would be no priest and rabbi story - and immediate calls for me to say something in response. Now I am not one for public speaking. My motto is 'if you're going to say something, say nothing.' But the gang would not take no for an answer, so I gave it a lash.

"As Paddy said, this is a sad day, an' a happy one," I said. "We'll be sad to be leavin' the Daymo after all these years, but we're very happy to be goin' out to Sunnyside, where everythin' is new an' shiny, an' we'll have the en suite an' everythin'."

This got a big whistle.

"Will ya have a beeday to wash yer arse in, Frankie?" Miley asked.

I decided not to dignify this vulgarity with a reply, largely because I could not think of a good one. I continued my oration.

"It's a great comfort to my wife an' I," I said, "tha' we won't be far from friends for long. It is marvellous tha' Paddy an' Mary will be neighbours," I said, noting Peggy's grip on the chair tightening. "An' o' course Joe Horgan an' his lovely family will be jus' across from us."

That chair was made of stronger stuff than I had ever suspected. The way Peggy was laying into it, I was surprised that it hadn't been reduced to splinters and sawdust by now.

On cue, Ginger piped up from somewhere over near the telly – where he was undoubtedly checking the connections.

"An' don' forget us," he said. "We're comin' too."

I almost couldn't carry on, drowning as I was in the milk of human kindness from my friends. There is a scene in the film 'It's a Wonderful Life' when Jimmy Stewart is surrounded by friends supporting him in rescuing the Savings and Loan business. It is a happy ending that would make a cat cry. Anyway, Jimmy gets a message from his guardian angel, saying that any man who has friends is a great success, or words to that effect. Well right then I felt like him. All I needed was Donna Reed gazing up at me lovingly, but Peggy was not available for the part, as she was still busy crushing furniture with her bare hands.

Ginger's words had hit her hard. She was like a boxer already woozy and down on his knees, with the referee counting up to ten, getting a whack behind the ear with a baseball bat. I could imagine her emotions racing after each other - surprise, pain, outrage ... to be followed - hopefully - by resignation that it was time to throw in the towel. I am a merciful man, and I reached for the matador's sword.

"I am also delighted to announce tha' Betty Magowan, o' Magowan's public house, known to some o' yis here, is also lookin' to establish a premises in Sunnyside. I for one, will be welcomin' this addition to the many amenities already available for the amusement an' refreshment o' the community."

There was a general chorus of interest and approval. If Moya was present, she would have done business. Peggy was only a shadow of the woman I knew before. She was now not so much clutching the chair, as slumped against it. She was staring into space, with a line of dribble coming out of her mouth. I was sad to have inflicted this, but it had to be done. I think they call it tough love.

I wound up my remarks with a very funny story about a golfer being short-taken out on the course, and having to use a fifty euro note - there being no Andrex Super Soft to hand. Before people had a chance to applaud, Ginger got stuck into 'A Nation Once Again', and that was that.

The rest of the evening passed in a warm glow. I remember thanking Paddy, Joe, and in particular Ginger, for their support. The beer ran out, and I was reduced to drinking cider and red wine. I like neither, but I found that if you mix them, they are not too bad.

★  ★  ★

When I woke up on the Sunday morning my mouth felt like I had eaten the bedclothes. My eyeballs were covered in grit, and it hurt to move them.

Marian and Susan had come back to help Peggy to clear up the mess. They were throwing empty bottles into a box, and from where I was hiding under the pillow, they seemed to be standing at the far side of the room, and lobbing the bottles in from there. Every one felt like it was landing on my head. Then someone fired up the Massey-Ferguson vacuum cleaner, to add timbre to the racket. I would have stayed where I was and suffered, but my bladder felt like it was attached to the mains water supply. If I didn't get up soon and have a slash, there was going to be a major eruption.

Susan was outside the bedroom door, as I emerged. In fairness, I was not at my most presentable. I was wearing my lucky Y-fronts that I wore at the 1992 Cup Final when Bohs beat Cork City one-nil. They were not new then, and at this venerable stage in their life, they had lost much of their original lustre. They were saggy and grey, but they were comfortable and they had great sentimental value. If Peggy owned them, they would have had a place of honour on the mantelpiece beside the ballerina.

Susan laughed and jumped out of my way, perceiving that I was in a hurry. When I came out, feeling much refreshed, Peggy was waiting in ambush. She pushed me into the bedroom.

"Wha' are ya doin' goin' aroun' in yer flitter for?" she asked.

"Wha'? Wha' are ya on abou'?" I asked back, although I was not really in the right form for debate and repartee.

"You! Look at ya!" she instructed.

Although there was a mirror handy, I preferred not to. My delicate state was not up to looking at what television newsreaders would describe as 'images which some viewers might find upsetting.' I knew that I would not win an award at an agricultural show.

"Have ya no shame?" she asked. "Poor Susan, havin' to look at ya half naked."

"Sure, she'd have no interest."

"Nobody'd have any interest," she said. "Get yerself dressed an' downstairs. I want to talk to ya."

She went out, banging the door behind her. I considered diving back into the scratcher, but thought better of it. There was no chance that I would be left there in peace, and the process of a later forced extraction would be painful. Having assembled the necessaries of socks two, shoes two, shirt and strides, I dressed, and dragged myself downstairs.

The work-party had downed tools, and were taking tea and toast. Order seemed to have been restored to the scene of battle. As far as I could tell, household items appeared to be in the places ordained for them. Marian grinned at me.

"Jaysus Da, ya look desperate," she said.

"Thanks very much," I answered.

"Did ya enjoy the party, Mr Flynn?" Susan asked.

"It was alright, I suppose. A refined an' respectable evenin' at home with one's family, friends, an' some dickheads," I said.

"Ya can sing tha' an' dance to it," said Peggy. "Did you invite Ginger Celtic?"

I conceded that I might have done.

"Tha' fella is a wild animal. He shouldn't be allowed indoors. Do ya know tha' he ate me flowers?" she asked.

I was not overly impressed. I have known Ginger to eat a rubber glove, a beer mat and a set of car keys. Not at the same time, mind you. But he was as likely to eat flowers as cabbage.

"Well ya had them in the middle o' the table with the food. Wha' did ya expect?" I asked.

Susan and Marian laughed. Peggy did not join in. I poured myself a mug of tea. There was no toast left, and I thought that I would allude to this, in the hope that a further supply might be commissioned.

"Is there any toast?"

"No," Peggy said, obviously not intending to do anything about that unsatisfactory state of affairs.

"I'll make ya some," Susan said, getting to her feet.

"He's well capable o' makin' toast himself," Peggy said. "It's about all he can do."

"Sure it's no problem," Susan said, bless her. In my invalided state, I doubted that I was capable of operating electrical machinery.

While the toast was toasting, Peggy sat opposite, looking at me. It was not lovingly – not like Donna Reed looking at

Jimmy Stewart. 'Glaring' would be a better description. Marian was still grinning like she had front row seats for the circus, and could not wait for the show to start. Susan came back with the toast and sat down.

I was concentrating on applying butter and marmalade, when Peggy broke the news. I will remember it always, like everyone remembers where they were when they heard that JFK had been shot (although I don't).

"I've decided tha' we're not movin' to Sunnyside," she said. Just like that.

I often think that fate is taking the piss, the way it fecks around with your life. It toys with you like a cat with a mouse, and then decides whether to disembowel you there and then, or let you loose, to fool around with you again on another day.

The moment should have been like in those court movies, where everything hangs on a word or two from the chairman of the jury: "We find the defendant ................... NOT guilty." There is jubilation, tears, embraces, and cries of: "Order in the court! Order in the court! I will have this court cleared, if there is any more of that!"

Of course we had none of that drama. Peggy made her earth-shattering announcement, and I took a slug of tea as the two girls watched me. I needed to play this carefully, in case it was some kind of trap. I didn't want to say something that might reverse what I thought I had heard.

"Wha's tha'? I asked, having first weighed my words carefully.

"Ya heard me. Ya're not deaf as well as thick," the love of my life responded.

"Yeah, but wha' d'ya mean? I thought ya were all for it. I thought ya were lookin' forward to it," I said.

"Ma's had a change o' heart," Marian explained.

"Yeah?" I asked, trying hard not to make it sound like 'WHOOPIE, YEEHAH and WAYTOGO!'

"As the move got closer, she could see everythin' that she'd miss from aroun' here. Isn't that right, Mrs Flynn?" Susan pitched in.

Peggy did not respond. I was still terrified that I would say something that would snatch defeat from the jaws of victory. I filled my mouth with toast as a precaution, in case I started talking shite by accident.

"Ya'll have to tell the agents – John-Paul an' tha' woman Moya," Marian said to her mother.

"I want to tell them – let me tell the bastards," I said – but just in my head.

"Yeah," said Peggy, "and the couple who want to buy this place."

"Ha!" I said - again just in my head, and I may have added a snatch of a tune. I think it was the 'Hallelujah Chorus.'

After I swallowed the toast, I very carefully sought confirmation that my winning lottery ticket was correct in all the details.

"So, do ya mean like tha' we're not goin' to move?" I asked. "Tha' we're stoppin' here?"

Peggy flared up like she was going to give me a kick in the goolies, but just as quickly, she subsided. She looked like Alex Ferguson graciously accepting defeat, and trying to come up with a speech of congratulation to the winning side. It was not easy for her.

"No," she said. "We're not goin' anywhere."

It was not much of a speech. It was not up there with the 'Friends, Romans and Countrymen,' or the 'I have a dream' stuff. But it was good enough for me. I allowed myself a suggestion of a smile – the slightest hint of a turning up of the lips.

"Ya needn't go grinnin' like an imbecile," she said. "There's goin' to be changes aroun' here. Now tha' we've got the place lookin' respectable, we're goin' to keep it tha' way. D'ya hear me?"

I nodded like a nodding dog on the back shelf of a rally car.

"It's prob'ly for the best," Marian said. "Sure yis would've been lost out in Sunnyside."

"Tha's right," Susan agreed. "Yis have everythin' yis need right here."

'Be it ever so humble, there's no place like home,' is my motto," I offered.

Peggy growled, but then softened.

"No, I suppose ya're right," she said. "I'll make more tea."

Okay, it was not quite the scene of unbounded joy that I had been looking forward to. That would have to wait until I made it to Magowan's, where I planned to shower the lads with gratitude and porter.

★ ★ ★

It would not be long before Peggy noticed that Joe, Paddy and Ginger were not, in fact, moving anywhere. I had not worked out yet exactly how I was going to explain that. I would cross that bridge when I came to it, drawing on my limitless resourcefulness. The important point was that, by the time it happened, the project would have been dismantled and rendered safe and inoperable. And hopefully it would be beyond Peggy's energies to recommission it, and start all over again.

In the meantime, I intended to take it easy for a bit. From the time of Marian's announcement, and my food poisoning, I had been under the lash. First I wore myself out growing vegetables, and then PJ nearly landed me in prison. After that I had the trauma of almost having to deliver little Margaret myself, I was handed the Santy job, and was within a whisker of being mauled to death by a mad dog. Then - as I was doing my best, as a dedicated family man, to become a motorist - I ended up on the Garda's most-wanted list. And as a backdrop to it all, I faced losing my home, and the community that I held dear. Job in the land of Uz had not got to put up with half of it.

But thanks to persistence, and the ingenuity of the Flynns, I had come through it all.

Now, I intended to put my head down and my feet up, because - this desperate life being what it is - I knew that it wouldn't be long before trouble would come calling again.

★ ★ ★